River Forest Public Library
31865003040960

D1087174

WHITE SMOKE

Also by Tiffany D. Jackson

Allegedly

Monday's Not Coming

Let Me Hear a Rhyme

Grown

Blackout (coauthor)

WHITE SMOKE

A novel by

TIFFANY D. JACKSON

KATHERINE TEGEN BOOKS
An Imprint of HarperCollinsPublishers

Katherine Tegen Books is an imprint of HarperCollins Publishers.

White Smoke

For information address HarperCollins Children's Books, a division of HarperCollins Publishers, 195 Broadway, New York, NY 10007.
www.epicreads.com

ISBN 978-0-06-302909-5

Typography by Erin Fitzsimmons
21 22 23 24 25 PC/LSCH 10 9 8 7 6 5 4 3 2 1

First Edition

To my puddin' pop baby brother, Duane Jackson,

who still hates horror movies

and will probably never read this book.

PREFACE

AH. THERE YOU are. They said you would be coming soon. All these years they left me to rot and ruin . . . to die. And now here you come. A family trying to replace me. To erase me. Us.

But that will never happen. Because this is my house. Doesn't matter how many new coats of paint or how many floorboards they replace . . . this will always be my house. You'll never take it from me. It's mine. Paid for with my family's blood. It will always be mine. Mine. Mine. Mine. All mine. They can't take it from me.

You'll learn soon enough: my house, my rules. Everything that is yours is now mine. And you will obey my rules until the day you leave. That's right, you won't be staying here long. I'll make very sure of that.

Oh, and look. You brought me a little friend.

ONE

ALARM: TIME FOR your pills!

I miss the warmth of the sun.

I miss cloudless blue skies, rocky beaches, mountain views, palm trees, and cactus thorns. The moist plant soil in my hands, the prickle of aloe leaves . . . the memories are sharp, fresh broken pieces of glass cutting through me.

Change is good. Change is necessary. Change is needed.

For the past three days, I've seen nothing but endless cement highways from the back row of our minivan, the sky growing grayer with every passing state. And dude, I'd give my right tit just to lay eyes on anything other than suspect motels, greasy diners, and gas station bathrooms.

"Daddy, are we there yet?" Piper asks from the middle row, a book in her lap.

"Almost, sweetheart," Alec says from the driver's seat. "See that city skyline? We're about five miles away."

"Our new home," Mom says with a hopeful smile, threading

her golden-brown fingers through Alec's pale ones.

Piper watches them, her jaw clenching.

"I need to go to the bathroom. *Now*," she says, with an air of haughtiness that makes it impossible to breathe easy in the packed van.

"Seriously, again?" Sammy mumbles under his breath, straining not to take his frustration out on a comic book. Buddy, our German shepherd mix, nudges Sammy's arm, demanding he continue to rub behind his ears.

"But we're almost there, sweetie," Mom says to her, beaming sunshine. "Do you think you can hold it a bit longer?"

"No," she snaps. "It's not good to hold your pee. Grandma said."

Mom winces a smile and faces forward. She tries her damnedest to defrost her, but Piper remains a block of ice no matter what you do.

Sammy, gnawing on an organic fruit roll-up, pops out an earphone, and leans over to whisper.

"This playlist should've lasted us the length of the trip according to Google Maps and I've already been through it twice. Should've added an extra day for Ms. Weak Bladder."

Piper stills, her neck straightening, pretending not to hear. But she's listening. She's always listening. That's what I've learned about her over the past ten months. She listens, stores information, and plots. Piper's a strawberry blond with copper freckles and pink lips that rarely form the semblance of a smile. From most angles, she is ghostly white. Enough for me to think that maybe we should've stayed in California, if for no other reason than so that the sun could powder her cheekbones.

"We'll get off at the next exit and find a gas station," Alec says to Mom. "No big deal, right?"

"Um, right," Mom replies, releasing his hand to wrap her long dreads into a high bun. She fidgets with her hair whenever she's uncomfortable. I wonder if Alec has picked up on that yet.

Change is good. Change is necessary. Change is needed.

I've repeated this mantra at least a million times as we've driven farther from the past toward an uncertain future. Uncertainty isn't necessarily a bad thing, just makes you feel cramped in a prison of your own making. But my guru told me whenever I start drowning in thoughts, I should hold tight to my mantra, a life preserver, and wait for the universe to send rescue, which has really worked over these last three months without my anxiety meds.

But then I see it. A black speck on my tan sundress.

"No, no no no . . . ," I whimper, convulsing, as the memorized fact washes over me.

FACT: Female bedbugs may lay hundreds of eggs, each about the size of a speck of dust, over a lifetime.

All the cars on the freeway collide and my body bursts into flames.

Hundreds of eggs, maybe thousands, are being laid on my

dress, on my skin, every passing second. Hatching, mating, hatching all over my body, can't breathe, need air, no, need hot water, heat, sun, fire, burn the car, get it off get it off get it off!

I snatch the speck with my nails, holding it up to the light, rubbing the soft fibers.

Not a bedbug. Just lint. It's okay. You're okay. Okay okayokayokay okay . . .

I flick it out the window and grip the glass terrarium on my lap before my bouncing knee can knock it off. I need a blunt, a brownie, a gummy . . . hell, I'd take a contact high right about now, I'm so desperate for numbness. Jittery nerves try to claw their way out from under the heavy skin suffocating them. I can't explode in here. Not in front of Sammy and especially not in front of Mom.

Grounding. Yeah, need to ground myself. *You got this, Mari. Ready? Go.* Five things I can see:

1) A blue city skyline, up ahead.
2) Burned-down church shaded by trees.
3) An old clock tower, the time wrong.
4) To the left, far in the distance, four white-gray windowless buildings that look like giant cinder blocks.
5) Closer to the freeway, some kind of abandoned factory. You can tell it hasn't been touched in years by the thickness of the weeds growing out the cracks in the parking lot and the art deco neon sign—Motor Sport—dangling

off the roof. The air whistling through all the broken windows must sound like whale chants.

Wonder what it's like inside. Probably some spooky decrepit shell of old America, hella dirty with World War II–era posters of women in jumpsuits, holding rivet guns. I hold my phone up to frame a shot before a text buzzes in from Tamara.

T-Money: Dude, u made it yet?

Me: No. We're driving nowhere fast. Think Alec's kidnapping us.

T-Money: Well, put on your locator so I can find your body.

Me: And I'm out of that gift you blessed me with.

T-Money: Damn!!! Already?

Me: Didn't even make it two states.

T-Money: On 2nd thought, tuck and roll out that bitch ASAP.

I miss Tamara. And that's about it. Everyone else back home can die a slow death. Aggressive, right? See why I could use a blunt?

"Daddy, is there something wrong with me?"

Piper's high-pitched voice can slice cracks in porcelain.

Alec eyes the rearview mirror at his daughter, her angelic

glow blinding him to reality.

"Of course not! What made you think that?"

"Sammy says I have a weak bladder. What does that mean?"

"What!"

That's Piper. She's all about the long game, waiting for the right moments to drop bombs. It's chess, not checkers.

As my little brother argues with the parental unit about name-calling, Piper sits with a satisfied grin, staring out at the city she'll undoubtedly take over.

You ever watch that first episode of *The Walking Dead*? You know, the one when Rick Grimes wakes up in his hospital bed, oblivious to the last forty-eight hours, then rides his horse through the apocalypse-ravaged streets, baffled to find the world has gone completely to shit? Well, that's what it feels like driving up the desolate freeway exit into Cedarville.

Piper leans closer to the window, eyebrows pinched. "Daddy, was there a fire?"

I follow her gaze to the array of burnt homes lining the avenue.

"Um, maybe, sweetheart," Alec says, squinting. "Or they're just . . . really old."

"Why don't they fix them?"

"Well, this city has had some . . . financial problems in the past. But it's getting better. That's why we're here!"

Sammy nudges me. "Mari, look."

On his side, more abandoned buildings, stores, even schools. Signage hints they've been closed at least since the nineties.

"Goodness," Mom gasps. This is a long way from the beach town she grew up in. Where I grew up. Where I can never go back.

Alec turns a corner, down Maple Street. I only notice the name due to the crooked street sign swinging in front of a three-story redbrick Victorian mansion, the steeple roof caved in, soot framing the boarded-up windows, dead vines crawling up its side.

The next house, even worse. A white one-story bungalow, the roof like a half-ripped bag of potato chips, a tree growing in its frame. The next like a creepy dollhouse . . . on and on it goes.

Mom and Alec share an uneasy look.

"Where . . . are . . . we?" Sammy mumbles, taking it all in.

"Oh!" Mom says, pointing. "There, up ahead. We're here!"

We park in front of a bright white carriage house, with a wide unfinished porch, bay windows, emerald grass, and a cobalt-blue door. A stark contrast to the rest of the homes on the block and the only one that has sprinkles of life as construction workers buzz about.

A white woman in a gray skirt suit waves from the front steps, a leather portfolio in hand.

"That must be Irma," Mom says, waving back. "She represents the Foundation. Be nice, everyone."

We slap on fake smiles, pour out of the van, and stand on the curb, looking up at our new home. But I can't help sneaking glances at the crumbling surroundings, waiting for a zombie to stumble out of the bushes.

Irma clicks down the driveway in her kitten heels, brown curls bouncing. Up close, she's older than her forced hair color gives her credit for.

"Hello! Hello! Welcome! You must be Raquel. I'm Irma Von Hoven, we spoke on the phone."

Mom shakes her hand. "Irma, yes, pleasure meeting you in person!"

"Congratulations again on winning the GWYP Residency. We are so happy to have you here in Cedarville!"

"Thank you! This is my husband, Alec; our son, Sam; and our daughters, Marigold and Piper."

"Stepdaughter," Piper corrects her.

Alec squeezes both of her shoulders with a chuckle. "Remember, sweetheart, we're a family now, right? Can you say hello to Ms. Von Hoven?"

"I thought *we* already did?"

Irma's eyes widen as she hugs her folder, then looks up at me. "My, aren't you a tall one!"

I sigh. "So I've heard a few million times."

"Uh . . . right. So how about a tour! Yes?"

"Yes, that would be great, thanks," Mom says, slightly deflated. "Sammy, leave Bud in the car."

"Come on in. And don't mind the contractors, they're just finishing up a couple of things here and there. We had a few hiccups some weeks back, but everything's running smoothly now."

The door creaks and we file into the foyer. Inside is massive. Three times the size of our beach shed, as my dad liked to call it.

"The house was originally constructed back in the early seventies but, of course, we've had it updated. Stainless steel appliances, some new plumbing, floors, the works. To the left, you have the living room, don't mind the tools. To the right, a formal dining room, great for dinner parties. They just stained this staircase, isn't it incredible?"

Wood. That's all I see. Wood everywhere. Fresh places for bedbugs to burrow. . . .

FACT: Bedbugs love to make their homes in mattresses, suitcases, books, cracks in the walls, outlets, and anything made of wood.

"Back here, a gorgeous kitchen that opens up to the family room. Great place for the children to play. This little breakfast nook gets tons of natural light. Walk-in pantry, plenty of closet space . . ."

A million cherrywood cabinets, wood-trim bay windows, glossy floors . . . wood, wood, and more wood.

With trembling hands, I set my terrarium next to a welcome basket of cured meats, cheeses, walnuts, and crackers. I grab the nuts and slam-dunk them in the trash, startling Irma.

Mom jumps in. "Sorry, Sammy's allergic."

"Oh, I see," Irma says, lashes fluttering. "Um, first door over here, a small library. Could make a nice little office space."

I knock on a wall. Hollow. The place got good bones but shitty insulation. I give the floor a stomp, an echo vibrating up.

Irma shoots Mom a pointed stare.

"Um, their dad is an architect," Mom offers sheepishly.

"Oh. I see."

I don't know why everyone's looking at me like I'm the crazy one. If winters in the Midwest are anything like they are in movies, we'll freeze to death come November! I punch a new alarm in my phone:

10:25 a.m. ALARM: Order heated blankets.

"What's that?" Sammy asks, pointing to a door under the stairs. The dark warped wood stands out among the stained and polished interior.

"Oh. Yes, um, that's the basement, but it's off-limits. Mr. Watson will explain; he's the supervisor. Shall we see about the bedrooms?"

We trek upstairs, congregating in the windowless hallway. A loud thump hits above us. Piper shrieks, grabbing hold of Alec.

"Not to worry! They're just working on the roof. Anyhoo, there're four bedrooms—three plus a master with bath. The master faces the front yard and has amazing light. . . ."

"What do you think?" Mom whispers to me, beaming. "Nice, right?"

"It's . . . a lot of wood," I mumble, scratching the inside of my arm.

"And over here, we have the upstairs bathroom. Giant, isn't it? That's a *real* working claw-foot tub."

As they pile in to admire the checkered tile, I drift away from the tour to call Dad. It's almost midnight in Japan, but he should still be up.

No signal. In the middle of a city? That's . . . impossible.

The floor creaks behind me, like a heavy foot pressed against the aged wood. Enveloped in the darkness, a chill crawls up my arms. Feels colder in here than outside. I turn in time to see a shadow pass under one of the bedroom doors.

Thought she said they were on the roof.

"Hello?" I say, creeping closer, keeping my steps light.

It's faint, but there's the slow inhale of breath as the shadow moves away. Then, silence.

I test the knob and the lock snaps. The door slowly swings open on its own, and I half expect to see someone standing right behind it.

But there's no one.

The room is empty. The walls white and bare. Not even curtains on the windows facing a backyard filled with tall pine trees, branches shifting in the breeze.

"Oh," I say, laughing at myself. Breeze, sun, branches . . . of course they'd paint shadows on the floor.

See why I need to relax?

The sun-drenched room with its small closet and lopsided floorboards is cozy, peaceful. My guru once said, "Home isn't a place, it's a feeling." Maybe this place isn't that bad. But in an instant, I'm distracted by the giant gaping hole in the molding of the window.

Well, not gaping. It's tight, but there's just enough space for bedbugs to set up shop.

I grab a credit card out of my wallet, gliding it down the crack.

Can probably seal this up with some caulk. . . .

Irma clicks into the room, my family behind her.

"And in here, we have . . . uh, dear? What are you doing?"

I straighten. "Um . . . checking for bedbugs."

Mom winces a grin. "Mari is very, um . . . proactive when it comes to house care."

Irma gapes but returns a fake smile. "Oh. Right, okay. Shall we convene in the kitchen?"

Sammy mouths "weirdo" at me with a smirk as we head downstairs.

"Oh, Mr. Watson," Irma sings, waving at the older gentleman standing in the foyer. "This is the Anderson-Green family. I was just giving them a tour of their new home."

Mr. Watson blows out some air, failing at hiding his

annoyance with Irma. He's bald with a thick graying beard and chocolate skin, standing a good six foot three. He takes off his hard hat and gives us a curt nod.

"Hello," he says. "Mind the water pressure. Don't work her too hard, she's new. Gotta check on the fellas."

He gives us another nod, slaps on his helmet, and slips out the front door.

"Oooook," Alec chuckles.

A man of few words. I like him already.

"Well," Irma sighs. "Shall we?"

Irma lays her portfolio out on the granite kitchen island, taking out various pamphlets and papers.

"Okey dokey. Here's the contract for you to sign. And for legal purposes, I must review the rules with you once more."

"Yes, of course," Mom says, Alec by her side, massaging her neck.

In an instant, Piper is behind him, tugging at his shirt. It would be comical, her endless need for his attention, if it wasn't so annoying.

Irma adjusts her glasses, reading off a paper. "As discussed, artists participating in the Grow Where You're Planted Residency, aka GWYP, are allowed to live in one of our restored historic homes free of charge for the length of the residency with the option to buy. Each quarter the artist, that's you, is expected to attend fundraising dinners, networking events, and galas, which will help promote the Sterling Foundation efforts to rebuild the

Cedarville community. At the end of the artist's residency, the artist must produce at least one major project, i.e., your new book. Terminating the agreement will result in immediate eviction and the artist must pay back the mortgage with interest plus any damages in accordance with the length of their stay."

"Daddy, what does *eviction* mean?"

Alec brushes Piper's hair behind her ears. "It means we would have to leave the house right away. But don't worry. That's never going to happen."

A warning laces Alec's words together tight.

Mom takes a deep breath. "So. Where do I sign?"

As Mom and Alec finalize the paperwork, I stand in front of a glass door leading to a narrow fenced-in backyard and try to call Dad like I promised, but my one bar of service can barely send a text. Outside, a construction worker stains the deck a dark cherrywood. His brushstrokes are hella rushed and erratic as sweat pours down the back of his neck.

Dude, nervous much?

Mom joins me, wrapping an arm around my shoulders. A warm aura of peace radiating off her skin.

"Plenty of space for a new garden. We can build some raised flower beds over in that corner, fence it in so Bud won't mess with it."

She's trying to show me the silver lining in all this, and I can't see a glimmer. But she's happy. I've always wanted her to be happy.

"Oh! You're into gardening?" Irma says behind us. "Cedarville has a terrific urban gardening program run through the library. Last Sunday of the month."

Following Irma out to the front porch, we survey the neighborhood and I half expect a tumbleweed to blow by.

"Ms. Von Hoven, no offense, but where is, um, everybody?" Sammy asks, scratching his head. "Is there like a BBQ in another state we weren't invited to?"

As far as little brothers go, I hit the lotto when it comes to Sammy. Mentally twice his age, with a wicked sense of humor and sarcasm for days, I can always count on him to break the tension by saying what everyone's thinking.

Irma giggles. "Well, you are our first artist in residence! But there will be many more. The Sterling Foundation owns all the property on this side of Maple Street. Come! Let me give you a quick rundown." She links arms with Sammy, heading to the end of the driveway. Piper slips between Mom and Alec, grabbing his hand as we follow.

"Okay! You, young sir, live on Maple Street, between Division and Sweetwater Avenues, in the Maplewood area of Cedarville," she says, pointing while she talks. "Which makes up about fifteen blocks or so. Population around two thousand. Three blocks up Maple Street is Cedarville Park. Behind the park is the cemetery. Take a left on Sweetwater, four blocks up and you're at Kings High School. Take a right, three blocks up and you're at Benning Elementary, right next to Pinewood Middle School. Now, take a left on Division for the local grocery and easy access to the freeways. You're about fifteen minutes away from downtown and the Riverwalk."

"There's a river?" Piper asks. For some reason, this interests her.

"Oh yes. Pretty walkway too. Lots of new restaurants, casinos, and an arcade. Now, a few tips for the parents, if I may. Sweetwater Avenue is like . . . the other side of the tracks, if you catch my drift. Your neighborhood is something of an up-and-coming area." Her voice deepens. "Lock your doors and windows every night. Never leave anything in the car or on the porch if you want to keep it, and don't let the children wander. Especially in these old houses."

You could hear a pin drop from a block over the way we all freeze.

Irma lets out a laugh. "But really, Cedarville is one of the friendliest cities in the country. A little dirt just adds character."

"That's one way of looking at it," Sammy mumbles.

"All right. I think that just about covers it. Next month, Mr. Sterling would like to host a welcome dinner at his house for you. I'll send the particulars. Contractors should be done with everything in the next week or two. You have my number, so if any issues arise, please let me know. And once again, welcome to Cedarville!"

Irma waves as she heads to her car, leaving us stunned, arms full of the information she dumped on us.

As she drives off, I beat Sammy to the punch. "So . . . we're not really staying here, right?"

Mom scoffs. "Why not?"

"Uh, for starters, have you looked around?" Sammy asks, motioning to the desolate street.

The brick house to our right choked in vines looks like nothing more than a giant hedge, wood slabs boarding up every window and door.

"Well," Alec says. "She did say there will be more families here. Soon."

"Guys," Mom pleads. "This is a great opportunity, and most importantly, it's a FREE house!"

"Yeah," I chuckle, crossing my arms. "And you get what you pay for."

"Free also means being *debt*-free," Alec adds, the accountant wheels spinning behind his bright blue eyes. "Think of it as an adventure. We'll be pioneers!"

"Don't you mean colonizers," I snap, "since all of these were clearly already owned by somebody before?"

It's now Alec's turn to wince, and it feels justified after the number of times Piper has made Mom uneasy.

Piper yanks at Alec's arm. "Daddy, can I pick out my room now?"

"Uh, sure, sweetie, sure. Let's go check them out."

Alec grasps Piper's hand as they skip back inside, not bothering to check if his other kids want to pick their room as well.

But who am I kidding, Piper is always going to come first.

Mom studies our faces and holds up both of her hands. "Okay. So, I know you're both . . . apprehensive. But look on the bright side: if it doesn't work out, we're only required to stay here for three years."

"Three years!" we scream.

"That's how the residency works. This will be a fresh, *debt-free* start. For *all* of us. Which is exactly what we need." She looks at me. "Right, Marigold?"

Ah, of course. *Debt-free* is needed since my stay at Strawberry Pines Rehabilitation Center wasn't exactly cheap. Just short of tuition at an Ivy League college. This is a test. Most scenarios will play out like this from now on. And I can't fail, or I'll relinquish the minuscule freedom they've promised to give me.

So I bite my tongue and spit out the practice mantra. "Change is good. Change is necessary. Change is needed."

Sammy rolls his eyes. "If you say so, Oprah."

Honk honk!

The moving truck pulls up behind us.

"Just in time," Sammy says. "Our old life has arrived."

Mom dusts off her hands. "Sammy, run inside and get Alec. Marigold, can you start taking stuff out of the van? I don't want those herbs to wilt and Buddy to melt."

The van doors slide open and Buddy leaps out, licking my face as if we've been gone forever. Gotta love dogs for their unconditional love.

"Hey," Mom says, approaching the drivers. "Thought you were supposed to be here this morning. What happened?"

One of the movers I recognize from California hops out of the truck as the others roll up the back door, unloading the ramp.

"Yeah, service is terrible around here! We stopped to ask for directions, but no one's ever heard of this *Maple* Street."

"Really? Who'd you ask?"

He chuckles and points behind us. "Your neighbors."

Up the road, across Sweetwater Avenue, life has sprung up in the form of bodies trickling out of houses, standing on the half-dead lawns, staring back at us in silence.

"Whoa," I mumble. Coming from a small white town, this is the most Black people I've ever seen in real life.

Gotta show Tamara!

I grab my cell phone from my pocket and Mom shoves my arm down.

"Marigold," she whispers. "Don't take pictures of people without asking them. It's rude."

"Don't you think *they're* being rude? They're staring like we're a pack of circus freaks."

"Maybe it's your beach cover-up, flip-flops, and hemp jewelry that's making them stare," Sammy laughs, jumping off the curb. He stands in the middle of the street and waves. "Hi!"

Silence. No response. Not even from the kids. Just a crowd of mannequins.

"Yikes," Sammy mutters. "Thought she said Cedarville was the nicest city in the country?"

"Yes, Sammy. Aren't you impressed by the welcoming committee?"

"Come on, you two," Mom chuckles. "Let's get to work!"

We help the movers unload the truck, lugging furniture and boxes inside. I supervised most of the packing and wrapping before we left, ensuring no bedbugs could hitch a ride to our new home.

DING DING DING

A chorus of alarms rings from upstairs, down, and outside. Phone alarms. Every contract worker has theirs set for the same time. Five thirty-five p.m. Tools drop all at once as the men scramble, sprinting out the door, diving headfirst into their cars.

"What's going on?" Sammy asks, pulling a suitcase through the living room.

"I . . . I have no idea," Mom says from the kitchen, unpacking a box of dishes.

Mr. Watson trots down the stairs and stops in the hall.

"Done for the day. Be back tomorrow. Cable and internet might be up late next week."

"Next week!" Sammy shouts, gripping his heart.

"Electric company had to rewire this whole part of the neighborhood. No one has lived here in thirty years."

"Really," I mumble. "You could never tell."

Mr. Watson nods once and rushes out the door. Car wheels squeal away.

"Guess they're in a hurry to get home." Mom shrugs. "Or maybe they're all heading to a party."

Doesn't feel like they're running toward something—rather, running away.

TWO

I'VE ALWAYS HATED the smell of other people's houses.

This house smells like wet wood. And not the kind you smell in the early morning dew, but the campfire burnt-logs-doused-with-water kind that no amount of paint and polish can mask.

The small tea candle under my oil dish flickers. Aromatherapy. One of the tricks I've learned to ease my anxiety. Soft music, plants, candles . . . you name it, I came ready. New places like this can tip my scales and I need to prove I can handle myself. Glad I bought an extra pack of incense and a vial of peppermint oil from my favorite apothecary shop back home.

But where do I go when I run out? Where's the nearest Trader Joe's? Yoga studio? Coffee shop? Vegan spots? A place to get my hair braided? Most importantly, where am I going to find weed? I'd probably be able to answer all these questions with at least one bar of decent cell service. Well, at least the Trader Joe's part. I grab my phone to set a reminder . . .

11:00 a.m. ALARM: Ask about stores.

Buddy jumps on the end of my bed, burrowing himself in blankets. He spends most of his time with Sammy but loves sleeping with me.

On my hands and knees, I crawl around the room, inspecting the baseboards with a phone flashlight, scrubbing them with hot soapy water, caulking holes, and adding a few drops of cinnamon oil.

FACT: Bedbugs hate the smell of cinnamon.

Heat treatment would be best for any eradication, but my blow-dryer and steamer are still at the bottom of a box somewhere, so these simple preventative measures will have to do for now.

Cough! Cough! Cough!

"Daddy! Marigold's smoking again!"

Alec's feet storm down the hall and hit my threshold, his mouth in a tight line, accusations dripping off his tongue. From the floor, I meet his glare with equal disdain. He sighs and about-faces into Piper's room across the hall.

"Sweetheart, she's not smoking. It's those smelly sticks we talked about, remember?"

She fakes another cough. "I can't breathe."

"You want me to close your door?"

"No! I'm scared."

I slam my door shut, taking a moment to appreciate having a handle again. Mom took the lock off my last door, leaving nothing but a gaping hole, privacy a laughable concept.

"Just for safety, baby," she had said, eyes full of pity. Couldn't even argue; I deserved it.

After another hour of cleaning, the house settles down and I switch to headphones, listening to a meditation app that helps quiet the mind.

Clink. Clink. Clink.

You can hear everything from my new room. Crying pipes. Breathing wood. Trees brushing against the ceiling. Cicadas singing in the backyard. Dishes rattling.

Someone moving downstairs.

Buddy sits up, ears perked, a low growl rumbling in his throat.

"Ugh . . . Buddy, chill," I grumble in a sleepy daze, throwing the covers over my head. "It's just the wind."

"Who left this glass out?"

Mom is holding up one of her Waterford crystal glasses in the kitchen, a wedding gift passed down by her grandmother. Well, first wedding. I don't even think she had a registry for her courthouse ceremony to Alec.

"Not me," Sammy says, grabbing his granola from the adjacent cabinet.

"Remember, no dishes in the sink. Everyone is responsible for themselves."

"*We* know that. But does everyone else?" Sammy laughs.

I shrug. "I don't know what to tell you, Mom. But someone was up walking around last night."

"Not me," Sammy says. "I was knocked out."

Mom looks at the glass, then at its home on the top shelf of the cabinet.

"It's too high for Piper. . . ."

"Maybe she climbed on the counter."

"No butts on the counter," Piper admonishes from the stairs. "Grandma said."

I chuckle. Of course she'd be listening from somewhere. She has an ear for dramatics.

Mom clears her throat and smiles. "Good morning, Piper. Sleep well? What can I get you for breakfast?"

Piper joins us in the kitchen with a mischievious grin. "Bacon and eggs."

Mom folds her hands. "Sweetie, we've been over this before . . . we don't eat that."

"Well, *I* do. And so does Daddy, when he's not with *you*."

Mom straightens, her smile dimming. She turns away, pouring herself a cup of coffee, probably to keep from reacting.

BEEP BEEP BEEP

8:05 a.m. ALARM: Time for your pills!

Damn, almost forgot.

"Marigold," Mom says, waving two of Sammy's EpiPens before placing them in the cabinet above the fridge. "Pens . . . here."

"Isn't that a little high for Piper without butts on the counter?"

Mom smirks. "Knock it off."

"Good morning, everybody!" Alec enters looking refreshed. Not like someone who's been up all hours of the night drinking out of Mom's crystal glass.

"Morning," Mom and Sammy say.

"It's a beautiful day in the neighborhood!" Alec sings into Mom's ear, and she giggles. Piper's face turns crimson, head ready to pop off her shoulders.

"Daddy, I'm hungry."

"Me too, sweetheart," he says, still holding Mom. "So, what's on the agenda today, babe?"

"Unpacking and more unpacking. I want to at least set up my office. I'm so behind on my deadline. How about you?"

"Well, I was going to take Piper to breakfast."

Mom blinks. "Oh. Really?"

"Yeah. Figured I'd take her to get a bite to eat, then do a store run."

She sips her coffee. "Hm. For everyone or just Piper?"

Alec straightens. "For everyone, babe! Of course. Um, do you want to write a list?"

"Sure."

"Uh, hey, Sammy. Care to join us?"

Sammy shakes his head and grabs the oat milk out of the fridge.

"No thanks. I'm still setting up my room. Wanna be ready for when the internet is up and running."

"Okay then." Alec looks to Piper. "Well, let's get going, sweetie."

Alec doesn't bother to ask me. He knows better.

As they back out of the driveway, the contractors pull up slow, each staring at the house with dread in their eyes, and somehow, I know the feeling.

"Morning, ma'am," Mr. Watson mumbles as he enters the kitchen. "You, um, happen to see a hammer lying around? About this big, red-and-black handle?"

Mom shakes her head. "No, I haven't."

Mr. Watson shifts on his back foot. "Oh. Uh, okay. Just one of the fellas . . . he must have lost it somewhere."

He rejoins the others in the front yard, delivering the news, which is followed by a tense yet hushed debate, each worker looking hella wary of stepping inside.

The rest of the day, I bounce around helping Sammy and Mom empty boxes. Being a newly crowned minimalist, I don't have much to unpack: a few shirts, shorts, and dresses, all either white or cream in color; white-plastic-framed photos; white comforter set; and Bluetooth speaker. Everything else was burned.

With Mom in her office and Sammy taking a break to play video games, I decided to focus on common areas of the house, spraying a mixture of rubbing alcohol and distilled water in the nooks and crevices, vibing to some Post Malone.

FACT: Spraying 91 percent solution isopropyl alcohol directly in infested surfaces will help kill or repel bedbugs, dissolving their cells and drying out their eggs.

The cozy living room is the ideal place for bedbugs to make their home. I launch an attack around the window frames and built-in bookshelves, being mindful of the staining.

CREAAAAAKKK . . .

I don't hear the creak, I feel it. The floorboard behind me bending under some heavy weight.

"I know, Sammy," I groan without turning. "I know this looks crazy. But you'll all thank me when we're not throwing our mattresses in a bonfire."

I pop out an AirPod and glance over my shoulder. I'm alone but not alone at the same time. Because I can still sense the essence of someone . . . lingering like a low fog.

"Sammy?"

A door squeaks down the hall. I speed through the living room and into the kitchen. Empty. The family room, the kitchen and nook, even the foyer.

"Mom?"

The door to her office is closed but Fela Kuti sings through the bottom sweep, meaning she's in the zone.

An icy chill taps up my spine as I make a U-turn, stopping short. The basement door is cracked open, a whistling breeze streaming through it.

Was this open before?

I test the door, its hinges squeaking softly, and peer downstairs into the endless darkness, clicking the light switch twice. Nothing.

"Hello?" I call, voice echoing, but only silence responds. Pushing it closed, I drift to the living room, unable to shake the sense I'm being followed when something in the corner moves toward me, fast.

"AHH!" I scream, stumbling back.

Buddy stands in the middle of the room, tail wagging, a goofy grin as if saying, "Hi! I've missed you!"

I laugh, rubbing his head. Been cooped up in here way too long. There's only so much you can do without contact with the outside world before you slowly start losing your shit.

One bar. Still. I've now tested all the corners of the house, searching for a signal. Buddy follows me around like we're playing a game, sniffing behind each spot I leave.

It's time to go exploring. The neighborhood seems pretty walkable. Helpful, considering Mom and Alec made it clear there's no way in hell I will ever get a car again. They barely let me walk to Tamara's house alone. That, along with an eight thirty curfew and mandatory bag inspections . . . you could almost mistake my situation for house arrest.

"Where are you going?" Sammy asks from the top of the stairs.

I clip Bud's leash to his collar and slip on my sneakers.

"Gonna take Bud for a walk. See if I can get better service on the corner or something. Wanna come?"

Sammy shrugs, thumping down the stairs. "Sure. Can't believe Alec's still not back with Piper yet. It's been hours."

"Dude, the longer that brat is gone, the better," I say, and throw the door open, running right into a fist.

"Mari!" Sammy screams before catching me as I fall back on my ass. Buddy barks frantically and I'm seeing white spots.

"Oh shit! Damnnn, you okay?" a deep voice says from . . . somewhere. The room is spinning too fast for me to place him.

Wait, him?

"Mom!" Sammy screams. "Mom, help!"

Mom rushes out of her office. "Marigold! What happened?"

"Aye yo, my bad! I was just about to knock, your doorbell's broke . . . and . . . yo, I'm so sorry! Here, let me help."

Two rough hands grip my arm, trying to pull me up, but I yank away.

"Dude . . . what the hell," I snap, eyes refocusing.

The man who punched my right eye wasn't exactly a man. Couldn't be much older than me, with light brown eyes and thick dreads hanging by his neck. I'm suddenly aware that I'm sprawled out in front of him like a chalk outline and quickly sit up. The room twirls as Mom examines me.

"Can I help you?" she asks, mildly annoyed.

"Uh, yeah. Yusef Brown. I'm with Brown Town Mowing Company. We, um, met your husband at the gas station around the corner. Said y'all looking to do some yard work and asked us to stop by."

He's a rich mocha brown. The hot chocolate with coconut milk on a chilly day by the beach type of brown. God, I hope these stupid flowery words dancing in my head aren't leaking out my mouth.

Mom huffs. "Help me get her to her feet, Sammy. We need to walk around, make sure she doesn't have a concussion."

"Nah, let me," Yusef insists.

"I'm fine, I . . ."

Swoooooosh . . . and I'm on my feet, a wobbly spin top.

"There ya go. You aight? And . . . daaaamn girl. You tall!"

"Thanks, Captain Obvious," I grumble.

Except he's tall too. At least six foot five. Didn't think they even made boys this size. In Cali, I just about towered over everyone in my sophomore class.

"Nice place you got here," he muses, walking me around the kitchen island. "How about some water? Whenever I get my ass beat, I always ask for water first."

"Yes. Water," I groan, unwilling to talk in full sentences.

Mom shakes her head. "Let me make an ice pack. Sammy, get your sister some water."

Sammy moves about the kitchen, the color drained from his face, feet dragging, never taking his eyes off me. Same look he had six months ago when he found me. Poor kid, I've scared him. Again.

"I'm fine, Sammy, it's okay."

He nods and gives me a cup of water, hand trembling. Yusef offers him a fist bump.

"What up doe, Sam. I'm Yusef. Aye, don't worry about your sis, she's a champ." He stops to wink at me. "I punched homie up the block yesterday and he still sleep."

Sammy's eyes widen. Yusef cracks a brilliant smile and pats him on the shoulder.

"I'm messing with you, man! Aye, you want some candy? Might be a little melted but I got a Snickers and—"

"NO!" I scream.

"Drop it!" Mom shrieks.

Yusef drops the Snickers, holding both hands up.

"Sorry, Sammy is allergic to . . . well, everything," I explain. "But especially nuts."

"That's probably why my husband reached out to you. I mentioned last night needing to keep the weeds down for Sammy's allergies."

"Oh. My bad. Ain't trying to take out both ya kids."

Mom chuckles while gently laying an ice pack over my eye. I hold in a whimper, wincing through the crisp cold.

Yusef studies me. One hand still holding my elbow, he leans forward and sniffs.

Is he smelling my hair?

"Mm. That smells good," he says. "What is that?"

"It's lavender," Mom says. "Will help with the bruising."

He nods and replaces her hand with his, holding the ice pack in place. So close, I'm able to snag a good look at him. He's cute, in a cute-and-I-know-it type of way. I'm allergic to nuts like this too.

There's a knock at the door.

"Oh, that's probably my uncle, wondering what I'm doing up in here."

"I'll get it," Mom says, jogging over.

"So, didn't catch your name," he says, grinning.

"Marigold Anderson," I answer flatly.

"Marigold," he muses. "An annual. Bloom, then die. Interesting."

I don't know how to take that, so I change topics. "You live around here?"

"Ain't far. Over on Rosemary and Sweetwater, by the middle school."

"Hey! That's where I'll be starting next week," Sammy chimes in.

"Oh, for real? I went there too. Watch out for Ms. Dutton. Miserable old bird!" He smiles at me. "So I guess you'll be starting at Kings High?"

I roll my eyes. "Guess so."

"New schools are tough, but at least you'll have one friend there to start."

Who said anything about us being "friends"?

Mom returns with an older bald-headed man, the

resemblance striking. Yusef's uncle takes in the room—the Snickers bar on the floor, his nephew icing some random girl's face—and huffs.

"Boy, what you get yourself into this time?"

"Hey yo, Unc, this here's Marigold and my main man Sam."

He chuckles. "Nice to meet y'all. I'm Mr. Brown."

Mom walks Mr. Brown to the backyard, showing him the hedges that needed trimming and Sammy takes Buddy out front to calm him, leaving Yusef and me alone. He keeps the ice pack pressed on my face, his eyes wandering from the ceiling lights to the floors, like he's taking inventory.

"You know I could handle this on my own, right?" I grumble.

"Yeah, but it's way more fun with me helping, right?" He leans over my shoulder, nodding at my terrarium. "That's a fly-ass succulent garden you have there. Biggest sempervivum I've ever seen. And that stone pattern pretty . . . what? What you laughing at?"

"It's just funny hearing a dude . . . I don't know, gush over terrarium patterns."

He shrugs. "Hey man, everybody's got their thing. Where'd your moms get this? These be costing a fortune online."

"I made it."

"Ha! For real? Look at you with the skills, Cali."

A nickname. Something blooms inside my chest and I rip it at the root.

"So, been working with your uncle for a while, huh?"

"Since I was a kid. He's more into the lawn care, weed whacking stuff. I'm the gardener. The artist."

"I used to have a garden," I mumble, surprised I'd blurt out something so . . . personal.

"Really. Well, maybe we can work on a new one together." He smiles. "You know I got all the right tools."

Cocky, arrogant, and knows he's good-looking . . . the exact thing I don't need right now. I yank the ice pack from his hand.

"Um, yeah, think it's time for you to go."

He laughs. "Chill! I was just messing with you!"

I cross my arms. "Shouldn't you go see if your uncle needs your help or something?"

Yusef's face falls as he weighs his options, whether to push it or let it go. He chooses the latter, shaking his head before brushing by me. The back door closes and I take a deep breath.

Don't overthink it, I coach myself, patting both my pockets. *He's not worth the trouble and . . . hey, where's my phone?*

If there was a positive of once having bedbugs, it's that I now can literally find a needle in a haystack with razor-sharp precision. I retrace my steps in the foyer, through the living room and kitchen. Must have fallen in all the commotion, but the floor is clear, the counters and surfaces bare. With no Wi-Fi, I can't use the Find My Phone app on my computer, but perhaps I can call myself with Mom's phone. That's if she has even a bar of service.

"Mom! Can I borrow your phone?" I ask from the deck. "I can't find mine."

"Sure, hun, it's in my room."

Yusef eyes me and I rush back inside.

Don't overthink it. You're not responsible for other people's emotions. Only your own.

At the stairs, my phone waits for me, lying neatly faceup on the middle of the third step, as if it planted itself there. I scratch my scalp, digging a bit too hard. It wasn't here. I know it wasn't here because I looked. I couldn't possibly miss this huge white dot on a slab of oak wood. Someone must have put it here.

Sammy. It had to be.

THREE

"FIRST FULL DAY in the big city and you get your ass whooped."

"Shut up, Sammy," I laugh.

Sammy splashes me with water as I dry off our dinner plates. If we were back home, I would've skipped dinner, headed down the road to Tamara's, hit a blunt, and recounted my run-in with Yusef. If we had Wi-Fi I would've at least FaceTimed her.

"Guys, you know we have a dishwasher, right?" Alec says, pointing to the machine by my legs.

"Oh right. I forgot," I say with a shrug. "We've never had a dishwasher before."

"And it's much more fun washing them together," Sammy says, splashing water again.

Piper looks on from the dining table, her face unreadable. Probably trying to find something to end our revelry. It's like she's allergic to happiness.

"Hey, hey, guys! Watch the floors!" Mom warns. "All right,

I'm off to bed. My back is killing me."

Alec rounds the table and massages her shoulders.

"You guys gonna be all right without me tomorrow?" Alec quips, kissing the top of her head.

"We were fine without you today when you sent stranger-danger here to knock out my sister and poison me."

Alec and Mom hit Sammy with the same look, before Mom pats Alec's hand.

"We'll be fine, babe. Don't worry about us. Tomorrow is a big day!"

When Mom was first accepted to the residency, Alec wasn't too pleased with the idea of moving. Money was tight and he had trouble finding work around town after my . . . incident. But then the Sterling Foundation hooked him up with a financial analyst position at one of their partner firms. He was full steam ahead after that.

"Daddy, can you read me a bedtime story?" Piper asks eagerly.

"How about you read me one instead, huh? Starting fifth grade soon!"

Piper winces a smile. She's not excited about starting school either. Something, for once, we have in common.

"Oh babe, have you seen my watch?" Alec asks. "I can't find it anywhere."

"Did you look in the tray in the bathroom?"

"Nothing there. Weird, I just had it."

Alec takes Piper to bed and Mom heads to her office, leaving Sammy and me to finish the kitchen. I stare into the hallway mirror at a welt the size of a large fist on my cheek and the bags under my eyes. This place has aged me overnight.

"Ew, Marigold!" Sammy wrinkles his nose.

"What?"

"You farted," he gags, covering his mouth.

"No I didn't!" I sniff the air and reel back. "Ugh, what the hell is that!"

The pungent stench makes it seem like we're living inside a porta potty. Pinching noses, we walk around in circles until Sammy stops at a vent, right below the hallway mirror under the stairs.

"It's coming from in there."

The next morning, Mr. Watson sniffs from a safe distance, then shakes his head.

"I don't smell anything."

It's not his lack of interest. It's the way he won't even go near the vent that makes me glance up from my coffee. Even Piper, swinging her legs on the stool at the kitchen island, slurping up her Honey Nut Cheerios, seems curious.

"Are you sure?" Mom asks, perplexed. "The kids said they smelled something."

"Could've just been passing."

"So random animals roll through here and fart often,"

Sammy chuckles. "Bud's farts are lethal but nothing like that. It smelled like something died in here."

Mr. Watson stiffens. It's slight but noticeable.

Mom wipes her hand on a dish towel. "It must have come from the basement. Should we check?"

There's a few silent seconds before Mr. Watson says, "We don't go to the basement."

It came out hard, violent even. Mom gapes at him. He tips his hat and quickly walks away.

Sammy nods his head. "Well, that went well."

CLICK!

With a loud snap, the TV is on, volume set to a thousand. An image of an old white man in a blue suit sitting at a mahogany desk fades in, the city's unmistakable skyline in the green screen background as he shouts.

"And so I say to you, cast the wickedness out of your heart for the good of thy neighbor, cleanse thy soul with fire!"

"Who's that?" Sammy asks, drifting into the family room.

The cable guy pops up from behind the TV stand, dusting off his hands.

"That's Scott Clark," he says, wrapping a cord around his arm. "He gives the daily sermon on local channel twelve."

"Daily?" I ask. "You mean he hollers like this every day?"

The cable guy frowns. "Y'all not Christian?"

"No. We're, uh, spiritualists."

"Like Scientology?"

"What? No! We . . . just believe in a higher power."

He rolls his eyes. "If you say so. Cable's up but internet's gonna take a little time."

"I see abundances in your future. God knows where the money is and he wants to give it to you. God wants to touch your life! But he needs your help. And if you call now, order your free HOLY SEEDS and follow the instructions, I promise, there will be an anointing on your life. Trust me. I would not lead you wrong."

Despite the rhetoric, I'm drawn into the skeleton-looking white-haired man who seems to be on death's door, shouting with his last breath. His neck is pulsing red, skin pasty, gray eyes bulging, blue veins like ivy vines on his temples. It's like a car crash you can't turn away from.

"Everyone in Cedarville watches him," the cable guy adds. "He's a mighty prophet around here."

BEEP BEEP

8:05 a.m. ALARM: Time for your pills!

"In the name of Jesus, you will be delivered from drugs, from debt, from wickedness and sin. . . ."

By late afternoon, we have the entire house unpacked and the place is starting to look like a real home. I stand by the vent a few more times, sniffing. Nothing.

Maybe it really was just a passing . . . thing.

DING DING DING

Scattering boots thump from every corner of the house, descending the stairs and out the front door. Mr. Watson doesn't bother to say goodbye this time.

We gather around the table for dinner, scarfing down a root vegetable medley and salad. Alec makes Piper a grilled cheese sandwich and fries.

"Mom, can you pick up some more oat milk?" Sammy says between bites. "We're out."

"What? Already? Alec just bought some yesterday."

Sammy chuckles. "Well, I'm not the only one in the house using it."

"I don't drink that nasty stuff," Piper declares.

Maybe that's why Piper's so pale, the lack of nutrients. I don't think I've seen her take so much as a gummy vitamin.

She catches me staring, eyes narrowing, and picks the crust off her triangle slice.

"I saw someone last night," she says, concentrating on her plate.

Alec snags a fry. "Who?"

"I don't know. Someone in the hallway."

"What were they doing?" he asks.

She shrugs. "Just standing."

"Was it Marigold?"

I narrow my eyes. "Why would you automatically think it's me?"

Alec doesn't spare me a glance. "Just a simple question."

Yeah, a simple *loaded* question, he means. I look to Mom, who shakes her head at me, hoping to avoid confrontation.

"It wasn't Marigold, it was . . . somebody else. She said she used to live here."

Alec smiles and gives Mom a wink. "Oh. Really? Is this a new special friend?"

Piper stays quiet and builds a small fort with her fries as if she didn't just mention some stranger was hanging around the halls while we slept.

You ever wake up in bed and feel like you're not . . . alone?

As I snuggle up to the wall, my eyes pop open, skin prickling at the whispering voices surrounding me, distant and muffled. *Someone is standing at the foot of the bed*, my senses scream. Standing there, watching me dream. I sit up quick, heart racing. I'm alone. My covers are on the floor, the room freezing, the voices silent. . . .

And my door is wide open.

In the hall, no one else's door is open besides mine. It's silent, the house still asleep. But there's a light on downstairs.

Buddy trots in an infinity loop around the kitchen and family room, nose to the ground like a hunting hound.

"How the hell did you get out?" I ask before a twinkle of light catches my eye.

The glass cup is on the counter again.

I pick it up, glancing at its home on the shelf, the inside still damp with murky water. Or maybe . . . milk.

"Weird," I mumble.

CREEEEEEEAK

Buddy freezes, his tail erect.

"It's nothing, Bud, chillax," I say, rinsing off the cup before shelving it. This place is old, full of old-house noises. My toes drum against the floor. Barefoot, I can fully feel that the house is strangely uneven, the ground tilting it forward, as if trying to feed its contents to the street. The cold bites into my bare legs. I check the time: 3:19 a.m.

"Bud, let's go," I order, and head for the stairs but hit a wall of a stench so violent I gag. It's rancid. A decaying animal, a rotting corpse.

CREEEEEEEAK

This time, the sound is distinct. Sharp. And close. Like it's right next to me.

Like it's coming from the hall closet.

A chill wraps my arms in ice, fear ramping up its engine.

CREAK

"Shit," I say, and take off, scrambling back to my room, Buddy at my heels.

FOUR

"ANYTHING?"

With a yawn, I hold my phone up like a sword toward the sun on the corner of Division and Maple. Sammy grips the leash as Buddy sniffs the edges of an overgrown yard.

Three bars and several text messages from Tamara roll in.

"Enough to call Dad," I say, relieved.

Sammy grins. "Do it!"

I press call and set it on speaker. The ring is full of static but as soon as he picks up . . .

"Finally! I thought you forgot about your old man."

"Hi, Dad!" we say in unison.

"Hey! Hey! Why does it sound like you guys are underwater?"

"No service in the house."

"No internet either," Sammy adds.

"Back in the Stone Age. All right, I got a meeting in fifteen, but tell me everything!"

We update him about our new home and the less than pleasant neighbors. Dad lives in LA but he's on a long-term project in Japan. He's a contract architect who designs condos and office buildings.

"I've heard about Cedarville," he says. "Most of those homes were foreclosed in the financial crisis, people leaving in droves. Pretty awful, but it's interesting what the Sterling Foundation is trying to do. Rename the city, buy up all the properties, and develop. Some of those homes were built back in the early 1900s. Too bad most of them burned up during the riots."

"Riots?"

"Yeah. I'll tell you all about it later, but right now, guys, I have to go. Say hi to Mom and Alec for me, okay? Love y'all!"

"Love you too, Dad!"

"Oh, wait. Marigold, take me off speaker for a sec, would you?"

I give Sammy a look and walk a few paces away.

"Yup, Dad, I'm here," I say, bracing myself.

"Is everything going okay?" Dad says in that "I'm dead serious" voice.

"Yeah, everything's fine."

"Okay. Remember what we talked about, we're giving this a chance . . . and then we'll see. But you have to keep your end of the bargain. No slipups. One mark on your record is enough."

"I know, *Dad*. You don't have to remind me."

Dad grunts. "I do it because I love you, kid."

Dad clicks off and I type "Cedarville" into Google. I don't know why I didn't do this before. Caught up in the prospect of leaving everything behind, I didn't even consider what hellhole I could be walking into.

"What are you doing now?" Sammy asks.

"Fact-checking." I sigh. "Dude, isn't it weird we're in the middle of a city and have such shitty cell service?"

Sammy shrugs as a grin grows across his face.

"Hey," he says, nodding over his shoulder. "Let's check it out."

I follow his line of sight to the corner house, its chipping white paint flaking over red wood. A ripped curtain waves at us through the busted bay window.

"You lunatic! No WAY am I going in there!"

"But it's an empty house. Like the ones Dad used to design."

"Those were brand-new homes. This is an abandoned one filled with other people's trash."

"Exactly why we should check it out! It'll be like exploring. Come on! I just want to see what it's like inside! Aren't you even a little curious? You can probably take some really cool pictures."

In theory, I should set a good example as the big sister and tell him no, that it's too dangerous. But I am hella curious. Who lived here before? And why did they leave everything behind? What was the rush?

My breath catches as I stare at the boarded-up door.

Probably thousands of bedbugs in there. . . .

Sammy measures my reaction. "As soon as we're out, I promise, we'll burn our clothes."

I nod. "Plus, hot showers and full-body scans."

"Done deal!"

Sammy ties Bud to a broken mailbox at the property line. We wade through the hip-deep weeds, bees and gnats fighting over their territory. Closer to the porch I stumble, tripping over a hidden step.

"Careful," I warn Sammy as we climb up, already having second thoughts but no way I'd let him go in without me. A little reefer would've made this adventure a bit more manageable. Sammy peers into the broken window as I scan the neighboring houses. There is an eerie silence when you live on an empty block. It's not a cabin-in-the-woods type of feeling. More . . . unsettling because you know there should be people nearby. You can almost sense a shadow of their presence. But there's no one. We're isolated.

The door is nothing more than an old piece of plywood, warped and weatherworn. Sammy shoves it with his shoulder. It huffs a breath and creaks open. The broken windows allow just enough light to shine into a living room, painted in volcanic ash. Or that's how thick the gray dust seems to be.

"Whoa," Sammy whispers. "It's like they just left . . . everything."

We split apart, navigating around cast-aside furniture,

crumbling paint chips, broken dishes, ripped lampshades, a two-legged table, empty bookcases, and an old wooden TV, its screen smashed in.

"Dude, this is way cool," I say.

Pulling out my phone, I angle and take the perfect shot. No one has seen these types of TVs in decades.

On the staircase leading to the second floor, every step has piles of random junk blocking the path upstairs—holey shoes, a mattress, rotting stuffed animals, and tires.

Sammy tests a locked door near the stairs. I rub the chill off my arms as we walk deeper in.

This place seems . . . familiar.

In the middle of the living room, a red sofa is cocked on its side, half-burnt, covered in mold.

FACT: Bedbugs lay eggs along the cracks and crevices of your sofa.

"Sammy, don't touch anything!" I shout.

Sammy jumps in his skin. "Ah! I'm not! Geez."

"Are you sniffling? Is it your allergies? We should go."

Sammy steps over some broken floorboards to check out a fallen mirror. "Dude, would you relax? This place is awesome!"

Something crunches under my foot. Crackers. A dusting of fresh ones. I follow their trail into the next room. Bright sunshine explodes from the open kitchen into a narrow dining room with a brick fireplace. In the corner is a green sleeping bag, aged and covered in dust.

Sammy creeps behind me.

"Squatters," I mumble, inspecting an open can of soup with the tip of my sneaker.

"What does that mean?"

"Someone, like a homeless person, was living here," I explain. "Sort of like camping out in a house that's not theirs."

"Someone was living in here . . . like this? Why?"

I shrug. "If you got nowhere else to go, why not take shelter in an empty house?"

Sammy gazes around. "Hey, this place kinda reminds me of our house."

There is charred wood in the hearth of the blackened fireplace, the dusty mantel carved with intricate flowers and some sort of family crest.

I snap a shot, testing a few filters before a creak above our heads makes my neck snap.

"What was that?" Sammy gasps.

Footsteps. Quiet ones, coming from upstairs. Someone's in the house! The sleeping bag, the open cans . . . shit, I should have known.

I push Sammy behind me, scanning the room for a weapon. A bat, rock, a glass bottle I could break, anything. Sammy clutches the back of my shirt.

Another crunch, a foot on broken glass. Much closer this

time. Heart surging, I take another step back, hiding us behind the kitchen wall. Broken chairs and scrap metal barricade the back door. With no clear path to the front door, we'll never make it out before whoever it is reaches the bottom of those steps.

"Mari," Sammy whimpers, and I bring a finger to my lips, pointing to the broken kitchen window. I could push him through, give him a chance to run for help. Sammy shakes his head, but I silently insist. He pleads again as I drape my hoodie over the broken glass to keep it from cutting him. And just as I'm ready to hoist him up, Piper rounds the corner.

"SHIT!" I cough out. "Piper!"

"You said a bad word," Piper shouts, pointing.

"What the fuck were you thinking, playing upstairs!"

"I wasn't upstai—"

"Dude, you're ten," Sammy laughs. "Back in my day, I threw a few curse words around without a second thought."

Piper narrows her eyes. "You shouldn't curse. Grandma says people who curse are stupid."

Sammy rolls his eyes. "Whatever."

"That wasn't funny, Piper! You scared the crap out of us," I snap.

"Yeah," Sammy adds. "And why don't you make noise when you walk like a regular human instead of creeping around like a cat?"

"I thought you were allergic to cats?" she shoots back.

"Ha, she got you there," I chuckle. "But really, what are you doing here?"

Piper struggles to come up with something but instead puffs her cheeks. "*You* shouldn't be in here."

"Oh, did your *grandma* tell you that?"

Piper's face falls, the wind knocked out of her. She toggles from Sammy to me, then back, eyes flooding with tears, before running out the front door. Sammy tilts his head back with a whistle.

"Dude, that was savage."

"I know," I grumble. "Low blow, but I'm sick of her shit."

"You know Ms. Tattletale is going to rat us out, right?"

I sigh. "Yeah. I know."

Piper sits on the porch steps for the rest of the afternoon, waiting for Alec to come home. Contract workers don't miss a beat, maneuvering around her like water around a rock, loading new building materials, racing against some imaginary clock.

Mom busies herself in the kitchen, making our favorite: black bean burgers on sweet potato slices with zucchini fries. Mom used to be a meat eater before Sammy was born and we learned he was allergic to the world. She switched gears, studied nutrition, and learned how to make everything from cauliflower crust to vegan butter.

"We should have internet by Friday," Mom says, grabbing a plate of veggie snacks with garlic hummus from the fridge, laying them out on the counter.

"Best news I heard all week," I mumble.

"And no wonder Irma's pushing for it," she says, scrolling through her phone. "I swear that woman has sent more than a dozen emails and invites. School district functions, board meetings, then a kickoff benefit. I haven't even written ten words for that *New York Times* piece due on Friday. Between the move, deadlines, and these contractors . . . Hey, have you seen my zucchini spiralizer?"

"No."

"Hm. I know I unpacked it. Feels like I'm going crazy, I keep misplacing things."

I glance at the porch, at Piper sitting upright on the steps, clearly listening in through the screen door.

That little asshole.

I move to slam the front door and see Mr. Watson in the sitting room, packing up some tools. It wasn't until he shifted the ladder propped on the wall that I noticed the intricate carvings on the fireplace, newly stained.

"Hey, Mr. Watson," I say, drawn to it.

He glances up, nods, and continues wrapping up his saw.

I trace a finger around the family crest.

Same as in the other house. . . .

If this house was in similar condition to the house on the corner, it would've been easier to just demolish and start from scratch. Except they didn't; they kept it. Almost as if they wanted it to stay the same.

"Mr. Watson, have you worked on all the houses in this neighborhood?"

He shakes his head. "Nope. First time I've been over here since I was a boy."

"Why did they decide to renovate rather than just tear this place down?"

He takes a swig of water, avoiding my eyes. "Don't know. Took over for Smith, who took over for Davis, who replaced all the pipes that were stolen."

"Stolen?"

"Yeah, folks like to steal house materials, bring them down to the scrapyard. You can get good money for copper pipes. Davis switched everything to plastic."

"So, there were three separate contract companies working on this house over the last year?"

"The last four months, actually. There were more."

"Why so many?"

He hesitates before shrugging and returning to his work.

A new boiler and plastic pipes mean the perfect water temperature for wash day.

As steam swirls, fogging up the bathroom mirrors, I detangle my twist out, examining the welt under my eye. Maybe I could cover it up with makeup, the thick kind I used to use when acne left craters on my face.

The last time I washed my hair was in California water, and the style survived the move. But no telling what it'll do here. Gonna need to try a few styles before school starts so I don't end up the butt of some stupid jokes. Bad enough I'm walking in there as the new girl during her junior year. I also want to kick myself for wondering if Yusef will be in any of my classes. Shouldn't be worried about boys while I'm on the road to self-healing. Boys are nothing but distractions.

Still, he's nice to look at.

I lift the knob above the faucet. The showerhead hums before water coughs out a steady stream. I step into the tub, pulling closed the shower curtain with a picture of a giant sunflower. Mom chose to decorate most of the house in bright yellows, blues, and oranges to remind us of sunnier, warmer days. My room will remain stark white, light enough for me to check for bedbugs.

The warm cascading water soaking through my hair is heaven on my scalp. That "ahhhh" feeling never gets old. I relish the natural massage with a few deep breaths, and just as I lean my head back and close my eyes, the water vanishes.

"What the hell?"

The knob for the shower is down, water racing out of the faucet, kicking the backs of my heels. I pull it back up and continue with my regimen—two washes with sulfate-free peppermint shampoo, fifteen-minute deep conditioner, then detangling with a wide-tooth comb before a cold-water rinse.

I'm elbows deep in suds when the shower shuts off again and a cool breeze hits my neck, making me shiver. Weird. It hasn't done this before. I lift the knob once more, jiggling it into place.

Just let me get through this last wash. . . .

It stays, giving me enough time to wash the soap out from roots to tip. I stick my head under the pouring water and take another deep breath, wishing it was ocean water instead of Cedarville's best tap.

Will I ever see the beach again? Do I even want to?

I open one eye to reach for the deep conditioner and see a shadow through the curtain as a shaky hand reaches for the knob.

"AHHHH!"

I reel back, hitting my head on the tile wall, and slip, catching air before landing on my ass. Ooof! Water shoots down on my face, filling my nostrils and mouth, until I scramble onto my hands and knees, shutting it off.

I snatch back the curtain, heart pounding. No one. The bathroom is empty. But the door is wide open, softly swinging into the wall.

Within seconds, I hop out of the shower, wrap myself in a towel, and rush into the hallway.

Sammy's back is to me, heading toward his room.

"Hey!"

He swivels, hands loaded with various snacks and an apple

in his mouth like he's a pig about to be roasted at the bonfire.

"That wasn't funny, Sammy! You scared the shit out of me."

"Huh?"

"Don't 'huh' me. That prank was hella weak."

He drops two bags of popcorn on the floor, freeing a hand to grab the apple silencing him. "Prank? Do I look like someone who has time for pranks?"

Soapy suds drip down my hair onto the carpet. My pulse a drum.

"SOMEONE was just in the bathroom. SOMEONE kept turning off the freaking water."

"Ew. Why would I be in the bathroom with you *naked*? That's all kinds of gross."

"Sammy, I'm serious!"

He rolls his eyes. "Okay, well, what did this *someone* look like?"

"I don't know! My eyes were closed."

"You saw someone with your eyes closed?"

"It's . . . hard to explain, Sammy," I gasp, realizing I was holding my breath. I grip my chest, trying to loosen the tightness in my lungs.

Sammy drops the sarcasm and the rest of his snacks, leading me into my room as I pinch my towel together, trying to gather air with a free hand. I sit on the bed, putting my head between my legs, and inhale the lemongrass essential oil I dab on my palm.

Sammy passes my inhaler, shaking his head. "You sure you didn't just get soap in your eye and freak yourself out?"

I take two puffs, letting the mist drift down my throat. Honestly, I hadn't thought of that. But even if the knob fell on its own . . . I know I wasn't alone in that bathroom.

Damn, I really wish I hadn't smoked that last blunt.

"No. Sammy, someone was there. There was a hand. . . ."

"Well, it wasn't me."

The thought hits us separately and we turn to Piper's open door.

Piper stares back at us from the edge of her bed, legs swinging. She doesn't say a word, but something makes it clear she's not even the least bit curious about what's going on.

She already knows.

FIVE

TAMARA'S BRIGHT SHINING face pops up on my MacBook screen after the third ring.

"Dude! Finally!"

"Hey, hey," I say, closing the door. "What's up? Service is still hella shitty but at least I can communicate with the outside world. Feels like it's been forever!"

"Dude, it's been decades!"

"Centuries."

"Millenniums."

"Eons!"

We laugh, and I notice a silver stud twinkle on her right nostril. A new piercing? Why did she wait until I was gone to do that? Did she go with someone else? Another friend? I scratch the inside of my arm and check my skin.

FACT: Bedbug bites appear as red, itchy bumps on the skin, usually on the arms or shoulders. Most bedbug bites are painless at first, but later turn into itchy welts.

"OMG, your room is huge," Tamara says, looking past me. "It's like three times the size of your old one. Are you guys rich now or something? I thought writers don't make any money."

"Shut up," I say, throwing popcorn at the screen.

"So! How's the rest of the house?"

"It's nice, I guess, but kindaaaaa creepy. Feels like I'm sleeping in someone else's bed, in their sheets, the toilet seat still warm as if they just took a shit. And I swear at night, I can hear things moving."

She chuckles. "You sure it's not just the fam or Bud?"

"No way. Even Buddy's on edge. And it doesn't help that we're surrounded by all these old decrepit houses. Oh, hey, before I forget, my dad said you can come visit us in LA during Christmas break."

"Um, yeah. I'll have to see," she says, avoiding my eyes as she checks her phone. "You know my entire family comes around then, so . . . you know how it goes."

Tamara has approximately one billion cousins, aunts, and uncles. I miss the warmth of her home, her mom's rice and beans and Mexican creamed corn. Living so close to one another, we were more like family than best friends. But I at least thought she'd be able to come for a few days. She knows I can't go back to Carmel . . . maybe ever.

"Anyway, so what else's been going on? And what the hell happened to your face?"

I give her the rundown of the last week, including being

knocked out by Yusef.

"Dude, he was totally hitting on you, literally! I mean, he talked *gardening*, that's practically foreplay. Better than David's cornball ass."

"DON'T say his name."

Tamara blinks. "Sorry. Habit."

The fan above my head spins with a click, underscoring the awkward silence. I clear my throat and change subjects.

"And of course, Piper is as annoying as ever."

"That's what little sisters are supposed to do, silly. But what are you going to do about your . . . uh . . . other problem?"

I lower the volume on my computer and lean closer. "You mean my lack of bud? I don't know. But from what I've read, drugs definitely hit this city hard, so I'm bound to find a hookup at school."

"Maybe your new boyfriend could help," she teases.

I point to the welt on my face. "Dude, this is not the best way to start a romance."

"You'll have a funny story to share on Insta for your one-year anniversary."

"I rather take my chances with strangers."

Tamara sighs. "Just . . . be careful, Mari. You don't want to get caught up again."

"I wasn't caught up, Tamara," I say, hard. "I was *poisoned*."

"Um, yeah. Right, sorry. Hey! You know . . . why don't you grow it yourself!"

I tilt my head to the left. "Dude, are you baked right now?"

"No, seriously, I was watching some show on YouTube about weed farmers, how they turned their backyards into the garden of good and evil. You could be your own supplier! Then you wouldn't have to worry about getting it from some stranger."

"Dude, I can't grow weed in my backyard. Mom would kill me!"

"Who said anything about *your* backyard," she smirks. "You said you're surrounded by empty houses. Choose one."

For a moment, I'm dumbstruck by the brilliance of her idea.

"I can't . . . or . . . well, I would need the right supplies. . . ."

"Ha! And it seems like you know the right man to give them to you."

I swallow, unable to hold the thought back any longer.

"Well . . . have you seen him?" I ask begrudgingly. "The cornball?"

Tamara nibbles on her lower lip, braiding her shiny black hair. "Just online. Track practice started up this week."

"What! They let *him* back on the team?"

"Well, um . . . he did make regionals last year."

"So did I! And I'm twice as good as that asshole!"

She shakes her head. "Why don't you just join the team there? You're fast as shit, they'll probably let you walk on with no prob."

I hesitate. "Nah."

She chuckles. "Okay. Then what are you going to do?"

Nothing. Absolutely nothing. After the past few months, all I want is freedom. Doesn't mean I want to go out partying at some raging kegger, smoke myself up to the moon. Just means I want to not be under my parents' thumbs 24-7 for a change. That's why the more chill I seem, the more chill they become, the more freedom I win.

The bedroom door clicks and slowly creaks open. Tamara frowns, leaning in to see past me.

"Uh, Mari . . ."

"Yeah, I know. Doors open here on their own all the time. The contractor said they're just 'old locks.'"

"Um, holy Ghostbusters, Batman. That's not normal."

I sigh. "I know."

"Piper, you feeling okay?" Mom asks. "You look a little . . . tired."

Mom watches Piper play with her cereal, a twinge of concern in her eye.

"I'm fine," she spits.

Piper does look tired. I've never met a ten-year-old with bags under their eyes. She also looks paler and slightly on the thinner side than I remember. Not that I've paid much attention to her.

As I slip on some shoes, my phones buzzes on the counter.

"It's Dad!" Sammy says, and presses accept. "Hi, Dad!"

"Hey, Dad," I say. "You're on speaker."

"Heyyy! Trying to catch you guys before the first day of school."

"Mom's here too!" Sammy chimes in eagerly, pushing Mom closer to the phone.

"Oh! Hey, Raq," Dad says. "How are our offspring?"

"You mean when they're not eating everything in the fridge? They're doing okay," Mom says, tickling Sammy's side.

"Sounds like they're taking after me."

Alec walks into the kitchen with his gym bag, kissing Piper on the head.

"Who's that?" he asks.

"Chay," Mom says. "Calling from Japan."

"Oh! Hey, brother! How are you?"

"Alec! Doing good! Just eating my weight in sushi. How's the new gig?"

I wish I was annoyed that Dad and Alec are sort of buddies, but . . . it's actually kinda cool. No weirdness or tension that I can see, but I once asked him about it during a game of chess.

"Hey, Dad, why are you trying to be cool with the jerk stealing your wife and kids?"

Dad laughed. "I love your mom, I want her to be happy. We weren't really happy together and no one deserves part-time love from a guy traveling all over the world. So if this guy makes her happy, then I want him to know that he's all right in my book."

Sammy's brows furrow, watching Alec talk. He's less than enthused.

"Oh, hey, Alec, did you get my text?" Dad asks.

"Yup! Just about to deliver it. Hang on, while you're on the line."

"Nah, man, you go ahead. I'll catch up with you later."

Dad says his goodbyes as Alec runs into the hallway.

"What was all that about?" Mom asks.

Alec opens the closet and retrieves a red shoebox from the top shelf. He walks back in, beaming, before holding it out to me.

"Here you go! Your dad asked me to surprise you!"

I stare at the box, blinking. Mom's face lights up.

"What's this?"

"New sneakers," he says, grinning. "For track! He thought you might need some."

Oh no.

Thoughts whirlwind and I lick my lips. "Um, thanks, but . . . I'm not doing track."

Alec's face falls. "What?"

"You can return them if you'd like. I'm sure they were expensive."

The rooms freezes around me. Too many questioning looks. I quickly grab my bag, duck around Alec, and head for the door.

"Mari," Mom says, following me, her tone clipped. "You don't want to do track?"

"I . . . just want to focus on my healing this year. I don't need any distractions."

Mom opens her mouth but I quickly cut her off.

"Anyways, gotta go, don't want to be late!"

• • •

Here's the first thing that I noticed about Kings High School: it's old. Like, seats attached to mini desks, green blackboards old. Lockers the color of liver; most of the textbooks coverless; a computer lab from the dinosaur ages. Not much wood to worry about, so at least I won't be a total freak inspecting my seat every day.

The second thing I noticed: the kids. On first glance, you'd think this was an all-girls' school. It's not that I'm looking for boys, but you could practically smell the estrogen permeating the air. By lunch, I counted no more than six boys, total. Yusef being one of them, surrounded by a pack of groupies, participating in some kind of fashion contest for his attention. I keep my head down and my distance.

The third thing I noticed: the smell. It didn't stink but it had a musty scent that reminded me of a nursing home. And yet, all day I spent sniffing the unfamiliar halls, classrooms, the dimly lit gym. Sniffing kept me occupied enough to ignore the few mumbles hitting my back.

"That's that new girl who lives on Maple Street. . . ."

"What happened to her face?"

But I wasn't smelling the school for a whiff of nostalgia. I was sniffing for . . . something specific.

Right before last period, with my nostrils full of dust, I catch a faint whiff of it. A girl with long braids and an oversized jean jacket wrapped in that familiar sweet, tangy scent mixed with fiery smoke.

Just the kind of smoke I'm looking for.

She treks down the hall in her headphones and I follow, straight into a narrow bathroom with two stalls. *Shit.*

"Uh, hey," I say at the sink, awkwardly washing my hands, realizing I don't have a game plan.

"Heyyyy," she says, squeezing drops in the corners of her eyes. The smell is even stronger with her bag open.

I'm trash at the whole "making friends with complete strangers" thing, so I blurt out the only thing I can think of.

"Um, you got a tampon?"

She chuckles. "Girl, that was weak as hell. You gotta do better than that." She faces me. "Did you know elephants are pregnant for two years and pretty much give birth through their butts? Imagine having to carry a load of shit for a whole two years." She pauses with a grin. "See? Now that's how you strike up a convo. Oh, the name's Erika."

Relieved, I smile. "Marigold."

"I know," she laughs. "There ain't no one in this school who doesn't know your name."

"I'm playing right into the New Girl in Town cliché, aren't I?"

"Yup. You're fresh competition."

"Competition?"

"If you haven't noticed, we're a pussy-heavy population."

"Glad it's not just my imagination. You're not threatened?"

She grins. "We're not playing on the same team, boo."

We walk into the hall and I'm comforted by her familiar scent. Comforted enough to ask for a hit. But . . . Tamara's voice is in my head, telling me to be careful. Erika is still a stranger, and if this move has taught me anything, it is to tread lightly with people you don't know.

With the day done, I'm pretty proud of myself for surviving unscathed and making at least one new friend. That is, until I hear a familiar voice call my name.

"Cali, what's up!"

Oh no. . . .

Yusef jogs in my direction, smiling, and the entire hallway freezes. The eyes of every single girl zero in on us. Erika raises an eyebrow.

"Welp, that's my cue," she chuckles. "Catch you later."

I squirm as she runs off, working fast to pack up my bag and grab my AirPods. A girl walking by bumps into my shoulder, a scowl on her face.

"Seriously?" Are we in middle school?

Yusef stops behind me as I slam my locker shut.

"Hey," I mutter, speed walking toward the front doors, but he follows.

"What up doe? Haven't seen you all day!"

"It's a pretty big school," I grumble, avoiding eye contact.

"Damn, girl," he says, finger circling my welt. "You bruise easy."

I shoot him daggers. "It's soooo not funny."

"Well, at least you came to school looking tough."

"Or looking like I got my ass beat."

He chuckles. "I'd lean them the other way and make 'em guess. So? How you liking it?"

We bust through the front doors with the entire population of Kings High watching us.

"It's school. What's there to like," I say, taking the steps two at a time.

"Good point," he laughs. "Walk you home? We can compare A and B day schedules."

I stop short to face him, keeping my voice down. "Dude, no way!"

"What?"

"Do you want me to get my ass beat for real?"

"Girl, what are you talking about?"

I glance over my shoulder, feeling the whispering voices on my back. Cliques of girls gather on the front steps, mumbling to each other, their eyes frosty.

"Just . . . stay away from me, Yusef. Seriously."

Yusef stares, dumbfounded. "Um. Okay."

Then I'm rushing away, fast. With a twinge of guilt threatening to catch up to me.

"And they have a science club. And a sci-fi club. And a code club!"

Sammy talks fast over a plate of carrot sticks, book bag still hanging off his shoulders.

"See? Told you you'd like it there," Mom says, sliding a bowl of oatmeal across the counter, his favorite afternoon snack. "And how was your first day, Piper?"

Piper doesn't look up from her Lunchable, remaining silent.

"Oooo . . . kay! And what about you, my other minion?"

I shrug. "I survived."

"Must feel . . . different," Mom says. "After the last few months of homeschooling."

"I guess," I mumble, popping a handful of grapes into my mouth. "They don't take cards in the lunchroom so I'm going to need some cash."

Mom stares for a beat, wheels spinning. "They . . . have a school account. I'll send a check."

"Seriously? I'm just buying lunch. You can't trust me to do that?"

Mom quickly pivots, putting the kettle on the stove. "It's just easier this way. Right?"

She still doesn't trust me with money. Guess I don't blame her.

"Gonna go for a run," I announce through gritted teeth.

I lace up my sneakers on the front porch and stretch my calves. Running releases toxins in the organs through sweating. It's not track meets, but it's a decent substitute. And I'm hoping it at least curbs the weed cravings gnawing on my tongue.

Across Sweetwater, the other side of Maple Street is idyllic compared to our side. There's at least some resemblance of life. Old men watering half-dead lawns, women on porches, kids playing in driveways, the smell of charcoal burning through the air, a casual afternoon. But the moment I jog by, all the reverie is cut short, shut off like a yanked TV plug.

The stares hit my skin and sink into my bloodstream. Reminds me of the day after my arrest. How the whole school stopped to watch me clean out my locker, flanked by police escorts. Megan O'Connell threatened to bomb the school and she was only sent to the nurse's office.

I turn my music up and push myself harder, trying to burn all the thoughts—the girls at school, Yusef's face, the image of that hand reaching into the shower—out of my frontal lobe. It was just my imagination, I keep telling myself over and over again. The exhaustion and new environment are playing tricks on me. There was no hand.

But . . . its skin was dark and charred like burnt plastic, nails black with dirt . . .

How could I make something like that up? If I was still on the Percs, I could've blamed it on a crazy trip. Damn, I could really use some weed. I know I made a promise to Dad, but it's the only thing that helps my anxiety. Surrounded by emaciated houses, with no cell phone service, a jerk of a stepfather, and strangers creeping in the bathroom—he can't really expect me to just deal in these types of conditions. Weed would at least take the edge off and make me a functional human.

My jog morphs into a sprint, muscles not warm enough, but I push them harder . . . with weed heavy on my mind.

Something is trying to break into my room.

It's scratching at my door, feverish and desperate. Hungry. I'm familiar with that type of hunger.

Okay okay okay if I can just get Mom's door open, I can get that sixty dollars I saw yesterday, then I . . . come on! Open!

I stir and blink in the darkness, lips dry, mouth parched. I sit up in bed, clenching my fists to keep them from trembling. The door shakes again, violently. Now fully awake, I crawl closer to the end of the bed.

Buddy is in downward dog, clawing at the door's sill.

"Ugh! Bud! You're killing me!"

New 10:00 a.m. ALARM: Buy Buddy new chew toys before I leave him on the side of the highway.

Buddy scratches harder, whining, staring back at me as if to say, "Are you really just going to sit there?"

"Buddy! Stop it. There's no one—"

But then I think of the friend Piper mentioned . . . and that hand in the shower. The door creaks loud as I open it a crack, peering into the dark hall. Buddy shoves his nose between my legs, and darts out, sprinting down the steps.

"Buddy," I shout under my breath, trying not to wake up the whole house. But there's a light on downstairs.

Thought I turned those off.

I tiptoe after him, following the light into the kitchen. Empty. So is the family room. No way my earth-conscious mom would ever leave the lights on like this. Must have been Alec.

The cup is on the counter again.

Buddy paces in front of the basement door, sniffing, nose jabbing at the bottom. Time on the microwave, 3:19 a.m.

Am I ever gonna get a good night's sleep in this place?

Who am I kidding? I haven't had a decent night's sleep in over a year.

Yawning, I pour myself some water. The windows facing the backyard are like black voids, a draft whistling through the cracks. Outside, something is staring at me. Or someone. I can't see them but I feel them there. Waiting . . .

Why is it always so damn cold in this house?

Buddy turns, giving me the classic puppy-dog eyes with a whimper.

"Forget it! I'm not going down to the cellar of doom in the middle of the night."

Buddy flops his tail, crying again.

"Ugh, Bud, there's nothing down there, look!"

I yank the basement door and it jerks me forward. Locked. Locked? It wasn't locked the other day. The knob is old, brass, screws loose, the keyhole ancient. I yank it again. Definitely locked, but feels like it's from the inside.

How is that even possible?

"Alec must . . . have the key or something," I tell Buddy, letting go of the handle.

That's when I smell it again. A mix of funk and . . . death. It's stronger now, like a cloud hovering over my face.

CREEEEAK

Am I losing it, or did something . . . just move behind the door?

I take two steps back, listening to the silence.

A loud THUMP hits the door, shaking it in its frame. A yelp escapes me and Bud whimpers. Something definitely shook that door. But that's crazy talk because there's nothing down there.

It's a draft. There's probably a window open. . . .

"Bud, come on," I snap, never taking my eyes off the door. "It's way past your bedtime."

I grab his collar and head for the stairs, but on step one . . .

"AHHH!"

Piper is at the top of the staircase in her pink pajamas, glaring down at me, face hidden in the shadows.

"Shit, Piper! What are you doing?!"

She stands there for several beats in silence. Just staring motionless. I take a step toward her and a large shadow behind her seems to shift. My body stiffens.

"Piper?"

A long, impossible noise echoes out of her mouth, like

crumbling metal. Ear-piercing and terrifying. Then she leaps, floating through the air, landing in a perch on my chest, slamming me into the front door. My head bangs against the wood and I briefly see stars before we slide down to the floor, Piper on top of me. Her eyes are black holes, bloody veins hanging out of their sockets like ripped roots. Black blood oozes from her mouth. I try to scream, to move, but I'm frozen.

Her little hands tighten around my throat, thumbs pressing against my voice box. She's strong, her fingers icy. I strain, unable to feel my legs, my arms, or anything. The room grows darker as my lips flap like a fish gasping for air.

And then I'm up, slapping air, gasping and sweating. Buddy looks up from his ball on the end of the bed, annoyed I disturbed him.

Dream. It was just a dream.

Heart pounding, I leap out of bed and lock the door, checking the hidden pocket in my book bag. The place I used to keep my stash.

Empty. I knew it would be but was hoping for a miracle.

God, I need some weed.

My bouncing knee rattles the metal kitchen stool as I stare at the basement door. It's locked. Just like it was last night. Usually, bedbugs are the star of my nightmares. So what if that wasn't a dream?

Stop it. You sound crazy!

"Well. What's her 'friend's' name?" Mom asks.

"Ms. Suga," Alec says, popping a handful of raspberries into his mouth. "It's cute. Says she's an old Black woman who likes to bake apple pies."

I need to smoke I need to smoke I need to smoke.

Mom cuts up bananas for our morning smoothies, a wrinkle of worry above her brow.

"Alec, she's ten," Mom says. "Isn't she a little . . . old to have imaginary friends?"

A blunt, a gummy, a bong, a hit. Anything. Everything. I need weed weed weed.

Alec straightens, quick to come to Piper's defense.

"With all the recent changes . . . marriage, the move, new school . . . I expected it to come out somehow. She had imaginary friends like this before, when my mother died."

"Yes, but . . . maybe we should have her talk to someone. I agree there's been a lot of changes, but given her close relationship with her late grandmother . . ."

weed weed weed weed

Alec places his coffee mug down, hard, before walking off.

"Sure," he mumbles. "We can send her to the same place Marigold goes."

The struggle not to react is real as I push away from the kitchen isle. I'm losing control. And if I lose control, they'll see it, they'll know . . . and they can't or I'll be back on lockdown.

My terrarium sits on the windowsill facing the backyard, where the light is less harsh. I used to have dozens of these, taking up all spare surfaces in our home. Every window, desk, and bathroom countertop had a piece of paradise I created. Now, this is the only one I have left that survived . . . well, me, and I'm clinging to it like a lifeline.

"You can build again," my guru suggested after I'd swept up the glass and soil.

Maybe I can. Maybe I can build a whole new type of garden.

At the edge of the backyard, I stab a trowel into the ground and scoop up a piece of earth, rubbing the soil between my fingers. It's moist, slightly clayish and stony. Even if Tamara mailed me the seeds tomorrow, the weather here is different than in Cali. I would need at least eight weeks before I could harvest, but an early cold front could kill all the seedlings in one morning.

I'll also need topsoil, fertilizer, a watering hose, containers, and an 8-x-4-foot raised garden bed to put this plan in action. Could probably find scraps of wood and nails from the nearby houses, but that'd only get me so far. If I had known I'd be back to gardening so soon, I would've never given all my stuff to Tamara's mom. I'll need tools, but I can't spend my own money with Mom clocking my every penny. I also need time away from Sammy and nosy Piper.

. . . every last Sunday of the month.

I grab my tote bag, rush for the door before anyone has a chance to join me.

"Going to the library!"

The Maplewood Library sits across the street from the elementary school, a few blocks from our house. It's an old redbrick building, the metal letters of the sign crying rust and there's cracks in the foggy glass door. By the entrance is a bulletin board with flyers of various business, outdated calls to meetings, and scheduled protests. A 'Brown Town Mowing Company' business card sits pinned on the top right corner. Below it, a flyer for the garden club Irma mentioned.

"Hello! Are you here for garden club?"

A woman in a bright blue T-shirt that matches her eyes and well-worn jeans smiles at me.

"Um . . . yes."

"Great, welcome! We're just about to start."

The meeting is being held in a conference room by the history section. Attendance is sparse. A few old women, four college students, and three old Black men. At the front of the room, setting up, is Yusef.

We catch eyes, and he gives me a hesitant nod. He's been keeping his distance, while I've been awkwardly avoiding eye contact just to keep girls from trashing me. I even dress down and try my best to blend into the background to avoid beef. This is supposed to be a fresh start.

Change is good. Change is necessary. Change is needed.

I sit in an empty middle row, near one of the grandmas. Okay, yeah, I know, the totally easier option would be to just ask Erika for a hookup, but like I said, I don't know Erika. Can't risk it. One more strike and I'll be shipped off to rehab like I have a real problem or something, which I totally don't. So desperate times call for desperate measures.

The woman who greeted me takes center stage.

"Hello, everyone, welcome! We have a new member today, so hi! My name is Laura Fern. Yes, that's my real last name, and yes, I love a good fern. Welcome to our urban garden club."

Laura gives updates regarding new developments in upcoming projects, trends in planting, and planned trips to a farm out in the suburbs.

"I'm also pleased to report that we are *this* close to approval for a house on Maple Street, which will host our nonprofit city beautification initiative, with a generous donation by the Sterling Foundation. Renovations will start as early as November."

Damn, the Sterling Foundation has their hands in every jar.

"And I think that's about everything. As usual, tools are in the shed."

A toolshed . . . perfect.

"We leave in fifteen minutes. Carpool assignments are on the board. See ya there!"

Class is dismissed and people congregate at the board. I turn to a neighbor, an old Black woman wearing a beautiful auburn wig and a bright smile.

"Um, excuse me. Where's the toolshed?"

"Out by the parking lot."

Slowly, I shuffle backward out of the room, trying not to draw attention to myself. Once outside, I speed walk around the building to a shed sitting in the grassy knolls at the edge of a crumbling parking lot. The padlock hanging off the side, I swing the door open and stand in awe. The tools are gorgeous. Brand-new rakes, hoes, garden shears, shovels in every size. Even a mower.

"Perfect," I mumble.

"So, uh, I hope you don't mind rolling with me?"

Yusef stands behind me, dangling the keys to his truck as folks from the meeting pile into each other's cars.

"All the other cars are full," he explains. "We weren't expecting a new member today."

"Rolling . . . where?" I ask.

"For today's project. We're planting some trees on the freeway."

"Oh, uhhh . . . sorry. Maybe another time."

Yusef frowns, his voice turning serious. "Yo, that's how it works, Cali. You volunteer, you get free use of the tools and all the compost and soil you want. So, you coming, or nah?"

I weigh my options with a huff. "You got leather seats?"

FACT: Bedbugs prefer cloth to leather.

We drive a few minutes in silence and I'm once again wishing alcohol was my drug of choice so I didn't have to jump through all these damn hoops. I hate hangovers and beer looks like foamy piss.

But I don't mind going for a ride, gives me a chance to really take in my surroundings—the trash in the abandoned lots, crumbling old churches, rubble of foundations peeking through tall weeds. For the briefest moments, I forgot I'm not on vacation, that I actually *live* here, in a whole other city, miles away from everything and everyone I've ever known, among the wreckage of . . . what? I'm not even sure. It's like a bomb exploded here that no one ever reported.

"Guessing you decided to start that garden after all," Yusef says.

"Uh, yeah," I admit, scratching my arm, out of habit.

"Well, my offer still stands. You gonna need a good cultivator to work that yard. We don't have one in the shed, but you can borrow mine from home."

I'm about to blow him off when it hits me: I need him. He knows how to work the land around here. Probably the best resource I could ask for next to Google.

"Yeah, that'd be cool. Thanks. And I, uh, sorry that it's all . . . weird and stuff at school. It's just that I'm new and really don't want any trouble, you know?"

He follows the caravan of cars down the freeway. "Yeah, I get it, I guess."

I laugh. "You guess that seventy-five percent of the girls in our high school *want* you? Humble flex."

He smirks, turning up his music. "It's not as cool as it looks."

Closer to downtown, we pull off near a stadium, parking behind a large truck with eight new baby trees in the bed. The garden club starts unloading stacks of soil and tools. From this position off the freeway, we're closer to those large gray cement blocks I saw when we first arrived in Cedarville.

"Hey, what are those buildings over there?" I ask Yusef. "They're, like, really huge! Are they factories?"

Yusef follows my gaze and his smile drops, jaw tightening.

"Those are prisons," he says, hard.

"ALL of them?"

He snatches a shovel out of the truck bed, storming away. "Yeah."

The garden club spends the afternoon digging deep holes and planting the new trees along the freeway exit, the place looking instantly better for it. It's kind of nice, doing something useful, being a productive member of society rather than a screwup. Or at least how I feel, how my parents' disappointment makes me feel. They don't say it, but I know. It's written on their faces.

Yusef is quiet, keeping his back to the blocks as we work. He strips off his hoodie and . . . damn. Dude is kinda ripped under that tank top.

Stop staring, you idiot!

When we're done, he gives me a tired smile. "Ready to go home?"

Yusef's tree-lined block is almost identical to ours, except the houses aren't abandoned relics. They're well lived in, peaceful, the porches perfect inviting spots for some fresh mint iced tea. But the calm is interrupted by the reverend's eerie voice, blaring out of open windows.

"And I say unto you, be mindful of sinners dressed like angels. For they will take you on a wrong path."

Yusef's house is in the middle of the block, a brown one-story colonial with a picture-perfect lawn, lush front garden, and a birdy on the mailbox. I recognize Mr. Brown's truck in the driveway, dripping dry after a recent wash.

"Is that the new girl?" Mr. Brown emerges from the shadows, wiping off his hands. "Thought I recognized you."

"Hi, Mr. Brown."

"Well, come on in. Want a pop?"

Inside is a sweet, homey trip to the past. A jar full of strawberry hard candies and white Life Saver mints greet us at the door. Pictures in brass gold frames hanging in the wallpapered hallway. A canary-yellow sofa set with a pea-green recliner facing an old TV, where I can see the top of a brown bald head as Scott Clark's voice bellows . . .

"Are you of faith? Are you of healing? Trust in the Church of Jesus Christ. . . ."

"Who's that there?" a rusty voice asks.

At first, I thought the old man was referring to Clark, but he swivels his recliner in my direction.

"Pop-Pop, this is Marigold," Yusef says. "Family just moved over on Maple."

The old man gives me a once-over. "Maple Street, huh? Humph."

Mr. Brown comes out of the kitchen with two cans of ginger ale.

"Here you go. You can have a seat."

The couch looks like it's from the early 1980s—worn cloth with a fading flower pattern. My throat tightens; I scratch my arm.

"Uh, no thanks. I'm good standing."

"Don't be giving away my ale!" Pop-Pop hollers with a hacking cough.

"Relax, Pop! We got plenty."

"Thank you," I say with a small smile, nodding in the old man's direction. He snarls and returns to his programs.

"Hear testimony from one of God's loyal children . . ."

The screen cuts to an image of a Black woman speaking on camera, seemingly at one of those megachurches with hundreds of people surrounding her.

"I was in debt for forty thousand dollars. I was dead broke and didn't have anyone to turn to. Then one day, I called the number and planted my HOLY SEEDS just like Pastor Clark told me. Three weeks later

they began to grow; next thing I knew I had forty thousand dollars in my account and God almighty, I was saved!"

The crowd cheers before the camera cuts back to Scott Clark behind his desk.

"You see that, children? GOD can move mountains! He is a deliverer! Cast away your sins and put all your trust in him and his prophets. I would not lead you astray. Trust me."

Mr. Brown chuckles, returning to the kitchen. "Better get dinner started before he starts hollering about that too."

I snort and whisper to Yusef, "What's up with the creep show?"

"Who? Pop-Pop?"

"No! That Scott Clark dude."

Yusef focuses on the TV and stiffens. "Oh, him. And his 'Holy Seeds.'"

"Yeah, what's his deal?"

He sighs. "Okay. It's like this: you call Scott Clark's hotline and put in an order. They send you this envelope that contains a pack of seeds and a letter that specifically tells you how to plant and water them. Even this prayer you gotta say over them. In return, you send the envelope back with your 'joyful' donation. The bigger the donation, the larger the blessing. If your seeds don't grow, you ain't praying and paying hard enough."

I chuckle. "Wait, nobody believes this shit, right?"

He shakes his head. "I can't tell you how many gardens I've

tilled just so folks could plant their seeds."

"Whoa, dude is like an evil genius! So what are they? Bean stalks to heaven?"

"Now you asking the right questions, Cali," he says with a smirk. "Nobody knows. You plant them and they may sprout a little something but then they die off quick. Ain't surprised, nothing grows around here except weeds. Ground won't take."

"Then how'd you get your stuff to grow, Mr. Gardner?"

"Give the land the right TLC, turn up the soil, mix it with some compost and plant food, and you can do anything. But them seeds, not even God himself could get those to grow. Believe me, we've tried. We're not in the three-generation gardening business 'cause we wanted to be."

Yusef nods at Pop-Pop, rolling his eyes. "Come on. This way."

As he leads me down a narrow hall, I hear music beating through the walls, enough to shake the framed black-and-white family photos. He opens the first door on the right and the music blows my hair back.

"Damn, conserve energy much?"

"My bad," he laughs, turning down the volume as I take in the spacious room—the football jerseys pinned to blue walls, the stacks of sneaker boxes, the three-monitor computer setup, giant floor speakers, and the souped-up deejay turntable.

"Whoa! You're a deejay? Dude, how many jobs do you have?"

"It was my dad's. He used to be a deejay. I'm . . . practicing, trying to take over another family business."

First time he's mentioned his dad. I note his discomfort and move on.

"So. What's your deejay name?"

"Haven't figured one out yet. But check out this set I'm working on. Found this cool song in my dad's collection." He clicks through a couple of buttons and the track plays. "There was a rap group back in the day called Crucial Conflict, had this track called 'Hay,' this beat is fire! Listen!"

He turns up the volume again.

The hay got me goin' through a stage and I just can't get enough

Smokin' every day, I got some hay and you know I'm finna roll it up.

Weed. It's a song about weed. My mouth waters.

"So, uh, you smoke?"

His face scrunches. "Nah. I don't touch that shit!"

"Right! Right, yeah, of course," I say, backpedaling.

He doesn't ask me, and I take it as a sign he assumes I don't either. My leg brushes against the frame of an unmade twin bed against the wall, sheets hanging on the floor. A wooden bed, a place for a million bedbugs to fester.

FACT: Although bedbugs do not have wings, they can jump short distances, catching rides to their next host's house.

I gulp air and step away, skin in flames. It's cool, keep cool, keep cool. Don't freak out. You'll wash your clothes when you . . .

I HAVE TO GET OUT OF HERE NOW!

"Um, so I gotta get home soon—"

"Oh, right! This way!"

The door at the end of the hall leads us back to the garage and a giant wall of tools. Some of the finest I've seen.

"All right. Let's see what we got." Yusef rummages through the shelves and I drift outside, admiring the rosebushes lining the driveway. Across the street, a woman stands on her porch, staring at me, unflinching. I shrink back inside.

"Hey, when does it start getting cold around here?" I ask.

"End of September."

"That's . . . really soon," I mumble, doing some quick math in my head. Last article I read said the vegetative stage for cannabis seeds can take three to four weeks, before the flowering stage, which can take another five. And with the tools I'm working with, I might not be able to harvest anything until November.

"Well, with all the global warming stuff, sometimes it's longer. Last year, didn't get under seventy until the third week in October. Frost not until Thanksgiving. So take it easy, Cali, you won't freeze to death just yet. But you better buy a good coat ASAP."

The nickname is growing on me. Only because it reminds me of home. I look out into his lush front yard. The woman still staring, now on her phone.

"Thought you said nothing grew around here except weeds?"

I ask, hinting to the rosebushes.

Yusef smirks. "Like I said, you gotta give the land some extra nurturing if you want anything to grow."

He pats a bag marked "Plant Fertilizer" next to him. I lick my lips.

"You got any more?"

SIX

THE ROOM IS pitch-black when my eyes peel open. I'm awake . . . but not fully. Everything is a fuzzy blur. My skin feels prickly, nerves tapping against bones. I blink and realize it's all I can do. Arms, legs, hands . . . nothing is moving the way it should. I'm stuck. Stuck. Stuck?

What's happening?

The door creaks open slowly, its eerie hinges singing. I try to roll over but remain frozen. It physically hurts to move as I struggle to talk. Who's there?

Someone. There's the faint outline of their body in the shadows. A tall body. Mom? Alec? Who is that?

My body throbs like a hit funny bone, invisible hands pressing me deeper into the mattress. Buddy sits up with a whimper, staring at the door. Then he lowers his head and lets out a low growl.

My mouth is dry from trying to force out words, fists clenched tight, gripping my sheets.

The shadow shifts. I can't see it anymore. Where is it going?

Don't go, help me. Please. I can't move.

Drool pools in the back of my throat. I'm choking, I'm drowning, I'm dying.

Things are crawling on me, bedbugs, get them off! Get them off!

With everything in me, I strain, pushing from the inside out. My spine cracks in my ear, neck muscles bulging as I let out a staggering exhale.

Buddy cranes his head around as I launch up, gasping for air.

What the fuck was that?

Panting, I look out into the hall, eyes now adjusted. The shadow is gone. But I know I saw something. Or someone.

Buddy sniffs around in the dark as I let the fridge light illuminate the kitchen. My skin still feels achy, hands tingling as I pour myself a glass of water.

Three nineteen again. The silence is deafening. Deathly.

Except it's not totally silent. Pipes still ping, wood breathes . . . but somewhere in the distance, I hear a growl, a rumbling.

Is that coming from outside?

Our street is a ghost town, quiet, desolate. We practically live on our own island. So when I peer out the front door window, I almost think I'm still dreaming. Because there's a truck sitting across the street, its lights off, engine purring, a shadow behind the wheel.

"What the fuck?" I mumble. Who the hell is that?

I ruffle the curtain as I grab the doorknob. The driver must have seen, because the truck quickly backs up, makes a U-turn, and skirts off.

"What! No way!"

Tamara's rejection is an awkward surprise. I reposition my computer.

"What do you mean? This was your idea!"

"I meant for *you* to find seeds there, in Cedarville. Dude, do you know, like, how much trouble I'd get into? Can't you buy them online or something?"

"My parents are watching my credit card and every dollar I spend. I would never be able to explain it."

Tamara rolls her eyes. "Oh, and *I* could?"

It's rare that we fight—at best we just avoid confrontation, letting steam blow over. Okay, so maybe asking her to commit a federal crime is a bit too much, but . . . her annoyance is unwarranted.

"But it's not even a big deal!"

"It is! And what's the rush?"

Oh, nothing, just crazy-ass dreams and night stalkers outside our house keeping me up at night. No biggie.

The door clicks, creaking open. I've grown accustomed to the creepiness . . . until it slams shut.

"Shit! What was that?" Tamara gasps, straining to see behind me.

Buddy jumps up and growls, his fur fluffed up. My eyes flicker from him to the door and back.

"I . . . I don't know," I mutter. "One sec."

It's quiet in the hall, as it should be at two a.m. All the bedroom doors are closed and I didn't feel a draft. I test the knob, inspecting the latch. Opening on its own is one thing, but slamming shut . . . makes no sense.

Buddy sniffs, trotting around in a circle, following his nose into the bathroom. The smell is back, the one from the kitchen, but not as strong. Is it drifting up?

Ugh! I don't have time for this!

I have more important priorities, weed being one of them.

"Everything okay?" Tamara asks.

"Um, yeah," I say, closing the door. "Anyways, so what do you think?"

"I don't know, Mari. I can get into a lot of trouble."

"I'm not asking you to send me a pack of blunts. Just some seeds! Pretend they're sunflowers or tulips if it makes you feel any better." I head straight to the punch. "Tamara, I need this. It's better than any other alternatives. Do you really want me to backslide? After everything that's happened?"

Tamara takes a deep breath.

Okay, I know it's hella shitty for me to guilt my best friend like this, but desperate times call for desperate measures.

"Fine. Where should I send it?"

I give her the address to the library.

• • •

"Happy anniversary, babe!"

Alec enters Mom's office with a huge bouquet of yellow roses.

"Aw, thank you," she says, kissing him. "My favorite! They're beautiful."

He ropes his arms around her. "Not as beautiful as you."

I want to gag on my guacamole, but honestly, it's nice to see Mom swept off her feet after two years of being single. As much as I love him, Dad definitely wasn't husband of the year. Gone months at a time, some would say he loved his job a touch more than being shackled down with a wife and kids. The divorce wasn't nasty; they were friends before and worked better that way, so his absence didn't faze me much. At that point, I was used to FaceTiming him on the road. Plus, there were Percs to keep me company. It didn't occur to me until much later that the only person who really felt they lost something . . . was Sammy.

Piper walks into the kitchen carrying her My Little Pony lunch box. She glares at Mom and Alec in the office, hesitates, then, surprisingly, resists the urge to break up their lovefest. Instead, she stomps over, laying her box open on the counter.

"Running away?" I joke.

She narrows her eyes at me before opening the fridge.

"Ready to go? Reservation is in twenty minutes," Alec says to Mom.

Piper proceeds to put cookies, chips, cucumber slices, juice boxes, and Lunchables in her box, packing them neat and orderly. She then takes two teacups and saucers out of the cabinet.

Mom laughs. "I told you, you didn't have to come home. I would've met you there."

"Nope. Definitely picking up my girl and taking her on a proper date!"

"I was homeless, smoking the crack. Was strung out for ten years. I prayed for a miracle. That's when I called Reverend Clark and ordered his FREE Holy Seeds. I planted them seeds in front of a home I wanted and it's like they grew overnight, they grew so tall. Two weeks later, the deed to that house was in my hands and I never touched the devil's candy again! Praise be to God."

I whip around. "Dude, turn that off!"

Sammy, sitting on the sofa, stares transfixed at the TV. "You missed it—a man just got up from his wheelchair and started break-dancing. The seeds cured him!"

Mom gushes as they step out of the office. Her hair is done up in a high bun, and she has on her favorite red dress with heels.

"Thanks, Mari, for watching the kids tonight. There'll be a little extra in your allowance this week."

"Oh goodie," I quip. "I can buy myself a cookie at school."

"Smart ass," she says, biting back a grin, then notices Piper's precision packing. "Piper, whatcha doing, sweetie? Where are you off to with my good teacups?"

She stops to face them and, in all seriousness, says, "I'm having a tea party with Ms. Suga."

"Ohhh," Mom says with a nod, winking at Alec. "Of course. Well, would you like more snacks for your party? I made some hummus earlier."

"No," she seethes. "Ms. Suga doesn't like bird food."

Mom blinks as Piper slams her box shut, balances the cups, and walks off.

We turn to Alec, waiting for an explanation.

"Uh, sorry," he says with a laugh. "She's very particular about her tea party menu."

If our house is 214 Maple Street, and the house on the corner is 218 Maple, that means the house next door is 216 Maple Street and the house across the street must be 217. So the one on the opposite corner must be 219.

219 Maple Street is the only vacant house on our block that seems to have a decent roof that won't cave when you throw a rock at it, a secluded backyard shrouded by tall trees, and most of its windows still intact. The corner gives several access points, easy to sneak in and out without being seen.

Carrying my new tools, I weave through the thick bushes, climbing over the broken fence to the back door, cracked open. I step inside a trashed kitchen and listen.

"Hello?" I call out, learning my lesson from that day with Sammy. "Hellloooo!"

Silence. The room is riddled with chips of plaster and dry caked mud. The cabinet doors are ripped off their rusted hinges, an iron sink on the floor, the walls kelly green, stained with mildew. It's warm, humid, the air stale. Sunlight hitting the glass creates a greenhouse effect.

Just what I need.

Without time to spare, I drag my supplies inside.

Every online article I read on how to grow cannabis advised to use containers, for a more controlled environment. I created ones out of old two-liter soda bottles, stuffed them into the 5 x 5 flower bed I built after my morning runs, using old boards and rusted nails. Almost broke my back sneaking across the street with the two bags of plant food Yusef gave me, blending it in with the rest of the trash until I was ready to use it. Germinating the seeds under my bed was risky, considering how nosy Buddy can be.

But it'll all be worth it.

As I give the seedlings, now planted in their new home, a healthy drink of water, I take a look around the place. A woman definitely lived here, maybe even alone, judging by the once-pink sofa, flowery frames, and array of broken porcelain dolls. A cracked ornate mirror sits above the fireplace, and despite the chipping white paint and thick dust, I recognize the same intricate mantel, like the one in our house with the strange family crest.

The same person must have built all these houses. Shame they've all gone to waste.

I step back to admire my handiwork. "And I shall call you the secret garden."

Mom pokes holes through the blisters on my palms and I suck air through my teeth to keep from whimpering.

"I've never seen anything like this before," Mom mutters, shaking her head. "You sure you were wearing gloves?"

"Maybe it's just . . . been a while. Different earth here and all."

Despite my work gloves, the intense labor at the secret garden wreaked havoc on my hands. Looks like I've been clawing at sharp volcanic rocks.

"Probably should take it easy for the next few days," Mom says. "Maybe let Yusef do more of the hefty lifting in garden club. Seems like you've made a nice . . . friend."

The accusations are like a bullhorn. "It's not what you think."

"I didn't say anything," she says in that annoying parental tone that says she's saying something. "I think you're smart enough to not fall for a boy's alleged offer to help. Again."

Parents have this unique way of reminding you of the ways you've disappointed them without spelling it out.

"Okay." Mom sighs. "Upstairs, under the bathroom sink, grab the salve ointment. I'll cut up some wraps."

I take my time on the stairs. Yes, my hands are ravaged, but that's just my outer injuries. Feels like I lost a wrestling match with Mother Nature herself. My lower back, feet, and arms ache. Without track keeping me fit, I have the body of a ninety-five-year-old woman.

But it'll be worth it, I keep telling myself just as I reach the top of the stairs, catching a snip of Piper's low whisper.

"Really? You'd do that? But what if they find out?"

Her pink lava lamp illuminates the dark hall. She's talking to someone much taller than her, but the wall by her half-open door is blocking the person from view. It's not Alec; he's downstairs watching TV with Sammy.

Stepping closer, I try to keep my feet light, but the creaking floor gives me away and her head snaps in my direction.

"Who are you talking to?" I ask.

She lunges toward me, blocking the entrance with her arms. "Huh? No one."

"You were just talking to someone."

For a moment, Piper appears unnerved before she quickly straightens, brushing back her hair, eyes going cold. "No, I wasn't."

"Yes, you *were*."

Piper sucks in a breath and smiles before screaming, "I said NO, Marigold! The money in Mr. Piggy is MINE!"

Heavy footsteps crush the floor as Alec bounds up the stairs.

"Hey! What's going on?"

"You little bitch," I mumble, and she smirks at me.

"Nothing, Daddy," she says, her voice light and innocent.

Alec rushes toward us, hard eyes switching from her to me, then back.

"What were you just yelling about?"

I point above her head. "She was talking to someone. In her room."

Alec glances at Piper, head cocked to the side.

Piper's eyes widen. She glances at me, then mumbles to the floor. "I was . . . talking to Grandma."

Alec's face drops as he falls onto his knees in front of her. "Of course you were, sweetheart. You used to talk to Grandma every day. And that's okay. It's okay. Even if she's not here in the physical sense, Grandma's always with you."

Alec pulls her into a tight hug. She sets her chin on his shoulder, a nasty smile smearing across her face.

We should put her in acting school, is my only thought. She'd make us millions, and then maybe we wouldn't have to live in this house.

SEVEN

"DO YOU REALIZE that books are just trees . . . with words?"

Erika gives me a lazy smile across the lunch table. She must have blazed sometime before gym and jealousy is steaming out my ears. She smokes almost every day, coming to class as calm and relaxed as I dream of being.

"Trees with words? That's deep," I say, stabbing my salad.

Erika grins, proud of the revelation. "Right. It's like, the trees are talking to us, but through the page. They sacrifice themselves to be heard."

In the corner of the lunchroom, Yusef is sitting at a table, surrounded by girls. They laugh at all his jokes, on cue, like mini robots, and he looks . . . kinda miserable. It's not in his smile but in his eyes. He glances in my direction and I flicker away.

Erika twists her neck around and spots him. "Heard you were over Yusef Brown's house the other day."

"What? Who told you that?"

"Oh, girl, please. You think the first girl to walk *inside* the Browns' home in years wouldn't make headline news? Ms. Steele told Ms. Merna who told my grandma who told the rest of the city. You're public enemy number one around here now."

I suck in a breath. "It's . . . fine. I'm used to being a social pariah."

She frowns. "Really? Even at your old school?"

Shit. This could open the door to the past I need to keep shut. This place is supposed to be a clean slate.

Change is good. Change is necessary. Change is needed.

"Doubt I'm the first girl. I couldn't possibly be the first," I say, changing subjects. "He's too cute to not sneak a couple of chicks through his bedroom window."

She brightens. "Ohhhh, so you *do* think he's cute! Well, I get it. I don't talk to him much in school either. But outside of school, we cool. He usually gives me a ride up to Big Ville."

"What's Big Ville?"

"The prison." She frowns. "My pops and brothers are up in there. So is Yusef's dad. So is just about everybody's dad."

"Whoa," I mumble. Across the room, a small group of girls stare at me. Not the way you'd scope out an enemy. Almost as if they're trying to figure me out.

The rest of the day, it's like that. More curious stares. More whispers. By the end of eighth period, for the first time since we moved to Cedarville, I'm excited to be walking through the front door of our house.

"Hey! I'm home!"

The silence is so unsettling in here, to put it mildly. Old-house noises, wind whistling through hollow walls, groaning wood, creaking floors . . . I freaking hate it.

"Mom?" No shoes by the door. Guess she went to pick up Sammy and Piper. I make my way to the kitchen, pulling out my phone to text her, and run right into an open cabinet door.

"Shit," I mumble, rubbing my throbbing forehead. "What the . . ."

My stomach drops as I blink at the scene.

Every single kitchen cabinet door and drawer is open . . . and empty. Food, dishes, pots, pans, silverware . . . all laid out on the counters. Everything is lined up neat like building blocks, size and color coordinated.

"Sammy," I chuckle, grabbing a box of granola.

Outside, Buddy hysterically whines on the deck, staring in as if he's been out there for hours.

The front door clicks open.

"Hey! We're home!" Mom calls. "Marigold? You here?"

"I'm in the kitchen."

Sammy runs in first full speed, sliding across the floor in his socks.

"Whoa . . . dude? What are you doing?"

I laugh. "What? Nothing, I haven't touched this little science experiment of yours."

Sammy frowns as Mom and Piper enter, carrying grocery bags, stopping at the entryway, stunned.

"What the . . . Marigold!" Mom shrieks.

"Huh?"

"What did you do?" She looks around the room in sheer exhaustion. "Are you . . . is this . . . were you looking for bedbugs again?"

"What? NO!"

But just the mention of them makes me start to itch, and to be honest, this does look like something I would do on my worst days. But I didn't.

"Look at this mess! I don't have time to clean all this up. I have to start dinner and finish another two thousand words tonight to stay on deadline."

Piper cautiously steps around the kitchen in awe.

Baffled, I glance at Sammy. "Wait, this wasn't you?"

"No! We just got home. . . ."

DING DONG DING DONG

Mom groans to the sky and drops her bags. "What now?"

As she stomps to the front door, I survey the kitchen, the room now off-putting. Something like this . . . would take hours, and they just got home. I rub my arms, a chill running through me.

"Are you Piper's mama?"

A harsh voice snaps from outside and I rush over to the kitchen doorway. On the porch is a Black woman, her long thick hair tied into a low ponytail. At her hip is the mini version of her. Big beautiful eyes, long lashes, staring into the house . . . at Piper. Piper calmly walks into the hall, stopping a few feet from the door.

"Um, yes. I'm—"

"Yeah, yeah. I'm Cheryl. So listen, I don't know what you folks do out in California or wherever y'all from," she says, hands waving. "But around here, we keep our children on a short leash, you understand? Now I ain't the one to tell a mother what to do with her children, but it just ain't safe for our babies to be playing in them damn houses."

Mom frowns, trying to compute. "Sorry, I don't understand?"

Cheryl juts her lips toward Piper. "At school today your little girl tried to convince my Lacey to come play with her in one of the abandoned houses!"

Mom whips around at Piper, who only stares at Lacey.

"Piper," Mom gasps. "Is this true?"

Piper doesn't flinch, her cream face still, lips in a hard line. A wide-eyed Lacey clutches her mother's jean jacket, trembling.

"She said she plays in them houses all the time," Cheryl continues. "Invited her over to have some sort of tea party. Do y'all know how dangerous them houses are? Besides them falling apart, you know what kind of people be in there squatting, smoking, and shooting up drugs? These girls could get raped and we'd be none the wiser!"

Mom is horrified. "Piper, what were you thinking! We told you not to go near those houses!"

"Marigold plays in them too," she shoots back.

The rug rips out from under me and I fall on my tailbone.

"What?"

"Oh. I see. It's a *family* problem," Cheryl huffs, crossing her arms.

Sammy and I exchange a shocked look. Indignant, Mom steps into her line of sight.

"Now, Cheryl, I know you're upset . . ."

But Cheryl ignores her, dragging Lacey down the porch steps, grumbling.

"You stay away from those people, you hear! Stay away from that little girl at school too. And tell your friends to do the same. Can't trust these new folks as far as you can throw them."

Mom slams the door closed, spinning to us. "Has everyone lost their mind! Piper, it's bad enough the whole neighborhood acts like we're lepers, now you want them to think we're unfit parents too? And why would you rope Marigold into this?"

"Because I've seen her go in there in the mornings. She's doing drugs!"

All the blood rushes to my feet as Mom shoots me a glare. But there's no way Piper could've seen me. I've been careful.

"Oh, really?" I sneer, calling her bluff. "So which house?"

Piper falters, pointing out the window. "The one next door."

Got her!

"She's lying! I've never been anywhere near that house!"

"And there's no way to get inside," Sammy adds. "You've seen it, Mom, the place is the only one on this block locked up like a fortress."

"Piper," Mom groans.

"No! I'm not lying!" She points in my face. "Ms. Suga's seen you! She knows what you're trying to do."

Mom pinches the bridge of her nose. "Piper . . ."

"I want my daddy! You can't call me a liar! I want my daddy!"

Mom rubs her temples. "Everyone go to your rooms. NOW!"

8:30 p.m. ALARM: Don't forget English homework.

I stare up at the ceiling, phone calling for my attention, but I can't stop replaying the afternoon over and over in my head. Even if Piper pointed to the wrong house, she was a stone's throw away from the truth. Was she following me, watching me from her room? There's no way anyone could see from that far. And—

Ughhhh! That freaking smell is back!

It must be coming from the vents, so there's clearly something dead and stuck inside the walls. Sometimes, I can't smell it at all. Other times, it's suffocating. Mom keeps calling Mr. Watson to come by and investigate, but he seems to be too busy and I'm nearly out of oils to burn. I can't go another night without sleeping. This calls for something stronger.

A puff of thick white smoke halos the burning sage as I wave it around my room. My guru always says when used properly, sage can help to cleanse the energy of a place. And we could sure as hell use some of that. Ever since we've moved here I've felt off. But it's not just me; Sammy too. And Mom, and Bud. Maybe the whole house needs to be cleansed.

I step into the hall, waving the sage in all four corners, then hit the bathrooms, the kitchen, the living room and dining room.

Sammy coughs, opening the front door to let in the cool night breeze. "Geez, are you trying to smoke us out too?"

"You'll live," I grumble, waving the sage inside the sitting room before heading back upstairs to do the bedrooms.

Piper is standing in the threshold of her room, lava lamp glowing behind her. She stares at me, her dark eyes following my every move.

"What?" I snap. "What's your problem?"

She takes a deep breath and boldly raises her chin. "This is Ms. Suga's house."

"Okay . . . and?"

"And she doesn't like this smoke stuff."

I roll my eyes. "Whatever, Piper! You'll get over it."

"She said she doesn't want you selling drugs in her house either."

I swallow to hold my composure. There's no way she could know.

"What are you talking about? Where did you—"

"She says you have to leave. The rest of us can stay, but you have to get out. She doesn't want a junkie in her house."

That's it. I'm tired of this little girl pissing me off.

I storm up to her, blood surging.

"Or what?" I challenge her. "What if I don't leave? What are you going to do about it, huh?"

The red glow behind her suddenly brightens, like a flare. But it's not coming from her lamp. It's an orange light coming from outside.

"MOM!" Sammy screams from downstairs. "The house across the street is on fire!"

Alec shoots out of his bedroom. "Raquel, call 911!"

"Daddy," Piper calls.

"Stay there, sweetheart," he shouts from the bottom step. "Stay with Marigold!"

I shove Piper out of the way, rushing to her bedroom window. 215 Maple Street is ablaze, flames bursting out of the windows, flicking into nearby trees. Alec runs out to the end of the driveway, stretching the water hose as much as possible.

Mom rushes downstairs. "Girls! Put your shoes on and grab what you need in case we have to evacuate."

That's when I look down. Piper already has on her shoes under her princess pajamas. There's fresh mud on her sneakers. We meet eyes, hers giving away nothing, and I walk back into my room, holding in a scream.

EIGHT

EVEN THOUGH 215 Maple is a blackened, charred carcass, with smoke still swirling into the sky, it doesn't look much different from any of the other houses. In fact, it looks more at home on our block than we do.

I stare from our front porch at the smoking pile of wet wood, biting my nails to keep my teeth from chattering.

I'm not cold. I'm shook . . . with the fire department investigating the ruins, mere yards away from my secret garden.

What if they go searching the other houses? What if they find it? Will they look for fingerprints? Am I in their system—

"How do you think it started?"

My head snaps to Sammy, standing beside me. "Huh? Oh, I don't know. Why would I know?"

"You think it was one of those . . . squatters?"

I suck in a breath, trying to hold off the image of a body beneath the rubble, fried to a crisp. "I . . . I . . ."

The front door clicks open and Piper peers out before

stepping onto the porch, standing on the opposite side. She doesn't acknowledge us, just stares at the house, face devoid of emotions.

I've been trying to rationalize the night to myself. That's what people do when faced with conflict. They take a beat, rationalize, then reconstruct what actually occurred. Piper had mud on her sneakers, but that could be from anywhere. She's a curious puppy, shoving her nose in everything with a sniff. She went out to the front yard maybe . . . but there's no way she started that fire. No way are we living with a mini arsonist. She's not that crazy.

"Hey! Where are you going?" Sammy calls after me.

"Stay there," I shout, speeding down the walkway. I need a better look.

Across Sweetwater, folks gathered at the intersection, craning their necks to see the wreckage but not daring to come any closer. Alec is talking to who I could only guess is the fire chief judging by a squad car, giving his account of the blaze.

The charred chimney stands like a tall redwood, ignorant of the carnage below. Pressing my belly against the yellow police tape, I stand among a few unfamiliar onlookers. My eyes water at the aggressive stench of burnt things. A porcelain tub that looks like it once belonged on the second floor, which is no longer there, sits in the center of the rubble, a white spot in a sea of blackness.

The cleanup crew is small. A couple of men in gear and two

Cedarville pickup trucks. They don't even seem official or that interested as they lazily fish through the soot.

Which makes sense considering how they cleaned up the rest of the houses in Maplewood. Why would anyone want their city to look like this?

"Was anyone inside this time?" one of the men beside me whispers.

"Not that they can tell," the other says with a sigh.

He looks down at the crowd gathering at Sweetwater and chuckles. "Gotta light a house on fire once for me to get the message. That's for sure."

It clicks why their faces and presence feels so off-kilter to me. These men, the fire department, and the onlookers, they were the most white people I've seen in weeks. And I don't know why, but I don't want them here. I can only imagine how my neighbors on Sweetwater feel.

I glance back at the porch. Piper smirks, then skips back inside.

"Hello! Welcome," Mom says cheerfully at the door. "Come on in, please!"

I recognize Mr. Sterling from his picture on the Foundation's website. He's short, with a small, somewhat wrinkled face, olive skin, bushy eyebrows, and shiny black hair with silver roots, his cologne flooding the room.

"Well, hello, Raquel," he says. His smile is so bright it

seems unnatural. "At long last, we finally meet."

"Welcome," Alec says with a sturdy handshake. "Glad you could make it."

"Thanks again for having us," Irma says, unwrapping the silk scarf choking her neck. "I just swore you were going to cancel, considering all the excitement you had last night."

"We heard about the house," Mr. Sterling says, peering across the street. "Close call for sure."

"Thank God you're all okay," Irma adds.

"Yes, speaking of 'all,'" Mom says, motioning toward the stairs. "May I present Marigold, Sammy—"

"And my Piper," Alec adds emphatically, and I have to resist rolling my eyes.

Mr. Sterling smiles at us. "Hello there!"

Sammy waves through the banister. "Hey."

"You're really dressed up," Piper says, regarding his suit, which shines like a new quarter.

Mr. Sterling bends to her eye level. "Why, you don't miss a thing, do you?"

This is going to sound kinda extreme, but I already don't like this guy. His flirty familiarity is somewhat off-putting. Or could be my inability to trust strangers.

Alec clears his throat. "Well, come on in! Make yourself at home. You own the place, after all."

Mr. Sterling chuckles but doesn't correct him with something like, "Oh no, Alec. This is your house now, friend."

Instead he and Irma follow Alec into the dining room.

"Kids, come on. Time for dinner," Mom says.

For the first time, we all sit at the long wooden table under the new chandelier, the room bright and sparkling. Alec and Mr. Sterling sit at the heads. Mom, me, and Sammy on one side, Irma and Piper on the other. After warm garlic bread and a hearty salad, the table is almost silent as we dig into our spaghetti.

"Boy, I tell you, Raquel, this pasta . . . rivals my grandmother's," Mr. Sterling says. "And she's from Sicily, the real deal."

Mom grins proudly, always a sucker for anyone complimenting her cooking.

"I was a bit worried at first," he admits, sipping some wine. "Heard you all were vegans, and I'm a meat and potatoes sort of man."

"Heh, so am I," Alec laughs. "Rough living, I've definitely lost a few pounds."

"And yet somehow, you're still alive," I mumble under my breath. Mom pats my thigh under the table but keeps her face unreadable.

Mr. Sterling wipes his mouth with his napkin, looking at me. Or through me, I can't be too sure.

Alec, ever oblivious, moves on. "So, boss, about what we discussed on Friday, I think—"

"Please, Alec," Mr. Sterling laughs. "We're off the clock. No shop talk in front of the women."

Mom's lips tighten and she blinks down at her plate. I dig my knife into my eggplant parm, just to keep from digging into one of his eyeballs.

"Besides," he continues, "I'm here to learn more about the Anderson-Green family."

"Okay, I just have to know, since I'm such a sucker for romance," Irma says with a giggle. "How did you two meet?"

Mom lets out a nervous laugh. "Uh, well, it's kind of a funny story. . . ."

"No, baby, it's a great story," Alec jumps in. "See, I used to live in Portland and was heading to a job interview down in LA. I was supposed to fly but there were some mechanical issues or something, all planes were down. But I just had to make it to this interview, you know. Me and Piper . . . we really needed a fresh start."

"And at the same time . . . I was covering a story on new CBD dispensaries in the area," Mom adds, pouring herself another glass of wine.

"Anyways, with the planes down, I figured why not drive! It'd take me, what, a day. It's a pretty scenic route, down the coast, on Big Sur. But when I get to the rental car center, I see this gorgeous woman . . . arguing with a rental car attendant. Guess a lot of people had the same idea to drive, and apparently, there was only one car left, which they had double-booked . . . and I tell you, she let that woman have it! Ha! Well, we got to talking, and since she lived in a town right off Big Sur, I offered to give her a lift. But that drive . . . that drive is like magic. All these beautiful beaches, cliffs, and crashing waves. We talked the entire way, and after I dropped her off, I couldn't get her out of my head. Been in love with her ever since."

Mom blushes as Sammy pretends to gag.

"Oh my goodness." Irma beams. "So that was it? You just up and moved!"

"Well, it took some convincing," he says, winking at Mom.

"I thought maybe we were rushing into things," Mom says sheepishly. "Bringing two households together. But Alec . . . he made me feel like the impossible was . . . possible. Everyone could use some of that."

Wow, I never heard Mom talk about Alec that way. It almost makes him seem like less of an asshole. I guess that's the point.

Alec reaches over and holds Mom's hand, smiling proud.

"Awww," Irma gushes.

"That is a wonderful story," Mr. Sterling says.

"Do they know what happened yet?" Piper asks, her voice cutting through the revelry, face red hot, eyes locked on their hands.

"What happened with what, sweetheart?" Alec asks.

"The house across the street."

"Oh! Well, it was an accident . . . someone maybe passed by and left a cigarette."

Can he hear all the cracks in his story? There's no way that blaze was caused by a forgotten little cig. And no one passes our block during the day, much less at night. Well, unless you count that weird mystery car.

"Those darn cancer sticks," Irma fusses. "Who'd think something so small would cause so much trouble! I heard they could see the fire from the park!"

"Well, thanks to Alec with his water hose and fast thinking," Mom says, "we were able to keep it from spreading."

"It's what happens when you survive a bunch of forest fires."

"I heard junkies hang out in those houses," Piper says, staring at me, and all heads snap in her direction.

"Where did you hear that?" Alec asks, frowning.

She shrugs, playing with a piece of lettuce on her plate. "School."

A shiver zips up my spine. Not sure where this conversation is headed, but I can already sense it is driving too close to home.

"Mr. Sterling," I start. "Can you tell us a little bit more about this house?"

"What do you mean?"

"Oh, you're not worried about all that gossip about the house being haunted, are you?" Irma laughs.

Once again, Irma has us all speechless.

"Haunted?" Mom says, setting down her glass of wine.

"Yes, all just a silly urban legend, grown out of boredom. But, as a precaution, I personally had our local priest drop by and give the home his blessing. Mr. Watson was here to witness."

"Um, okaaaay," I say, turning back to Mr. Sterling. "But I

was actually wondering who lived here before. And why did you pick this block, specifically, to start the residency? All these houses are empty. Why have us sit in the middle of all this?"

Irma softly sets down her fork, eyes darting to Mr. Sterling.

"That's really none of our business, Marigold," Alec warns.

"No, no, Alec. It's okay," Mr. Sterling says with a warm smile. "I'm all for curious minds. See, Marigold, I've lived in Cedarville all my life, and as you can see, our fair city has taken quite a beating over the years. Drugs, riots, crime . . . we've gotten a bit of a reputation. Thus, outsiders are hesitant to relocate here. Which is why I started the Grow Where You're Planted Residency. The hope is to incentivize nice wholesome families, like yours, to move into this area and help change our image so that more people will be willing to consider making Cedarville their home. This is just a start; soon all these homes will be remodeled, like yours, with a thriving community and booming industry."

"But wait, what about the people who already live here?"

"What about them?" he chuckles. "I'm sure you've noticed, we have a very slim population."

"What happened to everyone?"

Mr. Sterling nods, popping a piece of bread into his mouth. "They left. For work or other opportunities."

"But why leave so quickly? Why abandon everything you own? It's almost like they were . . . running away."

"Maybe running away from mortgages or property liens," he laughs. "But there's nothing scary about Cedarville. We're one of the friendliest cities in the country!"

"So you bought all these homes?"

He shrugs as if it's no big deal. "We've procured a number of foreclosed homes, yes."

"But if you own all of them, why leave them like this?" I wave toward the window. "It's almost like you want this city to look run down . . . on purpose. Which goes against your mission. So, if you want to change your image, why not start with the community that's already here?"

"We're only interested in working with people that want to see this city return to its glory," he says, a curtness in his voice.

"And you think the residents here don't want that too? Have you tried asking them?"

Irma's face grows tight, staring down at her plate. Mom takes a deep breath as Alec inhales, setting his fork aside.

But Mr. Sterling hasn't dropped his smile, doesn't even blink. It suddenly dawns on me, his face reminds me of one of those creepy dummies with skin made of fresh Silly Putty. Maybe that's why he seems so . . . fake.

After a long silent moment, Mr. Sterling wipes his mouth with his napkin and gives the table a gleaming smile.

"Well. It's been quite a lovely dinner."

NINE

KNOCK KNOCK KNOCK KNOCK

After watching the sun start to come up for the thousandth time, I had just fallen back to sleep when the knocking starts. Or I should say pounding. Like the police are at the front door. And that's the only reason I jump out of bed.

The house stirs, each door opening. I step into the hall just as Piper does, rubbing her sleepy face.

"Who is that?" Mom grumbles. "It's six in the damn morning!"

Alec throws on a shirt as he runs downstairs.

"Yes?" he says, opening the door.

An old Black man stands behind the screen door, his face in a deep scowl.

"Yes?" he snaps. "That's all you got to say? You gonna explain this?"

Alec steps out while we stay inside, protected by the screen door, crowding around each other to see.

On the porch sits a pile of various tools—a power drill, chain saw, even a little push lawn mower. None of which belong to us.

Alec and Mom give each other a look, still puzzled.

The old man points again at the tools, frustrated by something unsaid.

"Wait, are these yours?" Alec asks.

He scoffs. "You know damn well these are mine because you took them from my shed! I spent all morning driving around looking to see who stole my stuff all to find it here! And you didn't even bother to hide it!"

Alec, dumbfounded, glances around, as if an answer to the problem will appear.

"Um, look, sir . . . ," Alec says.

"It's Mr. Stampley to you!"

"Right. Mr. Stampley. We didn't steal your things."

"Then how you explain this!"

"I'm just as surprised as you! Maybe someone dropped them off at the wrong house."

"Pssh! No one would do some foolishness like this."

"Maybe someone was playing a little practical joke on you." Alec lets out a nervous laugh. Mr. Stampley only stares, fuming.

"Ain't nothing funny about stealing a man's things!"

"Did any of you see these here last night?" Mom asks us in a low voice.

We shake our heads. I was the last in after taking Bud for his evening walk and the porch was empty.

"Well, sir, I'm sorry but . . . I have no clue how your stuff got here," Alec says, hands on his hips. "But I'll be happy to load it back in your truck."

Mr. Stampley shakes his head, adjusting his cap. "I should've known. Only crazy people, troublemakers, would move to this block!"

He looks up at the house next door, visibly shivers, and starts collecting his belongings.

"Where's my ax? I know you have that too."

The school's track team has a meet today. I sit in the rusty bleachers, watching the 100 meter with my hoodie up. Don't know why I'm doing this to myself. Guess I'm a sucker for self-torture.

Monica Crosby is the team's star runner. She's toned, tall, slender build . . . and she's good. Almost too good for this school. If circumstances were different, I'd suggest she try out for a private school; she could totally score herself a scholarship, maybe even try out for a pre-Olympic team. She'd boost her speed if she focused on her core and tightened her strides. But here, in this new town, I keep my mouth shut and mind my business.

I can't believe Coach let David back on my old team. Then again, why would I ever think he would let me back? Especially after I fucked up. All the practices and meets I missed . . . with my record, no one should ever trust me on their team. I'll just screw up. Always do.

"That's the girl who lives on Maple Street," a girl whispers behind me.

"For real?" her friend gasps.

Tightening the hoodie around my face, I head for the stairs.

I was my old school's Monica Crosby. Now I'm nobody but a girl who lives on Maple Street.

Whatever that means.

"So what's the big deal about me living on Maple Street?"

The garden club asked for volunteers to help clean a piece of property in the hopes of converting it into a community garden. Yusef and I team up to comb through the perimeter with trash bags and sticks. But I'm already regretting it. Because a few yards away, I can see a moldy queen-sized mattress in the rubble-strewn field. An oasis for bedbugs. I can barely keep my eyes off it.

> *FACT: Bedbugs can live up to eight months without a blood meal, meaning they can survive on furniture until a new human host nears.*

Yusef wipes his forehead with his sleeve. "Why do you ask?"

"I mean, I get I'm fresh meat, but everybody at school keeps specifically talking about how I live on 'Maple Street,' like that means more than it should."

Yusef twists up his mouth a few times. "Nobody's lived on your block in a while."

"No shit," I chuckle. "But what else don't I know?"

Yusef sighs, squirming as if he is about to tell me the most embarrassing story.

"Aight, well. It's just that everyone surprised you're still alive, with your house being haunted and everything."

I snort and pick up an empty Coke can. "Oh. Is that all?"

"Nah, Cali, you gotta understand, your house . . . it has history," he says, following me. "No one thought you'd survive this long living with the Hag."

"The Hag? Who's that?"

"Not who, but what," he says, all serious. "It's this creature, a demon woman, who comes in the middle of the night while you're sleeping, cast some type of spell on you. You wake up, but you can't move or talk. You're, like, paralyzed."

"You mean . . . sleep paralysis?"

"Yeah, that's what it's called!"

My mouth dries, thinking of that night I almost choked on my own tongue . . . and the shadow in the hallway.

"And while you down, she steals your skin," Yusef says. "She collects other people's skin to wear during the daylight like she's normal. And when the skin gets too old and baggy, she has to find new skin."

"So, what you're saying is . . . people think that *I'm* the Hag, dressed in my skin, plotting to take theirs."

"Yup."

I shrug and pick up some empty food containers. "Cool."

"Cool?" he scoffs.

"Well, if everyone thinks I'm a demon, then they'll leave me alone."

He laughs. "I guess that's one upside."

"The best upside I could ask for."

"Oh, hey," he says, pointing. "You got something on your sleeve."

I glance at my arm and find three tiny red spots. The world comes to a screeching halt.

FACT: Bedbugs are small, flat, oval, brownish, wingless. They turn red after feeding on the blood of a human, like vampires.

"Oh shit, oh shit, oh shit!"

Yusef laughs. "Girl, it's just some ladybugs. Relax! They're harmless."

That mattress . . . I knew it! I knew it!

"I have to go, I just I can't no I have to go I um sorry there's not well I gotta go. . . ."

I'm babbling. I can hear myself babbling, but I can't stop myself from babbling because there are bugs on me and I don't know if they are bedbugs or regular bugs or harmless bugs or murder bugs, but whatever they are it doesn't matter because they're on me now and now they'll be on everything in the house.

"Cali? You okay?"

But I'm already running, full sprint, back home. Heart in my throat, ready to soak my skin in gasoline.

Back when my parents were still together, we were, for lack of a better term, hoarders. We collected and kept everything under the sun, our house full of junk too precious to throw away. Then my dad returned from a weeklong work trip to New York with bedbugs. We didn't know we had them. They hid in the crevices of our home, silently multiplying. Microscopic organisms with the uncanny ability to wreak havoc on your life.

I didn't think much of it when I saw the first bite. I blew it off as a mosquito bite. Until my legs were riddled like freckles and erupted into a rash that took over my whole body. At thirteen, everyone chalked it up to puberty, that I was overreacting to a simple allergic reaction. Nothing serious to worry about. I was given a million explanations but the right one. Then, one night, while combing through WebMD, I found an article, ran to pull back my bedsheets, and found the first of many nests. Hundreds of black dots and blood spots covered the bottom of my mattress.

FACT: Bedbugs are nocturnal creatures. They feast while you're sleeping, grazing on your skin like cows.

We trashed everything. Wooden dressers, bedframes, mattresses, sofas. It's what you have to do to truly get rid of bedbugs. They lay invisible eggs that can hatch at any moment, even after extermination.

But after months, I could still feel them crawling on me. I stayed up all hours of the night, hunting with a blow-dryer, re-bleaching clothes, fingers chapped from all the disinfecting. I saw bites that weren't there, black spots even when my eyes were closed, scratched my legs until they bled. Went to the top allergist in the state before they started sending me to shrinks, saying it was all in my head. Delusional parasitosis—the belief a person is infested with bugs that aren't there. Comes with a side of hypervigilance (like, obsessive cleaning), paranoia, depression, insomnia, and grade-A anxiety. I don't remember much from my freshman year of high school. Sleep-deprived, I failed most of my classes and exams. But no amount of affirmations and psych talk could get me to relax. Why should I believe anyone when they didn't believe me that something was wrong in the first place?

During the summer before our sophomore year, Tamara's cousin offered me my first blunt, and it was the palate cleanser I needed. But . . . it started to not be enough. The highs were fleeting, never lasting as long as I wanted. Then, I stupidly tore a muscle in track and was introduced to a lovely white pill called Percocet. Long after the injury healed, I found that snorting crushed-up Percs was the right concoction to stop the bedbugs from taking up all the space in my head.

• • •

Over the past few years, I've perfected the art of stripping and running, tossing clothes in trash cans, a solid distance from my house so bedbugs are not tempted to make their way inside. Standing in my underwear on the back porch, in a new town, makes me realize this might not be so normal. But I don't care. A thorough skin inspection is critical.

I rub a hand over my arms, picking at beauty marks I've seen a million times, taking deep breaths to keep myself from fainting.

You're okay, you're okay, you're okay.

Nothing out of the ordinary. But bites could pop up later. I need a hot shower immediately.

Sammy, sitting on the sofa watching TV, covers his eyes as I enter. "Dude, *why* are you naked!"

"Long story."

He waves one arm out. "GAH! I may never see again!"

"So dramatic," I laugh, running upstairs and find Piper standing at my desk.

"Hey! What are you doing?"

Piper flinches, then spins around, hiding something behind her back, struggling to come up with an excuse.

I bum-rush her, grabbing her arm and pinning it back.

"Ow!" she screeches. "Let go of me!"

It takes nothing to pry her little hands open. The incense I brought from home is snapped in pieces. Below the desk, my sage is crumbled up in the trash.

"You little shit!"

Piper yanks away, rubbing her wrist, tears swelling in her eyes. "I told you, Ms. Suga doesn't like that smell!"

Here I am standing half naked while bedbug eggs could be burrowing in my arm hairs, and Piper is busy vandalizing my things.

"Well, tell Ms. Suga to suck a dick!" I snap. "This isn't her house. It's not even your house. This is my mom's house. She won that residency, not Alec. If it wasn't for my mom, you two would be homeless! So maybe you can get your daddy to leave, since he does whatever you want anyways. And then you and Ms. Suga could live happily ever after."

Piper reels back, lip trembling. "I . . . I . . . you'll be sorry!" she sobs, then runs out of the room.

"And when you plant your seeds, you will start seeing miraculous deliverance. Thousands of dollars transfer into your account, cure from disease and sickness . . . those who cannot walk, will walk again once more!"

My eyes fly open at the sound of his voice, clear as day through my open door.

Three nineteen a.m. Again.

"Fuck," I grumble, throwing back the sheets.

I slump down the steps, yawning, and am almost used to the scene—lights on in the kitchen, same glass cup on the counter—except for one huge change that stops me dead in my tracks.

The basement door is wide open.

"You will always harvest what you plant if the Lord wills. As you sow, so shall you reap. Those who do not follow the Lord's will, will reap what they sow and burn in a fiery hell."

Something wedges itself inside my throat, mind going blank. The door leans against the wall like it's always been accessible, easy to open, as if I was just imagining yanking at it the other day. But seeing it from the inside, its rusted doorknob plate dented, its warped ancient wood with a hectic pattern of scratches that could've only come from fingernails . . . chills me to the bone.

"Hello?" I call out, like an idiot. Because honestly, who could be down there in the pitch-black dark? Then again, who opened it in the first place?

That smell, reeking of rotting fruit and spoiled meat, answers in the form of a fog drifting up the stairs. I reel back, eyes watering, preparing to slam the door shut when it slowly dawns on me: Buddy isn't by my side. He wasn't in my room when I woke up, and he's not in the kitchen or the living room. Which could only mean one thing. . . .

Oh God.

"That's why with your seeds, you will be working in God's favor. The seeds that blossom will bring anointing to your life and you will experience great abundance in areas you pray for. All you have to do is call the number below, place your order . . ."

Hands trembling, I gape down into the black abyss, a

never-ending hole, a bottomless well.

"Buddy?" I croak, bending slightly. "Here, Buddy. Come on, boy."

Oh no oh no oh no. I can't go down there I can't—

He whimpers. But it sounds a million miles away. Or maybe I can't hear him over Scott Clark's ranting. I race across to the sofa to switch off the TV.

"Trust in the Lord or perish in his wrath. He is coming for us all soon! Are you ready for salva—"

The sudden silence is relieving until something to the left catches my eye—outside, a figure ducks out of sight.

Was someone just peeping in? Or was that my reflection?

My head is swimming. A cup of caffeine would help me think straight, strategize how to extract my beloved dog from the depths of hell.

"This is my house," a voice echoes up from the basement. A woman's voice, raspy and distinct.

My jaw drops.

What the fuck was that!

The room is silent again. Maybe I was hearing things, in my groggy state. Or maybe this is another dream? 'Cause there's no way in hell I just—

CREEEEAK

The sound floats up from the basement, the sound of weight on wood, like someone taking a first step on the staircase. But that's impossible. This is just an old house. Old house, old-house noises. But . . . old houses can't form real words.

CREEEEAK

Another step.

Somebody is down there. And she has Buddy!

Soaking in dread, I grip the remote to my chest, heart thrashing, unable to tear my eyes away from the open door. I'm too far from the kitchen to grab a weapon. But I can make a run for it, past the basement, and scream for help.

CREEEEAK

"My house," the voice whispers. "Myhousemyhousemy-house."

"Mom?" I whimper. "I—"

Suddenly, a blast of music cuts through the walls, flooding the house, and I drop to my knees. Music? Coming from upstairs. I glance at the open basement door one last time and bolt for the stairs.

"MOM! MOM!"

"Mari! Mari?" Mom shouts over the music as she runs out of her bedroom. "What's wrong? What are you doing?"

Alec stumbles after her. "What's going on?"

Piper is already in the hallway, seemingly unbothered. She takes one look at me and covers her ears. "Daddy! It's too loud!"

Sammy tumbles out of his room . . . with Buddy.

"Buddy!" I gasp, diving on the floor for him, overcome with relief. Sammy, covering his ears, slips into my room and turns off the speaker.

"Dude, what the hell?"

"Someone's downstairs!" I sob. "Someone's in the basement!"

Mom gathers me up in her arms and looks at Alec.

He nods. "You guys stay here."

Piper clutches him. "Daddy, no."

"Stay here. I'll be right back."

Alec descends the stairs slowly, peering over the banister, then disappears out of sight. Piper fidgets on the balls of her feet, staring. We wait three long excruciating minutes before he reappears at the bottom step.

"Can you guys come here for a sec?"

Cautiously, we all march down and gather in the kitchen. Alec stands at the now-closed basement door and yanks it.

"It's locked," he says flatly.

Mom frowns, looking to me for answers.

"I swear, it was open! I swear!" My voice hits a hysterical peak.

Alec shakes his head. "I'm taking Piper back to bed. Come on, sweetheart."

Piper gives me a knowing smirk before taking Alec's hand.

"Mari," Mom starts, twisting her hands together. "Have you been—"

"Don't!" I snap. "Just say you don't believe me, but don't accuse me of anything else!"

Mom and Sammy exchange worried glances.

"Forget it," I groan, heading for bed, taking a quick second to peek outside, seeing that truck parked across the street and watching the house.

Again.

TEN

"BEFORE WE WALK in here," Alec says from the driver's seat in his suit and tacky tie, "let's just go over the rules again, shall we?"

I roll my eyes. "What's there to go over?"

"Well, we . . . just want to make sure we don't have an incident like last time with Mr. Sterling," Mom says delicately.

"I said, I won't say anything. And if you were so worried about it, you could've left me home."

"It'd look strange if the whole family came tonight and you weren't with us," Mom counters. "Might seem like you have a problem with Mr. Sterling."

"Which you don't, right?" Alec warns, glaring at me through the rearview mirror.

"Guess you should've brought Buddy instead."

"I don't have a problem with him, Daddy," Piper chimes in with a smile, her hair in bouncy pigtails.

"Can we just get this over with?" Sammy asks. "Some of us

gave up a gaming tournament to be here tonight."

As usual, I can always count on Sammy to have my back.

Alec and Mom share an exhausted look before opening the car doors, and we all pile out.

Tonight is the Sterling Foundation's first open house at their new office on the Riverwalk. The glass building is filled with historic Cedarville memorabilia: old black-and-white photos blown up poster size, an interactive timeline that borders the lobby, digital installations, art made by locals . . . even a 1920s car, apparently built in one of the shut-down factories.

"Wow," Sammy says as we make our way around the room.

Alec grabs two glasses of wine from one of the waiters carrying around a tray. "Pretty fancy, right?"

"Ooooh! Hello! There you are!" Irma waves from a distance, clapping her hands as she heads toward us.

"Hey, Irma," Mom says.

"Great to see you all! Raquel, can I steal you away for a moment? I'd like to introduce you to a few of our board members before the big speech."

"Yes, of course."

Mom raises an eyebrow at me before walking off. Another warning to behave myself. I don't know why she's acting all coy around these people. She's the one who raised me to ask questions, be curious, and speak my mind. So really, my keen observation skills and comprehension is her fault.

Alec parades Piper around the room, showing off his prize

possession to . . . well, I actually don't know who any of these people are. Only person I recognize is Ms. Fern, but no else from our side of town. A bunch of white people dressed up in fine threads and heels, the most I've seen since the house fire.

Hiding in the corner, I fidget in the dress Mom insisted I wear, stuffing my mouth with spinach quiches, while Sammy plays with one of the touch-screen setups, giving us a digital overview of Cedarville's history. On the opposite side of the room is a giant screen behind a large stage, I suppose to project a film or something during the presentation Irma mentioned.

This is fancy. Almost too fancy considering everything we've seen in this city. The budget for this event alone could've cleaned up a block or two.

I spot Mr. Sterling by the stage with Mom, talking to a group of people. Tonight's suit is crisp black, which brings out his dark eyes. Mom nods with a plastered-on smile, shaking hands. Despite looking a little unsettled, it's good to see so many people praise her.

"Hey, check this out," Sammy says, nudging me. "They have all the old schematics of the neighborhoods in Cedarville. Look, here's Maplewood."

I lean in and identify Maple Street, a line driving right into the park. Sometimes it pays to be the daughter of an architect. Dad had Sammy and me studying blueprints since we could walk.

"Look at all the old buildings that used to be there," Sammy adds. "This big one . . . I think that's that empty lot in front of the library."

"Huh. You're right," I mumble. "Wonder what that was?"

A squealing mic brings the room to attention.

"Hello, everyone, welcome," Irma sings from center stage. "Thank you all so much for coming. And special thanks to a few of our board members in attendance tonight: Eden Kruger, Richard Cummings, and Linda Russo. Let's give them all a round of applause."

The group standing next to Mom gently waves and nods, with glistening white smiles.

"Now I am pleased to introduce our founder and CEO of the Sterling Foundation, Mr. Robert Sterling."

The room erupts as Mr. Sterling takes the stage. He hits up both corners, waving like he's a rock star, which, judging by how hard everyone is cheering, he may just be.

"Thank you all for coming," he says, taking the mic from Irma. "When my father first moved to Cedarville, he was thirteen, alone, with barely a dollar to his name."

On the screen, a sepia-toned photo of a man who must be his father slides in.

"But he came here with hope," he continues. "And made a life for himself, later providing for his wife and six children. Our family's legacy is proof that any man can make a name for himself in Cedarville. We were once a booming industrial city, ripe with opportunities. Of course, things changed. Things that were . . . out of our control."

More photos of the changing landscape, pictures of homeless people and crime statistics. The audience shifts uncomfortably as something occurs to me: I haven't seen one homeless person since we moved here. Not on our block or walks to school. No panhandling at streetlights or outside grocery stores. The houses that they swore were filled with squatters all seem empty.

"But then my brother ran for office," Mr. Sterling continues as another photo pops up. "He believed in this great city and set out to revitalize it. And we're here to continue the work that he started."

The crowd stirs, growing curious.

"We've made some significant progress over the years with our endeavors, including our newest program, the Grow Where You're Planted Residency. In fact, we have our very first resident here with us tonight, Mrs. Raquel Anderson-Green."

Mom shyly waves as Sammy and I scream, hoot, and holler.

"But here at the Sterling Foundation, we're ready to pick up the pace. Over the years, we've taken it upon ourselves to buy investment properties in the hopes of a better tomorrow. And tomorrow, ladies and gentlemen, is on its way, sooner than you think."

"Does he mean the future that's happening in, like, three hours?" Sammy quips, checking his watch, and I bump his shoulder.

"That's why I am pleased to announce the To the Future

Campaign, a venture spearheaded by our foundation in conjunction with our esteemed investors, to bring Cedarville back to its former glory with a brand-new look."

The giant black screen glows white before the "To the Future" logo pops up.

"Our housing development and newly designed light-rail systems will give our citizens hope for a brighter future."

The screen zooms and flies into the "new" Cedarville animation rendering, featuring lush trees, deluxe townhomes, and happy animated citizens.

"Cedarville will be the prime location for start-up companies, tech firms, and alternative businesses that will guarantee a job growth rate of up to seventy-five percent. Groundbreaking will commence in three years' time."

There are oohs and aahs.

Dad makes these types of renderings for his clients. They're computer-generated 3D images of the intended construction plans and finished product, which, in this case, is a brand-new mixed-use development, with office buildings, retail spaces, and a giant park.

Wait a minute. . . .

I nudge Sammy out of the way and zoom back in on the schematic, lining up the shape of the park with their proposed rendering, and gasp.

The map takes over the entire area of Maplewood. It means they plan to flatten the neighborhood within a few years. Where do they think all those people are going? Or better question . . . what do they plan to do with them?

Mr. Sterling raises his glass, his eyes meeting mine. "A toast, everyone. To the future!"

"To the future!" the crowd cheers back.

"Who left the lights on?" Mom asks as we pull into the driveway, the entire house glowing like a firefly.

"Don't you mean, all the lights," Sammy says curiously.

"Not me," Piper chimes in.

As we climb the porch steps, Alec stops short, shooting his arm out to block us from moving forward.

"What?" Mom huffs.

He nods at the front door, cracked open. Through the screen, we can see a lamp knocked onto the floor. Mom gasps, throwing Alec a pleading look.

"Stay here," he whispers, and tiptoes inside.

"Everyone, back in the car," Mom whispers, shooing us down the stairs. "Now. Go!"

For ten minutes, we watch the front door from the back of the van, Mom standing at the steps, phone in hand.

"What's Alec doing?" Sammy asks.

"Guess trying to see if anyone is still inside."

Piper straightens, pressing both hands to the glass, her lips in a tight line.

Finally, Alec emerges and talks to Mom in a hushed voice. They both glance at the car before Mom dials 911.

• • •

There's no other way to describe it: the house had been through a tornado. We gingerly make our way through the rubble, glass crunching under our shoes. I recognize the pattern—Mom's wedding china blankets the floor leading up to the kitchen. Cookware, pots, and pans scattered about. My last terrarium, an anthill on the rug.

"They didn't take the TV," Sammy mumbles.

I'm surprised to see it still hanging unharmed while the rest of the house is in shambles.

"Weird," I mumble, then hear a sniffle coming out of Mom's office.

Mom stands on top of a pile of shredded papers, staring at her bashed desktop computer. Framed photos smashed, almost her entire collection of books ripped in pieces.

"My work," Mom whimpers as Alec ropes her into a hug, kissing her temple.

Sammy and I glance at each other and take for the stairs.

"Guys, wait," Mom calls with a sniff, but we're already on the first landing.

What's left of Sammy's Xbox is in the hallway, his headset snapped in two, Legos like scattered ice cubes thrown everywhere.

On the floor in my room, my laptop is smashed into tiny fragments. Clothing snatched off their hangers. There wasn't much to destroy; I didn't have much to begin with.

But across the hall, Piper's room is left untouched. Her lava lamp bubbles and glows blood red, illuminating her chilling satisfied smirk.

"Police are on their way," Alec says as we camp out on the porch.

Mom, holding Sammy on her lap, nuzzles his neck.

"I don't understand who would do something like this," she says. "Tear the place apart but not take anything."

As far as we can tell, no jewelry, money, or valuables were stolen. It's as if someone came in just to fuck with our things like trolls.

"You know who did it," Alec seethes, pacing in front of us. "Our 'friendly' neighbors. Thugs with nothing else better to do than cause trouble."

Don't know why he's all upset; none of his stuff was messed with. He and Piper are walking out of this unscathed.

"We don't know that for sure. It could've been anyone."

"You know what, I don't blame the Foundation for not trying to help these people," Alec carries on. "They don't even help themselves. Robbing and vandalizing their very own community. Why should anyone help them?"

Mom shoots him a look. "Alec, you have no idea what these people have been through. You, as a white man, couldn't possibly imagine."

Alec opens his mouth and shuts it quick, realizing he's gone too far.

"I don't get it," Sammy says to him. "Why did they leave your stuff alone?"

Alec shrugs. "Maybe the police drove by."

"Down this block?" I roll my eyes. "Yeah right."

Alec blows out some pent-up air and sits down on the steps, facing the street, Piper quickly joining him. What no one else can see is the way she seems to be holding in an amused laugh.

And I desperately want to know what's so funny.

ELEVEN

"IT WAS SUPER weird, Dad."

Standing on the corner in front of the same house we snuck into, I give Dad an update.

"It's like they had it all planned out and ready to go. It looked like a totally different Cedarville, with strip malls and stupid fountains. And they acted like all these people are going to leave tomorrow and as far as I can tell, no one is in a hurry to pack up around here."

"Well, that's what happens in cities that are controlled by investors. But I want to hear more about the break-in. Are you sure you're okay?"

"I'm fine, Dad. For real. Aside from my computer, I didn't have much they'd want."

"I would've thought they'd try to pawn off the computer," he muses. "Could've gotten a few hundred for it, easy. Why destroy it? And what's this I hear about you not wanting to join the track team?"

I glance at the house on the corner, the curtain waving hello again. Didn't want to tell Dad that this wasn't just a regular robbery. That it seemed calculated and targeted, like someone was trying to send a message. And I definitely didn't feel like talking about track.

"Yeah," I mumble, voice trailing off. "Hey, does Aunt Natalie still work for that nonprofit?"

"Yup. Still at it."

"But she always complains about needing to fundraise. How can a nonprofit like the Sterling Foundation afford to buy up a whole city?"

Dad laughs. "Ha! That's my girl. Always thinking through people's schemes. We couldn't even trick you into eating veggies."

"And look at me now," I chuckle. "Surviving on granola, tofu, and a prayer."

"You always get to things in your own time. But, Mari, I wouldn't worry too much about the people in Cedarville. It'll be a long time before they can push them out of their homes. However, to satisfy your curiosity . . . I would follow the money."

"Follow the money?"

"Yup. Once you know where all the money is coming from, you'll know who the real players are behind the scenes pulling the strings. It all may not be what it seems. What's the first rule of chess that I taught you?"

I take a deep breath, staring inside the broken window of the house.

"Every move is a setup for the next move."

After we finish cleaning up and Mom locks herself in her office, attempting to hit her deadline, I try calling Tamara for the sixth time. She hasn't answered any of my texts or Face-Times. What kind of best friend leaves you hanging during a major life crisis?

"Going for a run!" I scream before slipping out the door, first making a stop at the secret garden. It's only been a few weeks, but the seeds are starting to show some life. I give them a good shower and check the room temperature. You can smell fall in the air. Change of season means change of sunlight, so I pull the bins closer to the windows. It's a risk, since some-one could spot them while walking by, but seeing how no one comes down our block to begin with, I feel cool chancing it.

Except for that weird truck I keep seeing late at night. Maybe it's canvassing the place. Maybe they're the ones who trashed our house. But they didn't touch Piper's or Alec's stuff. Which is probably why I keep hearing Piper's words echo through my head.

"You'll be sorry."

With the garden tended to, I take off for my run, keeping to my routine to avoid raising any red flags about my where-abouts, Piper still in my forethoughts. Could she really have something to do with the break-in? I mean, she's just a little bratty kid. How much power could she have? She doesn't even have a phone.

"You'll be sorry."

I consider telling Mom about the car parked outside those few nights. But when you're known for being "the girl who cried bedbugs" at every crumb or red spot you see, you're not considered the most reliable narrator.

Deep in the groove, I don't even notice I've already made my regular lap around the park and am back in my neighborhood just as I hear a familiar voice.

"Damn, girl, who you running from?"

I spot Erika ahead, sitting in a broken lawn chair at the end of a driveway.

"Dude, are you cooked already?" I laugh between pants, slowing to a stop in front of her. "It's not even noon."

She gives me a glistening smile and checks the time. "It's that late already. But yooo, you're fast. You like the female Usain Bolt or something. You should try out for track team!"

I swallow back the acid threatening to erupt. "Eh. Not interested in school-run extracurricular activities."

She nods. "Don't want to work for the man? I feel you. Here, have a siesta."

She points to the chair opposite her and I take a seat.

"Want a pop?" she asks, digging inside a mini red cooler.

"Sure," I say, even though I should probably drink some

water after the miles I just put in. "Thanks."

I take a swig of the crisp ginger ale and glance back at Erika's house, its white shingles dripping off the side, rips in the screen door, an old fridge turned sideways in the dead grass. Inside, I hear Scott Clark.

"The Lord will send a blessing on your barns and on everything you put your hand to. The Lord your God will bless you in the land. . . . The seeds that blossom will bring anointing to your life and you will experience great abundance in areas you pray for. All you have to do is call the number below, place your order, and I will send you one pack of seeds absolutely free. Just follow the instructions in the detailed letter I will send to you."

"Sorry about your house," Erika says.

I almost ask how she heard but forget that quick. Everyone knows everything around here.

I wonder if they know they're about to be evicted?

"So, what are you getting into today?" I ask, changing the subject. "You always kick it in your driveway like a parked car?"

She pauses for a beat, her face losing all lightness. "Only on special days. Waiting for my ride up to Big Ville to visit my pops."

"Oh! Uh, cool. Um, can I ask . . ."

"What he did? Nothing, really. Wrong place, wrong time, that's all."

"Right," I say. "Sorry, I didn't mean to pry."

"You ain't prying. Nothing's a secret in the Wood. I bet you right now someone's on the phone telling somebody Leslie's daughter is kicking it with that new girl from Maple Street. Soon, they'll say we go together."

I trace my finger around my can with a shrug. "Well, you ain't bad-looking. I'd smash."

Erika narrows her eyes and scoffs. "Girl, don't go lying to me. I ain't no pity lay. Besides, you ain't my type!"

We crack up laughing and spend the next thirty minutes lighting each other up. Kinda reminds me of hanging with Tamara. It's the small slice of normal I needed, since she hasn't answered her phone, despite all the emergency emojis I sent.

Plus, I can smell the weed baked in Tamara clothes like the sweetest perfume and I'm ready to bury myself in her laundry.

"You visit your dad a lot?" I ask.

"Whenever I can catch a ride. It's like an airport up in there. Everyone coming and going." She sighs, kicking something invisible by her foot. "Them Sterling Laws fucked us."

"Sterling Laws?" I blanch.

"Nah, not the Sterling that got you that house. His older brother, George L. Sterling. He was the governor back in the early 2000s. He was like this holy roller, thought drugs were the devil's works. The moment he got in office, he doubled down and passed all these crazy laws. Mandatory minimum of twenty years if caught with just an ounce of bud."

I think of my secret garden and gulp.

"An . . . ounce of weed?" I choke. "But weed is, like, harmless."

"Well, he convinced them white folks that weed would turn people into addicts who would rob, loot, and kill, and they all believed his dumb ass. He dedicated the entire city's budget to 'cleaning the streets.' Everyone in the Wood was getting swept up. Police were riding around like an army, walking into houses, offices, restaurants, schools, hospitals with no warrants. After the first wave, they started getting greedy, planting drugs on folks . . . like my pops. Pops never smoked a day in his life, but they somehow found an ounce on him. I once read this stat that said in the two years after them Sterling Laws kicked in, the prison population grew nine hundred percent. That's why they had to build them giant blocks you could see from a mile away."

"Whoa."

"With the budget gone, school and hospitals started shutting down, folks took to the streets. And that was the first match that lit up the last riots."

I cock my head to the side, sniffing Erika again. "So . . . why would you risk smoking at all?"

"They got rid of the law about two years ago. As long as you not selling it, you good. But . . . they won't erase all them prior sentences."

"So everyone up in Big Ville is just . . . stuck?"

She takes a sip of her soda. "Pretty much."

"Dude . . . that's fucked up."

Her lips form a straight line as she stares off into space. I can't imagine what it's like growing up through something like that. Your whole world flipped, seeing your family and friends corralled into prison, practically kidnapped, on bullshit charges.

"But hey, it ain't all bad here, you know," Erika says, brightening. "There's this party tonight over on the east side. You should roll through. Yusef's gonna deejay. I give him shit but he's actually not that bad. And I think homie got a little crush on you."

Oh no. That's the last thing I need. Plus, won't that be a party with girls from our school?

But . . . it would be nice to do something normal for a change.

"Um, I'm not sure," I waffle. "Can I think about it?"

"Dude! What the hell!"

Tamara's face finally appears on my phone screen after maybe the thousandth time.

"I've been calling you all day," I shout, slamming my door closed and flopping on the bed. "Did the dozens of 911 texts not register to you?"

Tamara shrugs, seeming unfazed.

"My bad," she says, curt and not meeting my eye. "Didn't know if you were still playing that stupid-ass prank. It was hella annoying."

"Prank? What prank? We had, like, a real-ass emergency here!"

Tamara finally looks at me, her eyes narrowing, as if reconsidering something. "Well, maybe it could've been Piper. She did have long hair."

"'She'? What are you talking about."

"Someone kept FaceTiming me last night from your computer, but I couldn't see her face. She would just sit there in the dark, breathing all hard. I kept saying 'hello, hello' but she wouldn't answer. It was hella creepy."

"Tam, are you joking? 'Cause now seriously is not the time."

"I'm serious! She called like twenty times. I stopped answering after a while. Hang on, I took a screenshot. Check the receipts."

Tamara sends a photo taken from her computer screen and as soon as I open it, my whole body goes numb. It's a girl's silhouette, sitting at my desk, on my laptop, backlit by the light in the hallway, her face hidden by shadows.

She's too tall to be Piper. . . .

"Who IS that?" Tamara asks.

The Hag, I almost whisper back, but stop myself. Because that's ridiculous. There's no such thing as hags or any other craziness this town has cooked up over the years. But this must be the person who broke into our house. She was in my room, touching my things, pretending to be me . . . bile rises to my throat.

"Dude," Tamara pushes. "What is going on?"

How do I explain? Where do I even begin without sounding . . . nuts?

"Um. Long story. Lemme . . . uh, call you back."

TWELVE

WHEN ERIKA TEXTED me the address to the party, I expected a regular house. You know, one with running water and working electricity. Normal stuff. Instead, I follow a long extension cord down the cracking driveway of an abandoned relic on the opposite side of the park.

Inside, the house is flooded with red Christmas lights and cigarette smoke. Now, it's been almost a year since I've been to a party, and typically they're pretty standard no matter where you go: bottles and kegs, red cups and chips, drunk girls, horny guys . . . and all the hard candy you could ask for: weed, cocaine, oxy . . . maybe even a little Molly.

This party is different. For starters, it's almost impossible to miss the huge holes in the ceiling and moldy furniture pushed in the corners, dust collecting on everyone's kicks. Next, there's, like, a really weird mix of people. Not just kids and college kids, but there's some real-ass adults weaved into the crowd too, as if it's completely normal to do shots with someone's grandpa. Yet no one seems to find any of it strange. Just like the rest of Cedarville, everyone accepts this as normal when it's anything but.

Licking my lips, I scan the crowd, but no Erika in sight, and tonight I'm desperate to find her. She has what I need most. Something deeply unsettling is corkscrewing itself inside me. A familiar feeling when I'm close to the edge and about to do something . . . stupid. I have no way of texting her. Didn't bring my phone since I know Mom still has that stupid tracker on it and my weak "going to the movies with friends from school, might be home late" lie wasn't exactly my best work.

What if she doesn't show?

I follow the extension cord straight to a dining room filled with people. And standing behind the deejay setup is Yusef, his father's speakers set up on either side of him. He looks . . . legit and in the zone. I hang back, watching him from afar. With his Beats headphones, laptop, and a lit-up turntable, he flawlessly blends hit after hit, the party loving him, the vibes chill, and for a moment, I forget that I'm in a dilapidated house and lean against a nearby windowsill. But within seconds, it cracks under my weight.

"Ah!" I scream, falling on my tailbone. Yusef's head snaps in my direction. So does the rest of the party.

Nice, Mari. Way to keep it low-key.

"Cali!" Yusef says, helping me to my feet. "I didn't know you were coming tonight. You okay?"

"Yup, yeah. Totally fine! I'm used to embarrassment," I say, dusting myself off. "But, uh, is this place safe? The walls aren't going to cave in or nothing, right?"

He laughs. "Naw, they have parties in here all the time!"

"Oh. Nice." And I know it came out hella judgmental, but I'm still picking paint chips out of my twist out.

"Well, I'm glad you came," he says, beaming.

I squirm under his joy and the curious eyes watching us.

"Hey, I heard about what happened at your house," he says. "You want a drink?"

"Sure, but don't you got to, like, work or something?"

"I left it on a mix, we should be good for a few."

We walk through the crowd into the kitchen. Well, what used to be a kitchen since there's clearly no appliances and barely any counters. Yusef pours us two vodka and orange juices. It's the cheap stuff but definitely helps soothe my nerves. I'm not used to being at parties sober. Not saying I don't know how, but I feel like an out-of-place puzzle piece. Or it could be the whole "house being vandalized, strange noises, neighboring house set on fire, lack of sleep, and some random girl playing pranks on my now-smashed computer" ordeal that has me feeling so . . . off.

Change is good. Change is necessary. Change is needed.

"Hey, you okay?" Yusef shouts near my shoulder. "You seem out of it."

"Oh, yeah. I'm fine," I say, faking a laugh. "Um, you're pretty good at that music stuff."

He grins. "For real? You think?"

"Yeah, I'm sure your dad is, like, hella proud of you!"

Yusef's smile dims as he averts his eyes to sip his drink.

Damn, Mari, foot in your mouth much?

"I'm sorry. I didn't mean . . . well. I was just saying . . ."

"It's cool," he says, waving it off. "I actually saw him today."

"Really? How is he?"

He shrugs. "The same. He got his whole squad up in there with him, so it's not like he's missing much. Except being with his family. But maybe someday he'll get to see for himself how good I am."

"He will," I assure him. Knowing how close I am with my dad makes me want that so badly for him.

"Heyyyyy! You made it!" Erika bursts through the crowd. Eyes low, grin wide. "What up doe!" She dances in our direction, cup in hand.

I laugh. "What's up?"

"This party is lit, Yuey," she sings. "Glad they gave the kid a chance."

"Yuey?" I repeat, raising an eyebrow at him.

Yusef groans. "Bruh, for the thousandth time, stop calling me that!"

Erika shrugs and slips a blunt from behind her ear, sticking it between her lips before lighting up, the sweet and tangy smoke puffing around us. My mouth waters. It's almost pornographic how good she makes it look.

Erika notices me staring and smiles. "You want a hit?"

Tongue pulsing, I lean toward her. Yusef waves smoke out of his face.

"Nah, E, chill. She's not into that."

Erika purses her lips at him. "Did she tell you that?"

Yusef glances at me, as if to say, "Back me up here." And I can't. Because there's nothing I want more.

"So? You want a hit or nah?" Erika asks.

My eyes toggle between the offered spliff and Yusef. He crosses his arms, eyes focused on me, and although I shouldn't care what he thinks, it's hard not to when his judgment is swallowing up all the air in the room.

"Um, yeah," I say, a little too eagerly. "I mean, sure, why not."

I grab the spliff, inhale hard, letting the smoke take up every corner of my lungs before exhaling with an "ahhh." It hasn't even had a chance to work through my system, but just having it in my hand makes me feel whole again.

Yusef snarls. "Yo, you really fuck with that shit?"

"It's just a little weed," I say with a shrug. "No big deal."

"No big deal?" he shouts. "Tell that to everybody up in Big Ville!"

His bitterness is a cold slap in the face. I want to say something, defend myself, but nothing comes up.

"Yuey, chill," Erika says. "Why are you coming for her neck?"

Yusef shakes his head, slamming his cup on the cracked counter. "I gotta get back," he says dryly. "Later."

He storms away, disappearing into the crowd without a second glance. Erika waves him off.

"Don't sweat it, he'll get over it. Big-ass sensitive baby."

"Right," I mumble, taking another hit to ease the guilt.

Okay, I know what you're thinking. I still don't know Erika that well and I shouldn't be smoking at all and Yusef may never speak to me again, even though he's been hella cool . . . but right now, after everything that's happened the last few weeks, I need this hit more than anything.

I take another pull, letting myself float into outer space. The party light-years away.

Erika and I find a corner to post up, still in view of Yusef. He looks good. Really good.

Shit. Hope I didn't say that aloud.

"I'm . . . hungry," I mumble, licking my lips.

Erika turns to me, her eyes low. "Yo, do you realize that we have eggs inside us and lay eggs like chickens every month? We ain't nothing but some birds. Being a chick is some wild shit, bruh."

I stare at her and blink before a fit of giggles bubbles up. "Dude, what? Where did that come from?"

"You said you were hungry. And I want a steak and eggs. Hey, pass that roach."

I hand over the blunt and sigh, letting my body dissolve into the wall. I wasn't always this way, this desperate, this thirsty, the type of person who needed weed to maintain some sense of sanity. I can remember everything before we had bedbugs. Before every speck of dirt made me do a double take. I was once a normal kid, with normal cravings, like a casual drinker. But weed, it lifts the heavy anxiety that blankets all my thoughts and for the briefest of moments, I feel free of it all. No fixation or paranoia, no questions. Light as a feather, I float and keep floating . . . until I no longer notice life crumbling around me. Once you have a taste of that feeling, once you experience it, you'll find yourself chasing after it for the rest of your life.

I'm going to sleep so damn good tonight.

That's all I can think as I stretch into a T-shirt and joggers. I can tell just by the way my muscles have loosened off the bones, the weed is deep in my system. It wasn't the best weed I've ever had, but you know that moment when you've been starving for hours and you have some chicken, and you don't know if it's the best chicken you ever had in your entire life or you were just really hungry? It's like that. Not that I eat chicken. Thinking of chickens . . . I stifle a giggle.

Erika is fun! We definitely need to be besties.

Buddy is sleeping with Sammy tonight, so I have the whole bed to myself. I click on the space heater and slip under my comforter. Why does everything feel so good when you're high? These cotton Target Essentials sheets are like Egyptian silk.

Still can't shake Yusef's expression out of my head, but this is the best I've felt since moving to Cedarville. Well, I guess that's not all the way true. I would've had fun tonight at the party regardless. It was good to be . . . normal for a change. Think I'll ask Erika for her connect tomorrow. I can't wait on my secret garden any longer.

With the weed baking me, I close my eyes and doze off within seconds. But it's the teeth chattering in my mouth that wakes me up, like my brain went off-roading. The room still dark, now cold enough to see my own breath as I let out a groan.

That blunt should've knocked me out for hours. How the hell . . . shit, it's freezing!

My blurry eyes strain to adjust to the dark as I pat around me. The comforter is gone, goose bumps riddle my arms, feet are blocks of ice. I sit up, my head heavy. The door is open, a draft of cold air blowing in.

And there's a man standing in the corner near my closet.

He's facing the wall, head down as if in old-school punishment. If it wasn't so sparse in the room, I wouldn't have noticed him. In my haze, he would've been just another shadow among shadows. Except for the fact that he's fisting the end of my comforter.

I blink twice, rubbing my eyes. He's still there, shivering, mumbling, head twitching every few seconds. The room drops to negative twenty.

I turn away, sitting so still I can be mistaken for a piece of furniture.

This isn't happening. This is a trip. I'm tripping. Another crazy-ass dream.

But do dreams have such a violent smell?

It's the funk of forty thousand years that Michael Jackson song warned us about. I hold in a gag, my neck muscles clenching tight. I need to get out of here, but I don't want him to know I'm awake. I don't want him to look at me because one look will eviscerate this numbness and I'll scream.

Gently, I place one foot on the floor, then the other. Doing everything I can to control my breathing, I calmly walk out of the room, as if I don't see him, as if he's invisible, because that's exactly what he is. A hallucination, an apparition. And if we just ignore each other, maybe he'll go away.

I step out into the hallway, phone trembling in my hand, back rod straight.

"It's just a dream," I whisper, closing my eyes.

This is what you do. You see things that aren't there. It's been a while since you've smoked. You're out of practice.

But I can still hear him muttering.

"Just a dream," I breathe. "Ground yourself. Ready?"

1) Piper's unicorn door sign I want to shred into a billion pieces.
2) Stairs . . . that lead to the door, where I want to run straight through, out of the house, back to California.

The mumbling stops. The house falling silent. But I can still smell him, and I can't force myself to move.

3) The rug Mom bought online.

4) The attic door. . . .

Footsteps, heavy and staggering, echo out of the room, charging in my direction. My stomach lurches and I hold both hands over my mouth to keep from screaming.

Mari, wake up, wake up, wake up! Please please please!

The bedroom door slams shut behind me and I jump twelve feet in the air.

Draft. Just the draft, the wind. That's all. The door always closes on its own.

But why can I still smell him?

Mom and Alec's door remains closed. It didn't wake them up. If it did, they'd take one look at me and know I'm high. They'd never believe that some strange man has taken over my bedroom. They won't even bother to look. So I tiptoe into the bathroom and dial the only person I can think who would.

"Yeah?" Yusef snaps; his voice is groggy and horse.

"Okay, okay, I know you're all mad at me and stuff," I whisper, sliding down into the tub. "But can you come over?"

"Girl, do you know what time it is?"

I know what I'm about to say is going to make me sound crazy before I even say it, but I say it anyways.

"There's . . . there's a man in my room."

"A what?"

"Or a something," I babble. "Maybe a demon. It's in the corner, holding my blanket."

Yusef sighs. "See, and this is why you should stay away from that shit."

"Can we skip the 'I told you so' speech for five seconds because the killer is literally standing in my room and I'm scared."

Yusef takes a deep breath, sheets rustling. "Cali, it's just your imagination. I shouldn't have told you that stuff about the Hag. It got you seeing things."

"I'm not lying. I swear."

"Where are your folks?"

"Are you crazy! I can't wake them up. They'll *know* and they'll flip. I'll get in so much trouble."

Even as I say it, I realize losing my freedom is scarier than the stranger in my bedroom.

"Okay, okay. So where you at now?"

"Um . . . in the bathroom."

"Did you hear anyone . . . or the 'thing' come out of your room yet?"

I listen to the house breathe. Nothing but silence. "No."

"Did you close the door?"

"No. It closed on its own."

"Hm. Okay, you got a pen and piece of paper handy?"

"Um, I can get some. But why?"

"Okay. Here's what you do: get a piece of paper and draw a happy face."

"A what?"

"Draw a happy face."

"This isn't funny, Yusef," I snap. "There's some deranged lunatic in my bedroom and you're making jokes?"

"Who's joking?" he says, an edge in his voice. "Especially not at three thirty in the damn morning when I just got in bed and have two houses to work on tomorrow. So you want my help or nah?"

I chew on my bottom lip and stumble out into the hallway, grabbing a pen and pink Post-it note off the console.

"Okay, now what," I whisper, drawing a quick face. Can't believe I'm even doing this.

"All right, slip that paper under the door."

"What? Why?"

"'Cause demons hate anything happy, it'll scare it off. Then, in the morning, when you sober up and go to your room, you'll find something silly to greet and remind you that this was all just a bad dream."

I freeze for a few beats until a giggle escapes my lips.

"Uh-oh, was that a laugh?" Yusef says with a chuckle.

"No, you're hearing things." I sigh. "I'm being ridiculous, aren't I?"

"Nah. You just need to drink some water and sleep that shit off. But . . . glad you came to the party tonight. You looked . . . happy."

"Don't I always look happy?"

"Nah, not really."

"Damn," I huff, pressing my lips together. Do I really look that miserable here? "Well, um, thanks for your help."

"You want me to stay on the phone until you fall asleep?"

"You'd . . . do that?"

"Yeah. Just in case he comes in, then I'll hear you scream. Or just snore."

"I don't snore."

He sucks his teeth. "Quit playing, girl, you know you snore."

"Ugh. Okay, fine, I snore! But it's not that loud."

"Dude, what are you doing?"

Buddy happily licks the toes on my one foot hanging out the bathtub as Sammy stands over me.

"What?" I stir, rolling over. But one look at Sammy, I unfurl from the towels I used as blankets and scramble out of the tub.

"Uhhh, why were you sleeping in the bathtub?" Sammy asks, eyebrow raised.

"I . . . um, wasn't feeling good. Thought I was going to throw up or something. So I stayed in here."

Sammy inspects the tub, then shrugs. "Oh. Well, can you get out? I have to pee!"

In the hall, I check my phone. Yusef must have stayed on the call until way after I fell asleep. How . . . sweet of him. Especially for some crazy new girl who calls in the middle of the night, talking about demons.

Oh! The Post-it note!

I burst into my room, excited to see the pseudo love note to myself (or kind of from Yusef), relieved he would be right about the whole silly fiasco. I glance down and the Post-it sits by my bare foot, but it's not facing the way I slipped it under the door. It's been flipped, sticky side up. And there's a drawing, but it's not in the same pen I used. It's in marker, bleeding through the paper. My skin goes cold as I grab it. Someone . . . or something drew another face. Not a smiley face, an angry face, the mouth made to look like sharp teeth.

And it's in childlike handwriting.

PIPER!

Piper is eating her cereal at the kitchen island as I storm downstairs, slamming the Post-it in front of her.

"You think this is funny?" I roar.

Piper nonchalantly glances at the note, then back at me, mouth forming a sly half grin.

"What's that?" she asks in a cheerful voice, and I want to shove her off the stool.

"Mari," Mom says, setting her coffee down on the counter to step in between us. "Take it easy. What's the matter with you?"

"She put this in my room!"

Piper's face remains stoic. "No I didn't. Ms. Suga did."

Mom examines the Post-it, baffled. "What's—"

"What's going on?" Alec snaps, standing behind Piper.

"I think Marigold is sick, Daddy," she says, full of fake

concern. "She was sleeping in the bathtub last night."

Mom crosses her arms. "Why were you sleeping in the bathtub?"

I fix my mouth to tell them about the man in my room and explain the Post-it note, until I look at Piper's smug grin and realize, I can't say shit. If I tell them what I saw, it'll be a major red flag. They'll use it as an excuse for me to take one of those at-home drug tests Mom keeps in her bathroom she thinks I don't know about. I'll fail it, instantly.

Mom stares at me, as if trying to take a read, as if she's seen this part of me before. I straighten, snatching the note out of her hand.

"Food poisoning. But . . . I'm fine."

THIRTEEN

"DUDE, THAT'S SERIOUSLY fucked up."

Tamara and I are having our weekly FaceTime veg fest, including snacks and music. Mom and Alec took the kids to the movies, giving me a much-needed night alone and some quality girl time.

"Tell me about it," I groan, sitting cross-legged at my desk. "IDK, maybe it was bad weed that sent me on a trip. And Piper must have overheard me talking to Yusef."

"I told you to be careful, you don't know those crazy people. I've been reading up on Cedarville . . . it was like a war zone back in the day. Crack had people walking around like zombies. Trust no one!"

That's Tamara. My own Veronica Mars, she's good at researching shit. She can pinpoint an address based on an Instagram pic. I told her she should open her own private-eye business. She'd rake in some serious cash and could buy herself a car.

"Yeah," I say. "Guess you're right. Clearly, I'm letting this town and their weirdo ways get to me."

Even though I can't stop thinking about what Erika told me regarding the Sterling Laws. It's pretty fucked up and explains what really happened here more than any Wikipedia page could.

"You better get something to flush that shit out your system," she warns me. "And quick. You don't want your mama sending you to a farm."

"Oooh! Good idea," I agree, and set a new alarm.

11:00 a.m. ALARM: Buy detox kit.

Buddy, chewing on a bone by my bed, raises his head with a sniff. He stares out the open bedroom door, a low, deep growl rumbling from his throat.

"What's up with Bud?" Tamara asks.

"Nothing. He's just being a spazz. But seriously, what am I going to do about Piper? She needs to pay for this shit."

Tamara sighs. "Mari, maybe you should just let it go. Take it easy on her."

"Are you seriously coming to that little bitch's defense?"

"Dude, you're my girl, for real. But Piper . . . is just a kid. A kid who's been through a whole lot. I mean, she lost her mama and found her grandmother dead after school. You would be seriously fucked up too, if that was you."

Shame bubbles up, twisting my stomach in knots. Mom told me when Piper came home from first grade that day and found her grandmother unresponsive in her recliner, Piper sat by her feet and watched TV for five hours, until Alec came home. Maybe Piper really is just acting out after all she's gone through.

"Well . . . when you put it that way," I grumble. "Ughhhhh. I hate it when you're right."

Tamara frowns, leaning closer to the screen. "Hey, I thought you said you were home alone."

"I am."

Her face drops, her eyes bulging. "Dude . . . ," she stutters. "S-s-s-omeone just walked by your door."

I chuckle. "Very funny, asshole."

But Tamara's paling face makes my muscles clench.

"Mari, I'm not kidding," she whispers closer to the screen. "Someone really just walked by your door. Like, for real."

It takes several seconds for my brain to click into gear. I spin around and stare out into the empty hallway, listening to the silence.

"What did he . . . or she look like?" I ask, not taking my eyes off the door. It's one thing for me to see something that's not there. That would be a normal day. But it's another when Tamara is seeing something too.

"I don't know," Tamara says, flustered. "It was like a tall shadow. Mari, maybe you should . . ."

A door slams from somewhere down the hall and I leap to my feet, blood freezing solid.

"What was that!" Tamara yelps, completely freaked.

I involuntarily touch my trembling lip.

Be cool, Mari, it's nothing. You're going to lose it and you don't have weed to chill you out this time.

But what if someone broke in? Again?

"Umm . . . it's, uh, probably them, home early."

"Are you sure?" Tamara presses. "Shouldn't you call the police or . . ."

"Yeah. Got to go. I'll hit you later."

I press "end call" and spin back to the door. Don't know why I hung up so quickly. Guess I didn't want my best friend witnessing my potential murder, scarring her for life.

"Mom? Alec?" I call out in a shaky voice. "Sammy?"

Footsteps. Fast ones. Like tiny feet running down the hall. The flame on my candle flickers with the passing breeze. Buddy's fur spikes. He growls, backing up into my legs.

"It's . . . just a draft," I tell Buddy. Heart beating my chest blue, I take one wobbly step toward the door.

"Hello?" I croak, jaw clenching. But then his voice echoes from below.

"Your salvation, children of God, is at stake! The devil preys upon the weak. But he put the power in your hands to right the wrongs. Power in the hands of the righteous. Will you not defend your beliefs? Will you not defend your God?"

Buddy and I are greeted by an empty first floor, Scott Clark the only sign of life. It's cold, like twenty degrees colder than upstairs. I recheck the front door, deck door, and all the windows. Locked. The basement is still sealed tight. So why can't I shake the feeling that I'm being . . . watched? The residue of someone lingering, tainting the air . . .

ZzzzCLICK!

In an instant, I'm dipped into darkness, the whole house blacked out. Breath catches in my throat, strangling a cry, feet stuck to the floor. A full moon bleeds through the back woods. Something is moving in the living room . . . or is that tree shadows? Whispering . . . or is that the wind? I grab on to Buddy's collar to ground myself as he whimpers . . . or is that me crying? Suddenly, Buddy stands erect, his tail a sharp line.

THUMP!

My head snaps up to the ceiling. Why did it sound like a bag of hammers dropped on the floor?

It's just the heat . . . turning back on. That's all.

Rationalizing does nothing to stop my thin, shallow breaths from slowing down. Then there's a small creak before the tiny footsteps return, running above my head.

Someone's in the house?

WiiizzzzzCLICK!

The lights come on all at once, a dizzying effect—TV blaring, ice cubes clicking out the fridge door, stove and microwave clock blinking 12:00. I cough out a breath.

Logic begins filtering through the panic: *Be cool, Mari, don't freak. They did a shitty job with the electrical. They were rushing, remember? If it happens again, you check the fuse box, just like Dad taught you.*

But the fuse box is in the basement.

Don't be a hero. Call Mom.

Sprinting upstairs, I fly into the room and let out a yelp.

The phone. It's not on the desk where I left it. It's on the floor, lying in the middle of my room, facedown.

Was that the noise I heard? But how did it drop? Unless it grew legs, how did it flip itself all the way over here? Could it have rolled? Squares don't roll.

You're spiraling, Mari. Control, focus, control.

Heart beating out of my chest, I nibble on my lip. If I call Mom, she'll read right through me. She'll start bringing up rehab again and I won't have much to prove the opposite of what she's already thinking: that I'm losing my mind. She'll also make me pee in a cup and it's barely been twenty-four hours. That blunt is still in my system.

"Energy flows where attention goes."

That's what my guru would always say. Maybe that's it, I'm overobsessing about this creepy house, causing all this weird stuff to happen. Thoughts become things, and all that crap. I need to get out of here, clear my head. . . .

I snatch the phone from the floor. The screen isn't damaged, and nothing is noticeably different. Maybe it really did fall. Doesn't matter, I still call him.

"Hey, what up doe," Yusef says, lowering his music. "Took you long enough. Was wondering when you were gonna give me an update on your little situation from last night."

Sounds like he's driving with the windows down and the music on high.

"Um, hey," I mumble, a tremor in my voice, staring at the door. Too afraid to turn my back to it.

"Yo, you okay? Why do you sound like—"

"Oh! Bruh, is that New Girl?"

Her voice is a shock to the system. "Erika?"

"Man, put that shit on speaker! Hey, girl! What's up? You want a Coney dog?"

I cough out a laugh, relieved. "A what?"

FOURTEEN

"BRUH, I CAN'T believe you don't eat meat," Erika says, slurping an extra-large Coke in the passenger seat of Yusef's truck. "That's, like, sacrificial."

"You mean sacrilegious," I laugh, throwing a fry at her from the back seat.

"That too," she says, eating the fry. "Coney dogs were, for real, made in heaven. You need to try it at least once."

Erika definitely has the munchies. Eyelids hanging low, she ordered three Coney dogs, one cheeseburger, and a large chili cheese fries.

"You really missing out, though," Yusef agrees, biting into his dog, mustard dripping down his chin, chopped onions falling into his lap.

"Um, yeah. I'll take your word for it."

We're parked outside what looks like a busy no-frills diner/gas station with the best greasy food in Maplewood, full of signs of life. Exactly what I need to shake the tremors out of my hands.

"And then," Erika continues her outrage, hot dog in hand. "You go and get fries but not the chili cheese fries. Dry-ass fries looking like the Sahara."

I purse my lips. "Are you done?"

"No. 'Cause what we supposed to do with you? Expect us to take you the nearest bird feeder or something?"

"That's a good question," Yusef says, turning to me. "What d'you feel like getting into? This night is young!"

"Well, we do have school tomorrow," I point out.

"Whatever," Erika says. "We need to make moves. We can't sit here all night."

I could. Any place is better than being at home. I would have no problem living in this car for the rest of my life. Plus, Yusef has a pretty fire playlist.

"Y'all feel like going down to the Riverwalk?" Yusef offers.

"And risk running into members of the 'Yusef Stan Club,' get our poor sweet new girl fucked up? Nah, we gotta go somewhere where we won't be seen."

Yusef nods, thinking, before a giant smile takes over his face and he starts the engine. "Bet! I know a place."

"And girl, would you keep your head down," Erika scolds, buckling her seat belt. "Anyone see you in Yuey's car, at night, they'll know something's up even if it's not."

I slide down in my seat as Yusef pulls out of the parking lot. "Feel like I'm being kidnapped."

"Don't worry, we're not far," he says, turning to give me

a sympathetic smile. "Plus, I've been meaning to take you to this spot for a minute."

Erika mouths a "told you" with a mischievous grin. My cheeks burn as I slide lower. Yusef rolls down the windows, letting the cool air glide in as he speeds down the freeway.

"So, I don't get it," I say, putting my head between the front seats. "How is it okay for you two to be friends, and not us?"

Erika groans. "What I keep telling you? I don't pose a threat. Although I have brought a few ladies to my side of the park, if you know what I'm saying."

She wiggles her eyebrows and I can't help laughing.

"Well, I'd happily play your girlfriend just to avoid all the heat."

"For the last time, you are not my type. You're also tall as fuck. I've chopped some trees down before, but never a damn Amazon."

"That's her gentle way of letting you down easy," Yusef quips.

"Besides, I need to be free for all the pretty girls who plan on dressing like sexy nurses and housemaids for Halloween."

"So, what are you going to be?" I ask.

"Sick." She fakes a cough. "With a dirty house."

"What are you gonna go as?" Yusef asks me.

"You should be a damn ghost," Erika says, kicking her feet up on the dash. "With your house being haunted and everything."

The word *ghost* hits hard, ringing louder than any word I've heard all night.

"Who . . . who said my house was haunted?"

Erika smacks her lips. "Girl, you live in the Hag's house. Of course your house is haunted!"

"Dude, that's just some old-ass story. We don't have a ghost," I say, looking to Yusef for backup.

He takes a deep breath, avoiding my gaze. "Um . . . I don't know."

"You don't know? Dude, you've been to my house. There's no floating women or chairs sliding across the floor."

There are doors that open on their own, though, a small voice inside me says, but I ignore it.

Yusef rubs the back of his neck, focusing on the road but clearly holding something back.

"Your spot went through a lot of contractors. And they all complained about . . . just a bunch of weird stuff happening."

"Weird stuff happens at lots of construction sites," I counter, feeling defensive. "My dad worked on a property where every single piece of equipment broke down. But he didn't rush to call the Ghostbusters."

Erika turns to face me. "All right, let me ask you this: Anything missing?"

"Well . . . yeah. But we just moved. Stuff gets lost in the shuffle."

"Pssh. Yeah right," she scoffs, shaking her head.

Yusef tries to take it easy on me. "Cali, there wasn't one construction worker who walked out of your house with everything they walked in there with. No matter how hard they searched. Shit kept vanishing."

I think back to our second day in Maplewood. When Mr. Watson was looking for a hammer. Swallowing, I try to keep a straight face.

"My house isn't haunted." The statement came out cold and weak.

Erika laughs. "Girl, the Hag is chilling in your living room as we speak."

Darkness shrouds the car as Yusef parks and turns off the engine.

"We're here," he says.

"Is it safe for me to come out?" I whisper, unnerved by the silence.

"Girl, ain't nobody here," Erika laughs, opening the door.

I pop my head up and see we're in an empty parking lot facing a beach dipped in moonlight. Behind us, a blackened road is surrounded by high trees, hills, and grassy knolls. Jumping out of the truck, I'm speechless.

"Where . . . are we?" I gasp, drawn to the water.

"This is Cedarville Park," Yusef says, standing next to me. "And that's the Cedarville River. Dope, right? See, we got beaches here too. In case you thinking of heading back west."

Erika cackles, skipping ahead. "Don't go listening to him. This ain't no real beach. Feel the sand, we might as well be standing in kitty litter. And look at that water! Bluer than blue. Walk in there and it'll tie-dye your skin."

As soon as my feet touch the sand, tears prickle the corners of my eyes. It's not that I thought I'd never see a beach again, but just the sight of it floods my muscles with instant relief. I take a deep breath and smell . . . chlorine?

"Whoa," I mumble, creeping closer. Across the river, houses line the shore, their lights twinkling in the water. I guess that's a neighboring city. Haven't exactly had a chance to look at a map, but we should be pretty close to Canada.

"Watch," Erika says, grabbing a nearby pebble and chucking it into the water. "Dang, I thought it'd do that skipping thingy like in the movies."

Yusef rolls his eyes. "The Sterling Foundation did this massive cleanup of the river and parks a few years ago. Commissioned this new sandbank. I've seen people chill here during the summer. No one from the Wood, though, they remember too much of what the river used to be like."

"What was it like?"

"Let's just say if you stuck a toe in, it'd probably burn off."

"Bruh, the shit was slime green, had three-eyed fish and killer eels," Erika adds.

"Dude, that's gross!"

"Yusef drank some once. That's why he got a tiny peen," she

snorts, shoving him before taking off.

"Yo, quit playing!" he shouts, chasing after her.

Watching them run around the beach, I bend down to grab a handful of sand. It's heavy, a little damp from the rain, no broken coral or shells. It's like we're playing in a kid's sandbox. I sit, patting the area around me. Bedbugs hate the beach, which is probably why I felt so safe there.

The rippling currents softly lap the dark blue water. Nothing like the crashing waves back home, but the setting reminds me of all the bonfires we used to have after winning track meets. I can almost feel the sand in my toes, taste the trash beer, smell the smoke in my hair. I shake the memory away, trying to remain present.

Change is good. Change is necessary. Change is needed.

I'm in a new city, with new friends. That old life is gone . . . all thanks to my ex-boyfriend. Well, who am I kidding? It was my fault. All of this is my fault. And everyone knows it. So, I deserve to swim in slime-green water at a fake beach. Thankful for the darkness, I wipe away a stray tear. Until I stuff my hand in my pocket and hit my phone. Crap, I forgot to leave it. But maybe Mom's not watching like usual. Maybe she's so caught up in the movie and actually trusting me for a change, she won't bother to check my whereabouts. Besides, I'm just at a beach, with friends, like a normal girl. She can't be mad at that.

Yusef and Erika run over, bookending me. The three of us gaze out at the water, light dancing across the tide.

"This is kinda nice," I admit. "Why aren't there more people out here? I would be here every day if I could."

"The park used to be full of people," Erika says. "Having cookouts and family reunions. At night, the place was like a parking lot. Folks flossing in their whips and new fits. Just kicking it and vibing to music."

"My dad used to deejay from the truck," Yusef adds, pointing a thumb over his shoulder to his rust bucket. "Had the turntables set up in the bed. I came here once with him. I was real little, but I remember."

"My pops used to have this fly-ass aqua-blue Cadillac with white leather seats and chrome rims," Erika laughs, shaking her head. "Mom said he looked like a can of Ajax."

"Then what happened?" I ask.

Erika's face darkens as she stuffs her hands into her jacket pockets.

"Them Sterling Laws, that's what happened," she grumbles. "Started locking everyone up until folks were afraid to walk outside, the city coming up with any law you can think of just to arrest you for breathing."

Yusef tenses beside me, staring at the water.

"Damn. That . . . sucks," I mumble.

We fall into a heavy silence. I twist a finger around a strand of hair, wishing I had something profound or comforting to say.

"Welp. Excuse me, kids," Erika says, hopping to her feet.

She dusts herself off and walks in the direction of the tall grass by the shore.

"What's she up to," I chuckle. "Is she about to pee in a river?"

Yusef shakes his head. "Nah. Probably gonna go smoke."

"Really?" I say, fast. Maybe a little too fast, as I whip in her direction, about to follow, but stop, cocking my head back at Yusef. "Wait a minute, why are you okay with Erika smoking?"

Yusef purses his lips.

"Don't get it twisted, I still hate that shit," he says, then sighs. "But Erika, well, she hasn't had it easy. Almost her entire family is up at Big Ville. It's just her and her grandma left and they barely making it on grand's Social Security. So, guess I make some exceptions."

"Oh," I say, staring in the direction she disappeared.

"Guess we . . . kinda understand each other in that way. Our family trees got hacked to shrubs. Drugs, Sterling Laws, not to mention the fires. The Wood can't seem to catch a break."

"So why don't you leave? Go start somewhere fresh."

He shakes his head. "I ain't leaving until my family gets out. Don't want them coming back to a place full of strangers."

The schematics of the New Cedarville come to mind. I don't know why I can't tell him about what I saw, what they're cooking up. Maybe because I'm afraid of the never-ending questions to follow that I have no real answers for. Maybe because I feel guilty being a part of the very people that they plan to replace him and his family with.

"Thank you for bringing me here," I say. "This is dope."

He smiles. "I wanted to bring you here the first day I met you."

I gulp. "Really?"

"Yeah. I mean, what kind of Cali girl would you be without a beach?"

Yusef's softening eyes sparkle in the moonlight, a crackling flame.

I clear my throat and divert my gaze. "Uh, so, you never said what *you're* going to be for Halloween."

He chuckles. "Oh naw, we were just joking about all that. No one does shit on Halloween."

"Why?"

"'Cause of the fires," Erika says, emerging from the grass with a slow stroll, smelling sweet and tangy.

"What fires?"

Yusef winces, debating something. This isn't the first time someone has mentioned "the fires" but they never explain further. What are they not telling me?

Erika plops down beside me. "Come on, Yuey. She needs to know."

Yusef rest his chin on his knee, staring at the sand. "All right, the story goes like this: a long time ago—"

"Not THAT long ago. Keep it real!"

Yusef rolls his eyes. "Fine. Back, like, thirty-something

years ago, after the riots and the recession, all the abandoned houses used to be filled with squatters. Homeless people. Or drug addicts . . . still strung out."

His eyes toggle to Erika and back. Erika stares down, digging her heels into the sand.

"They weren't . . . in they right mind, you feel me?" he continues. "Anyway, one Halloween, some little white kid, Seth Reed, got separated from his friends, stumbled his way into Maplewood. He walked up to one of them abandoned houses, I guess maybe to ask for directions. . . ." He takes a deep breath. "They found his body the next day. Don't even want to talk about what he went through."

"Shit," I gasp.

"The city came down hard on the Wood; some say his death was the beginning of the end. After that, the tradition goes that every year, on the night before Halloween, folks set fires to the abandoned houses to smoke out any squatters, keeping the streets safe for trick-or-treaters. They called it Devil's Night, because the way the Wood was burning, looked like hell itself."

"But they didn't always smoke them out," Erika adds, her voice toneless. "Some people died in them fires, too high to notice the smoke. They say some of the burnt-down houses still got bodies in them."

My mouth drops. "Holy shit! That's arson. That's . . . murder! How could any of this be okay?"

"'Cause they think they doing right, keeping kids safe," Yusef says. "And no one around here is gonna snitch. Problem is, some of them fires would burn out of control, spread to regular lived-in houses, and then folks lose everything they own. No way to rebuild when they don't have money to start with."

I think of the house across the street and shiver. "Wait, who was setting the fires?"

Yusef palms his fist, blinking away. "Um, no one really knows."

"Why doesn't the police stop them?" I ask, eager to understand. "Or the fire department."

"You expect them to care about the Wood," Erika scoffs. "Girl, bye. They be the ones handing out the gas cans and matches."

"That ain't nothing but a rumor," Yusef jumps in.

"Bruh, my cousin saw them!"

"Whatever," Yusef grumbles. "But that's why no one goes anywhere on Halloween. Everyone's home, protecting their house. My uncle still sits outside, one hand on his gun, the other on a watering hose."

I rub my temples. Can't believe I live in a town that doesn't celebrate Halloween. But then again, that almost falls right in line with the rest of the madness in Cedarville.

"That's insane," I mumble. "And this still happens today?"

"Sometimes," Erika spat. "There just ain't enough people left in the Wood to burn."

I lean away, feeling the heated anger radiating off her skin. Erika hops to her feet and strolls back to the car. Speechless, I look at Yusef, and he only shakes his head.

"The fires scare her. Real talk, they scare everybody. 'Cause if you lose your house, there ain't nowhere to go."

Nowhere to go. Does the Foundation know that? I rub my arms, a chill sweeping in.

"You cold?" Yusef asks.

"A little," I admit.

"I got another hoodie in the car. You can layer up."

"Aww. You willing to share your hoodie with me," I tease, bumping his shoulder. "I MUST be special."

He stares before giving a shy shrug. "Yeah. A little."

There, in the flicker of that awkward pause, I feel it. An extra heartbeat, melting the ice it's wrapped in.

Yusef rises to his feet, reaching a hand out. "Come on, let's be out."

I take his hand, the rough patches on his palms connecting with my own, and stare up into smoldering eyes. We can come to the beach every day, just the two of us. Picnics and bonfires and—

Stop it, Mari!

Yusef is a friend, nothing more than that. If I wrap myself in heat again, I'll be the only one left burned. Resisting his warmth, I wiggle out of his hold, glancing up at the sky.

"Oh, uh, thought I saw a shooting star," I say with a nervous laugh, taking an inconspicuous step away.

Yusef shakes his head with a chuckle. "Um, I hope you bought a real coat."

"This IS a real coat," I say, pulling at my fleece jacket.

"That's a sweater with a zipper. It gets real cold here, like negative fifteen. Snow so thick you can't see in front of you."

"Ugh! Dude, you don't have to threaten me with such violence. I'll take the damn hoodie!"

As we head back to the car, I think of Sammy, walking Buddy on his own.

"Do you think there's still squatters living in the houses on my block?"

Yusef chuckles. "Doubt that. Ain't nobody wants to be near the Hag's house."

Back at home, I find myself doing exactly what Dad suggested . . .

"Follow the money."

Because throwing people out of their homes after they've already been through so much can't be legal. Going to jail practically for life because of weed shouldn't be legal either. But I have to pick my battles; I'm an army of one. The new girl, a stranger. And if I can find out who's planning on ripping the rug up from under my neighbors, then maybe I can tip off the community and we can all rise up together.

I'm also trying to avoid any and all thoughts of ghosts.

Sure, the house is old, this block is creepy, and yes, some major weirdness has been going on. But to lay it all on a ghost is just . . . ridiculous. And daring to bring up that type of crazy talk around Mom or Sammy will score me a one-way ticket to the nearest psych ward.

The Foundation's website is bright and inviting, but there's not a single picture of what Cedarville really looks like. No wonder so many people were enticed by the residency offer. I click through the various pages until I find what I'm looking for: a list of board members.

—Patrick Ridgefield, heart surgeon

I guess that makes sense. Some doctors can make six figures at their practices.

—Richard Cummings, retired football player and community activist

That's . . . interesting. Maybe he made a lot of money in the NFL. But his hair is white. He's clearly been out of the league for years.

—Eden Kruger, philanthropist

Generic title. She must be a trust fund baby or a rich man's wife.

—Linda Russo, partner at Kings, Rothman & Russo Law

A lawyer. That seems fitting.

—Ian Petrov, CEO of Key Stone Group Real Estate

Hm. Why would some random Russian real estate bigwig be interested in Cedarville?

Even with their combined incomes, it doesn't seem like

enough to fund an entire citywide buyout. Where is all this money coming from?

Curiosity piqued, I type "Maplewood Devil's Night" into the search bar. Only four photos appear. Strange, considering the way Yusef and Erika went on about it. They made it sound like the whole city burned down, and judging from these photos, there were only a couple of old homes being put out by fire departments. The only other fires mentioned were the riots, which seemed more to do with justice than anything else.

Maybe they were exaggerating. But the look on Yusef's face . . .

Against my better judgment, I type in one more name: Seth Reed.

The first article is from the *Cedarville Gazette*:

> Reed, age 10, was found in an abandoned lot in the Maplewood section of Cedarville. His body, discovered by one of the search party members, Richard Russo, a business owner, was said to be covered by a beige carpet. The manhunt for the alleged child killer has sparked community outrage. Over twenty homes have been set ablaze . . .

Wow. He was the same age as Piper.

Wait . . . Russo? Like Linda Russo.

Russo seems like a common last name . . . but is it possible he's related to Linda?

Searching Richard Russo, I come up with dozens of them,

but a few have businesses. One of them is a window replacement company. They even starred in their own commercial. And they must do a lot of windows that cost some serious cash, because they are flossing like millionaires. With Versace glasses, gold watches, rings, stacked chains . . . all with black hair so shiny it looks wet in the light. Now, I don't want to be judgmental or anything, but these clowns are giving me hella mobster vibes. I keep digging, searching all the businesses with Russos attached—a flooring company, carpet cleaners, air duct installers, electrical engineers. On LinkedIn, there's a bunch of Russos who work for Cedarville Electric. There's even a Russo working as an SVP of the local cable provider, Sedum Cable. Another Russo, the president of the local union, was in the news last year.

> The Local 83 has reached a $2.5 million dollar settlement with the city of Cedarville. . . . The union was represented by Kings, Rothman & Russo Law firm.

Bingo!

The phone buzzes. Yusef.

"Hey," I say, trying to hide my surprise. "What's up?"

"What up doe. Just, um, making sure you got in okay."

"Uh, yeah," I chuckle. "You watched me walk in the house."

"Oh, right," he says. "Well, guess I'm making sure homeboy isn't chilling in your room again."

My stomach clenches at the gesture. He's being nice, I tell myself. People are allowed to be nice. Even boys. But the other side of me fidgets. I don't deserve nice. Not after . . . everything.

"Hello?" Yusef says, seeming worried.

I sigh. "Dude, if you just wanted to hear me snore again, you can just say that."

He laughs. "Damn, you caught me."

BEEP BEEP

7:00 a.m. ALARM: GET UP!

Shit. I should have nixed the alarm last night. After all the research and chatting with Yusef, I'll be operating on two hours of sleep today. Going to need coffee and lots of it. The absolute worst way to Monday on a Monday.

"Nice going, Mari," I grit through my teeth, throwing back the blanket to roll out of bed. The room is like a freezer. I slip on some cozy socks and head to the closet in search of something warm and comfortable to wear, which will most likely be the sweats everyone has seen me in five thousand times now.

BEEP BEEP

7:03 a.m. ALARM: Don't forget your pills.

Ugh! There has to be a better way of fighting acne than pumping my body full of hormones and . . . wait. That alarm is hella early. Usually doesn't go off until after breakfast. Must have set it wrong. Maybe?

Whatever.

I grab a clean T-shirt, bra, underwear, and jeans instead from the dresser, catching a glimpse of myself in the mirror. I'm a wreck. Didn't wash and twist my hair yesterday. Guess I'll be going for the high bun look all week. This is too much chaos for a Monday.

BEEP BEEP.

"Huh? Now what?"

7:20 a.m. ALARM: Pack your calculus textbook.

Oh right, test today. One I absolutely plan on failing since I didn't study. Another thing I forgot to do. Feeling scattered, I stop to take a deep breath, in through the nose, out through the mouth. This day is already off the rails and I haven't even taken a piss. If I skip my run, it'll give me about thirty extra minutes to look through my notes. I also need to make sense of all the stuff I found out about the Russo family. They're definitely holding the city hostage. And if they are, the others must be too. But it's hard doing all the research from my phone. Maybe I'll stop by the library after school and use one of their computers.

Lotioned up and dressed, I'm battling with my hair when an alarm goes off again.

BEEP BEEP

"Are you kidding me?" I groan, snatching the phone off the dresser.

7:25 a.m. ALARM: Where is Buddy?

Weird. I mean, yeah, I have a bad memory. It's why I leave

little notes with my alarms. But why would I ask myself where Buddy is?

"He's right here," I mutter, glancing at his empty spot on the bed—Buddy didn't sleep with me last night. I went out and left him home. Alone.

The room wobbles, motion sickness tiptoeing in as I set the phone down.

"Don't be ridiculous," I chastise myself.

He's probably downstairs with Sammy already. Relax!

Still, I slip on a hoodie as fast as I can. Need to see with my own eyes. Like, I know this is anxiety talking and I'm going to laugh about it later, but when it comes to Buddy, I don't mess around. Just as I snatch my watch off the dresser . . .

BEEP BEEP

My stomach tenses, staring at the bomb ticking on the desk. I don't want to pick it up. I'd rather throw it out the window and run it over with a car. But I cross the room, lead weights around my ankles.

7:26 a.m. ALARM: Did you remember to lock the door behind you last night?

I drop the phone as if it combusted and scalded my hand. The hairs on the back of my neck spike with frost and I spin around. Felt as if someone was standing right behind me, breathing down on me. But there's no one. I'm alone. I've been alone all night. Haven't I?

BEEP BEEP

My body jolts at the now-terrifying sound piercing the air. A hectic and raw ring. Straddled over the phone, I swallow before looking down.

7:27 a.m. ALARM: Someone may have gotten in. Again. 😈

My pulse thumps against my eardrum as I try not to scream. That devil emoji takes me back to the Post-it note. I squeeze my eyes shut, trying to regain some sort of composure. Because this isn't happening. It can't be happening.

"This is a dream," I say softly.

BEEEEP BEEEEP

I jump five feet in the air, then snatch the phone up from the floor.

7:28 a.m. ALARM: Did you check the closet?

The closet?

I whip around, breath quickening. The accordion closet door is half-open, and from my angle, there's nothing but neutral-colored clothes and shoes. If someone . . . or something was in there, I would see them. Still, holding my breath, I gingerly step closer, licking my dry lips, hands clammy.

Ready? One, two . . .

On three, with a quick shove, I push the panel aside, its wood creaking at the force. Empty. I clutch my chest, heart hammering.

"What the fuck—"

BEEP BEEP

The phone, now buzzing in my hand, lights up.

7:29 a.m. ALARM: Did you check under the bed before you went to sleep?

My stomach plummets to the basement, throat too dry to let out a scream. I peer over at the unmade bed. The sheets and comforter askew, the bed skirt . . . unmoving.

BEEP BEEP

7:30 a.m. ALARM: Looks like you didn't.

There's someone under my bed!

No way. There's no freaking way someone is under my bed. Unless . . . there is. Unless this was their game all along.

And if there really is someone, I'll only have seconds to run. But if there isn't, I'll be causing an insane amount of commotion for no reason. I have to look. I have to see.

One step, two steps . . . I creep toward the bed, scanning the rest of the room, which feels so much smaller than before. Grabbing the lamp off the desk, I raise it high, readying myself to smash it down and make a mad dash out the door. Hands shaking, I'm nearly hyperventilating as I slowly bend beside the bed, gathering a corner of the bed skirt with one hand. Heart jackhammering, I still myself.

Ready? One, two . . .

On three, I rip back the skirt and poke my head under. Nothing.

"Ugh. You gotta be shitting me . . ."

BEEP BEEP

The phone lights up the dark space as I read the message.

7:31 a.m. ALARM: Did you check for bedbugs?

At that moment, the scream stuck inside me shoots out.

"AHHHHH!"

The spot on my arm erupts, and I hit my head on the metal bedframe, crawling backward.

"Mari?" Mom's voice calls from downstairs. "You okay?"

I spray my arms with rubbing alcohol, stripping, scanning my body in the mirror for bites. Black spots gloss over my eyes and I fall onto the floor. My chest is a tightening fist, the room wavy. I gasp for air, scrambling to find my inhaler. With two puffs, I slump in front of the fan, tugging at the bra digging into my sternum, waiting for my heart to ease.

I know I didn't set that alarm. I wouldn't be crazy enough to set any of those alarms. But someone did. Someone knew I went out last night. Someone was playing with my phone. Someone was trying hard to scare the shit out of me.

And there's only one person I know who would be that cruel.

Piper!

Anger injects adrenaline straight into my system. Flinging open the bedroom door, I fly down the steps.

"Morning, Mari," Mom says, smiling. But I stalk past her, toward Piper, aiming for her neck.

Piper's eyes widen the moment she realizes and jumps from her stool, screaming.

"DAAAADDYYYYYY!" she shrieks, and takes off running. But I'm already on her tail, close enough to grab a handful of her hair, jerking her back like a yo-yo.

"AHHHH! DADDY, HELP ME!!"

"You little shit! You stupid little—"

"Mari! What are you doing?" Mom shouts, snatching my wrist, trying to shove me off with her shoulder. "Let go of her! Right now!"

But I'm seeing red and out for blood. I yank harder.

"DADDY!"

Piper squirms, squeaking as Alec comes rushing down the stairs.

"Oh my God," he shouts, yoking Piper. "GET OFF HER!"

But my grip is firm, leaving Piper caught in a brutal game of tug-of-war.

"LET GO! LET GO!"

"DADDY, PLEASE, DADDY!!"

"Mari?"

A shell-shocked Sammy, standing in the living room with Buddy, breaks my concentration. I loosen my grip, and Mom and I fall back onto the floor.

Alec consoles a hysterical Piper, patting her scalp. Mom pulls me to my feet, shaking my shoulders.

"Mari, what the hell is going on?" Mom screams. "And why do you smell like rubbing alcohol?"

"She's been messing with my phone, trying to scare the shit out of me!"

"What? What are you talking about?" Mom says.

Alec, shoving Piper behind him, towers over me, a finger in my face. "If you lay one hand on my daughter again, I'll . . ."

"You'll do nothing!" Mom roars, slapping his hand away. "Because we don't TOUCH our children. Right?"

Alec is enraged. "Raquel, you can't possibly let this stand. She assaulted Piper!"

"Because she was in my room," I snap. "Leaving strange creepy messages on my phone!"

Mom stands in front of me, using her body as a shield. "Messages? This is all over some messages, Mari?"

"It wasn't me," Piper shouts. "I swear! Ms. Suga did it!"

Alec and Mom whip around to Piper.

"What?" they say in unison.

Piper's mouth drops before she snaps it shut and quickly tries to throw the focus back on me.

"You're always on that phone," she shouts, then tugs on Alec's shirt. "She tells her daddy that she hates it here and hates you and sends dirty messages to that boy she likes!"

Mom frowns at me.

"Are you kidding me? NONE of that is true! Ask Dad if you don't believe me, because I know you don't. But let's not lose sight of the real problem here, and that's that she's fucking with my shit! She's creeping around with no respect for people's things, going through my phone, and is now blaming it on her stupid imaginary friend she's too damn old to have in the first place. It's a total invasion of privacy! So what are you going to do about it?"

Alec and Mom exchange a tired glance before Mom crosses her arms and cocks her head at Alec, as if to say, "Well?"

Alec's face softens, staring down at Piper.

"Well, it's not nice to talk behind people's backs," he says mildly.

Mom's mouth drops as Sammy's eyebrows hit his hairline.

"Unbelievable!" I scream, and storm off.

FIFTEEN

STARING UP AT the ceiling is how I do my best thinking. The vast blankness helps me sort out all kinds of stuff. Like how to chuck my little stepsister into a nearby dumpster without anyone knowing.

Piper refused to apologize for the phone fiasco, and Alec "doesn't feel he should force his daughter to do anything she's not ready to do" or some bullshit like that.

But if I'm honest, there's a small piece of me that wonders if it really was her. Unless she snuck in here like some super ninja while I was sleeping for those measly two hours, I can't see how she pulled it off. And I had my phone with me the entire night.

Except . . . when I went downstairs and the lights turned off. It was just lying on the bedroom floor so perfectly, as if placed there.

Ice prickles around my neck and I pull up my hoodie. So much happened in the last twenty-four hours. But none of it would bother me if I was high. I'd gladly give Piper all my passwords to any device she wanted just to have some numbness.

Which reminds me, I need to go check on the secret garden.

Mom opens the door just as I change into my run gear. "Yep?" she asks, full of eagerness.

I tilt my head, pulling my shirt down. "Yep what?"

She frowns. "You didn't just call me?"

"No."

"Huh? I guess I must be hearing things."

"Ugh, don't go losing it, Mom. You can't leave us alone with Alec."

"I'll try to keep that in mind. Her smirk turns serious. "You feeling okay? Anything you want to tell me?"

I can tell this morning's fight with Piper has Mom on red alert. I plaster on a fake smile.

"I'm fine. Totally in control."

"Hm. Well, where are you off to?"

"A run."

Mom nods, impressed. "You've been really on top of your game here."

"Have to be," I say, doing a quick stretch.

"So why won't you try out for the track team again?"

Immediately, I want to run in the opposite direction of this conversation.

"It's just not my thing anymore," I say, keeping my voice light, hoping she'll drop it.

"Mari, what happened with David and school . . . don't let it railroad your whole life. It's okay to let go. It was an . . . accident."

"Yeah. But I was the only one punished for it," I snap. Unintentionally, but I couldn't help it. Just the mention of his name makes me want to break the floorboard with my heel.

Mom twists her lips. "You're right. It's not fair. Life is not fair. But we keep moving forward. We moved to this new town so you could have a fresh start. And a fresh start also means doing the things you used to love. Like track."

She's right. We only moved here because of what I did. If it wasn't for me, we would still be where I loved and was once loved.

She kisses the side of my head. "Just . . . think about it, okay?"

"Sure," I mumble, and head out the door.

"If I haven't said it, I'm very proud of you, Marigold. You have made some significant improvements while we've been here. I just want you to start thinking about your future. Don't be so stuck in the past. There's nothing back there for you."

Guilt pinches at my side like a cramp. I paste on a fake smile.

"Thanks, Mom."

She smiles, giving me a hug. "Oh, by the way, have you seen the broom? I can't find it anywhere!"

The plants are starting to flower. Much faster than I anticipated. Meaning my one-room secret garden smells like a two-acre weed farm. The blooming sweet fragrance hits me as soon as I open the door.

This is both good and bad. Good, as I'll probably be able to harvest before Halloween. Bad, in that *anyone* could catch a whiff of this place from a mile away through the cracks in the windows. If I spent more than five minutes in the house, the essence would bake into my clothes and hair. Might as well wear a sign on my forehead that says what I'm up to (and thank God I keep a pair of clothes to change into). A quick Google search and I learned a carbon filter would minimize the scent . . . if I had read that far.

The janitor's closet at school was surprisingly helpful. It had plenty of the supplies I needed to build a makeshift filter system—charcoal air filters, duct tape, tinfoil, and clear plastic sheets.

The duct tape I stuck on the back door as a poor man's security system is still in place, but the moment I step inside, something feels . . . off. The house seems smaller, air putrid and dusty. Windows still closed, I glance at the duct tape. No signs of someone messing with it. A few cautious steps in and I stop short. The dining room is now crowded, as if every piece of moldy furniture in the house had been moved, rearranged, and shifted. Acid rises to my throat.

"H-hello?" I call out, and listen close. No movement.

Slowly, I backpedal into the kitchen, gripping the bags tighter. The plants sit, seemingly undisturbed. But on the floor surrounding them . . . red muddy footprints circle the table. I can count the toes from their bare feet. . . .

Someone was in the house.

I slam the door, burst through the brush, and run off in a frantic zigzag, looking over my shoulder every five seconds.

Someone was in the house. Someone saw the secret garden. Someone knows!

It dawns on me as soon I hit the porch steps that I'm still carrying the materials I stole from school.

I slink around the house and find a man standing in the backyard.

"Mr. Watson!" I yelp.

His head snaps up and he looks neither surprised nor happy to see me. Just a chronic state of indifference. In his hands are the overalls and shirt I leave under the deck.

"What are you doing here?" I ask.

He glances at the clothes in his hands, inspecting them, checking their tags.

"Your mother called," he says nonchalantly. "Asked me to replace the gutters. I was just taking some measurements. Are these . . . yours?"

I swallow, keeping my distance. "Yeah. They're my garden gear."

"Oh," he says, handing them over, his nose twitching. Can he smell the bud baked into the jeans? Is he going to tell Mom? What was he doing digging under the deck in the first place?

"Shopping?" he asks, noticing my bags.

"Yeah. I have a . . . science project to finish."

"Hm," he muses, then points next door. "You ain't . . . going in any of these houses no more, are you?"

How did he know about that?

"No," I say impassively. "I've learned my lesson."

Mr. Watson frowns. It wasn't the answer he was expecting. "Well, just be careful. These houses are dangerous."

He nods and walks away. I follow, unsure how I missed his Volvo parked out front. Guess my mind was too preoccupied with the idea of going to prison.

"Yusef, that's . . . a completely ridiculous idea."

I laugh until the point of tears during another one of our late-night chats I've almost become accustomed to. They're better than pretending to sleep while waiting for police to come crashing through our front door.

"Nah, you just ain't got vision," Yusef insists.

"A gardening competition show?"

"Yeah! It'd be like a showdown to see who could come up with the dopest layouts and landscape arrangements. Like, imagine they dropped our team in some random trash backyard and gave us two hours and a thousand-dollar budget to turn it into an oasis."

"*Our* team?"

"Yeah! You'd have to be on my team. You got terrarium skills. And don't think I didn't peep the way you arranged those tulip bulbs in GC. We'd smash the competition."

My heart flutters. Gardening compliments seem to have more meaning coming from him.

"Dude, who is going to watch this show?"

"Everybody! People love them baking shows. Making flying cupcakes and crap in less than twenty minutes. Why not ours?"

"Because cake is everything! Sugar over dirt any day."

"Like I said, you just don't got vision."

CREEEEAK

The door clicks, its hinges wailing, before opening just a hair, as if whoever stands behind it is deciding whether to enter. Chest tightening, I chew the inside of my cheek.

Relax. It's just a draft.

"You okay?" Yusef asks.

"What? Oh, yeah. I'm fine."

"You lying. Tell me. What's up?"

I take a deep breath, turning away from the door. "It's . . . nothing. Think I got a little cabin fever, that's all. You know, the other night, when we went to the beach, that was the farthest I've been from this house in weeks. Think I'm just . . . spooking myself."

"It *is* the spooky season," he counters.

"And I haven't even seen one pumpkin or witch on a broom!"

"Hm. Wanna get out the house tomorrow. Take a drive?"

CREEEEAK

It's nothing. It's nothing. It's nothing.

"Um . . . uh, sure? Where to?"

SIXTEEN

FALL IN CEDARVILLE is like one from the movies, where the air is crisp, the trees turn amber, and the streets are littered with crunchy brown leaves. The most idyllic way to spend my first change of season. Yusef pulls his truck into a muddy lot, parking right in front of a giant sign with a pig dressed in overalls welcoming us.

"An apple farm?" I ask, raising an eyebrow.

"You said you wanted to get out the city," he says, turning off the ignition. "The garden club takes trips out here every year."

"I love apples!" Sammy cheers from the back seat. I brought him along since he could use some fresh outdoor life as much as I could.

Mr. Wiggles's Farm is swarming with families and kids running about. It has a corn maze, photo booth, hayrides, a pumpkin patch, and a farmer's market.

"Mari," Sammy gasps, gripping my arm. "I need to ride that horse!"

He points to a run-down stallion, making loops with kiddies on its back.

"Dude, that's, like, for babies."

He holds up a hand. "I don't care. She will be my noble steed."

Yusef chuckles. "Go on, bruh! She's a hater."

I shrug. "Ride like the wind."

We watch Sammy run off to the animal farm in silence.

"Um, want some hot cider?" Yusef asks.

"Sure."

Yusef doesn't seem like his normal self as we stand in the fresh doughnuts and hot cider line. He barely said a word on the hour-long drive. Just let Sammy flip through his playlist. Smiling, but somehow it seems forced.

After another five minutes of silence, he finally speaks.

"Hey, you got a man back home?" Yusef blurts out as if he has been holding his breath.

Ugh. And I was having such a good day.

"No," I say flatly. "An ex."

"Oh. What was he like?"

I sigh. "White. Rich. Oblivious."

"Damn," he chuckles. "Then why were you with him?"

I pace in place, kicking myself for not wearing something warmer. Sixty-two degrees is like twenty degrees to my California blood. But I can't seem to find my new cream cable-knit sweater. Laundry must have eaten it with my tube socks.

"He was . . . fast. Like one of the fastest runners on our

team. I mean, the way he ran, he could've skipped across water. I found that . . . fascinating."

Yusef nods as the line moves up. "Still, doesn't seem like you had a lot in common."

He's right. Other than our love of weed, which is how we even started to begin with, we didn't have much in common. But the way Yusef acted at the party, I thought it best to leave that part out.

"I guess that's why we broke up," I laugh. "What about you? You have a girl?"

Yusef smirks. "Nah. Not even an ex to complain about, though many would say different."

We move up in the line, the air rich with cinnamon sugar and baked apples.

"That's impossible. You've *never* had a girlfriend? Don't tell me you're out here breaking hearts all over Cedarville."

"Not at all," he laughs as we reach the counter. He orders two hot apple ciders and four doughnuts. And like a classy gentleman, he offers to pay.

"What's up with all the questions about my ex?" I ask, following him.

Yusef shrugs. "No reason. Just wondering what you were like, back home. Feels like I don't really know anything about you. You're like a big-ass lockbox."

"So, is this some *Mission: Impossible*–style quest to try to open me up?"

He squints. "See? You're doing it again."

"Doing what?"

"Deflecting. Every time anyone gets a little close, you freeze up with Dad jokes."

"Hey, that joke was good, my dad would be proud. And why are you trying to get close to me anyways?"

"Because . . . we're friends!"

"Friends?" I catch the hurt in my voice and clear my throat. "I mean, right. We *are* friends."

Yusef nods as if to say "duh" and walks ahead. It's not like I wanted Yusef, or any boy, for that matter. But I'm not going to lie, it felt good knowing he wanted me. Nice stroke to the ego. Who knew reverse friend-zoning would come with such a sting.

"All right," he says, stopping at an archway made of hay bales. "Ready to pick your pumpkin?"

The pumpkin patch is massive, the size of at least two football fields. We walk through the endless rows, sipping our cider, inspecting pumpkins along the way.

"Are you sure we're even allowed to have one of these? We're not going to get arrested bringing it home?"

He shakes his head. "You so extra. What about this one?"

Yusef lifts a narrow-shaped pumpkin up in the air.

"That looks like Mr. Potato Head."

"Okayyyyy," he says, and huffs. "How about this one?"

"Bumpy face? Dude, no way!"

"Yo, don't be disrespectful. Bumpy face got feelings! He can hear you."

We laugh, maneuvering through the rows, the sky a gorgeous baby blue, the fresh air sweet. I can spot the apple orchard in the distance. Maybe Mom can make her famous vegan apple crumble or a pie. This was just what the doctor ordered, a normal Saturday afternoon.

"Yo, you hear that the Sterling Foundation is trying to tear down the library?"

I nearly trip over a vine. "Uh, no. Didn't hear anything about that."

Yusef nods and keeps moving. I don't know why I lied. It seemed easier than telling the truth. And the truth: there's no stopping what's already in motion. Yusef just has no idea.

"Ain't that some shit," he grumbles, inspecting another pumpkin. "Instead of them fixing shit, they just want to tear everything down."

"Well," I start, trying to keep my voice light. "Would that be so bad?

He whips around. "What?"

"Okay, not to shit on your home or nothing . . . but Maplewood is a bit of a mess. Our high school alone could use some serious upgrades. Maybe it's time for some changes in the neighborhood."

He stares at me, his eyes growing harder by the second, then crosses his arms. "Yo, you ever watch that show *Midnight Truth*?"

"Yeah! It's one of my faves!"

"Okay, remember when they replaced the actor that played Logan with some new guy, 'cause the original Logan kept coming to set drunk?"

"Ugh! Don't remind me. New guy was so blah-looking."

"Right, the show went on, but it wasn't the same. That's what 'change' sometimes be like. Take the whole soul out of something. Not all change is a good thing."

Change is good. Change is necessary. Change is needed.

My breath catches and I'm not sure why I feel so exposed. Nervously, I dunk the last of my doughnut in the apple cider.

"So you rather the Wood stay like it is now? A mess?"

"No! I never wanted the Wood to be this way. No one did. I'm just saying, they didn't throw away the Sistine Chapel because the paint started to flake. They renovated that shit! Took them some years and some serious cash, but they got it done. Why can't our city do the same for us? They got all that money for the Riverwalk but can't spare a dime to fix the pothole in front of Ms. Roberson's house."

I stop to glance up at him. "Okay, not going to lie, I'm hella impressed with your Sistine Chapel knowledge."

He smirks. "Heard someone say that on one of those stupid baking shows."

"Told you, sugar over dirt!"

"You right, you right," he laughs. "Well, Unc and I, we're thinking of starting a Maplewood historical society."

"Really?"

"Yeah. We have to start saving our legacy before it's all washed away. Pop-Pop took lots of pictures growing up. We can maybe raise some money for a museum or something."

I smile. "I love how . . . passionate you get about Maplewood."

"It's my home, why wouldn't I?"

"I don't know. Guess I don't really feel attached to much of anything . . . anymore."

"Why not?"

Because my old town is full of jerks, and my old house kept the memories of bedbugs, my ex-boyfriend, and my parents' divorce alive. Plus, there's the whole nearly dying on my bedroom floor thing. But I didn't want to get into all that.

"No reason," I say with a shrug before spotting the perfect pumpkin right by my boot.

"There! Got one." I lift it up in the air. "And I shall name you Sweets and I shall carve out your eyes and smile with a steak knife."

He shakes his head. "Well, that ain't creepy at all."

Yusef offers to carry Sweets to the car as we head back. Sammy waves at us from his horse, practically moving in slow motion.

"Yo, we should've brought your sister," Yusef says. "She would've loved this too."

I roll my eyes. "Dude. That little bitch is not my sister. Besides, I would've been too tempted to tie her to a scarecrow."

"Whoa," he says, face turned up. "Yo, do you talk like that around her? Not cool."

"You don't know what's she's like. She makes life . . . miserable. More miserable than it has to be."

He rolls his eyes. "She's a kid!"

"She's ten," I snap back.

"She's. A. KID! Give her a break. She ain't got it easy."

"How would you know?"

"Come on now, it's the Wood. Everyone knows everything about everybody. Word is nobody talks to that girl. She's straight-up canceled. Think of all the looks you be getting at school, multiply that by a hundred. That's what she's dealing with."

Guilt starts to eat at my hard candy shell. I didn't know she had it that bad. Didn't seem like she cared either way if she had friends or not and totally fine staying up under Alec. But maybe that's her defense mechanism, pretending everything's fine and she doesn't give a damn.

That's at least one thing we have in common.

"Still don't give her the right to take her issues out on us," I mumble.

"Girl ain't getting no love at school, no love at home . . . seems like there's nothing left to do but be a little asshole. But even assholes got a heart and a turning point. Just got to give her a chance. I'm sure folks given you second chances when you've fucked up."

My stomach muscles tie in knots.

Does he . . . know?

Sunday. Wash day.

As I stand in front of the mirror, detangling my coils, my thoughts drift back to the secret garden. Could I be imagining things? The room felt . . . off, disturbed. Didn't seem like anyone broke in there; the door was exactly as I left it. So how could the furniture be moved around yet the door never be open? And if someone was snooping around . . . why didn't they mess with the plants? Maybe they're waiting for the right time to blackmail me.

"Mari! Mari!" Sammy calls from downstairs.

In the beginning, this whole plan seemed so foolproof. Now I'm exhausted living this double life and, what's worse, not even close to the type of high I want. Scratch that, need.

"Mari! Mari!"

"What?! I'm doing my hair!" I shout through the door, hands covered in deep conditioner.

"Come here! Quick!"

"Dude," I groan, and stuff my wet curls in a plastic cap.

"Mari, are you coming?"

"I'm coming, I'm coming. Hang on," I say from the steps, water already leaking down my neck, soaking the collar of my T-shirt.

"Hurry up!" Sammy excitedly waves me on, grabbing my

hand and pulling me into the family room.

"What is it?"

"Come here! Look at Buddy!"

Buddy is sitting back on his hind legs, paws in the air. For a silly slobber dog, he's completely stoic, motionless.

"He's been like that for, like, five whole minutes," Sammy laughs. "He hasn't moved. Even when I offer him treats!"

Sammy snaps his fingers, but Buddy doesn't blink. Tail erect, eyes focused, he's a tense living statue. The same way he looks when he spots a squirrel; his wolf instinct returns and he's nothing but a predator glaring at his prey.

I follow Buddy's eyeline to the basement door.

"Buddy?" I say slowly.

A low growl seeps through his teeth, transfixed on one spot. Hairs prickle on my neck like hundreds of tiny knives.

There's nothing there. There's nothing there. There's nothing there!

With two quick strides, I bolt across the room, pushing Buddy sideways, and he yelps.

"Dude!" Sammy yells. "What'd you do that for?"

Stunned, Buddy shakes his head, looking up at me with a happy pant, tail wagging.

"It's . . . uh, it isn't good for his joints, sitting like that," I say, plopping on the sofa, trying to keep it cool. "You want him to get arthritis?"

"He's seven," Sammy scoffs before his voice trails off, and he turns, staring at the basement door. I lean forward.

"What is it?" I gasp.

For a moment, he stands staring just like Buddy, entranced, unmoving, but exhales, turning back to me.

"Oh. Nothing," he quips with a shrug. "Thought I heard something,"

"Something . . . like what?" I ask, inching forward, prepared to catch his secret.

"I don't know," he laughs, blowing me off, and gives Buddy a good scratch behind the ears. "It's nothing."

I bite my tongue to keep from pushing further. I want him to hear something. To see something. I want him to jump on the crazy train with me, so I don't feel so alone.

"Where's Piper?" he asks, rubbing Bud's belly.

"In her room, I guess."

"You guess? Some babysitter you are."

"Believe me, this is one job I did not sign up for and quit regularly," I moan and flop on the sofa, leaning my head on the sofa arm with a yawn. Insomnia and early morning gardening has me wiped out.

"She was just sitting down here in the dark, doing nothing. No TV or anything. Weird little kid."

Considering my talk with Yusef, I try to see things from Piper's perspective. Through the eyes of a little girl living with cold strangers who doesn't have a friend her age in the world. I glance at the freshly carved Sweets on the counter and smile.

"Hey, did you have fun apple picking? I mean, after you rode your pony?"

He narrows his eyes. "She was a retired racehorse. And

yeah, I did. Yusef's really cool."

A memory flashes of David and Sammy playing video games in our living room while I did homework. Sammy loved David. He took the breakup pretty hard, enough to find David's number in Mom's phone and secretly call him sometimes. It made our breakup complicated.

"Well. Don't get too attached," I blurt out.

He snorts. "I could say the same thing to you."

"Touché . . . ," I chuckle. "Ugh. It's so annoying having a younger twin."

He points at my head. "You're getting your hair mayo on the sofa."

"Shit," I mutter, jumping up. Last time I tried to do a hot oil treatment, I fell asleep watching *The Great American Baking Show* and oil leaked out my shower cap, staining the cushion. I flipped it over and it's been my little secret ever since.

"Hey, what's that?" Sammy points behind me, frowning.

"What?"

"On your pants."

I slide a hand down my side before looking, expecting to touch something wet, but instead come across something dry, minuscule . . . and hard.

Sammy's eyes grow wide, shooting his hand out. "Wait, Mari . . ."

But it's too late. I glance down and see a sprinkle of black dots on my pants and pinch one in between my nails.

"Oh God," I whisper before snatching the cushion up, exposing my oil stain . . . as well as black spots in the sofa lining.

The scream that bubbles up is agonizing. The scream of a siren. Sammy covers his ears as I back away, tripping over Buddy, my arm in flames.

Bedbugs. We have bedbugs. Bedbugs bedbugs bedbugs . . .

Sammy moves closer to investigate.

"NO, SAM! Don't!" I sob, reaching out to grab him. Buddy, unnerved by my screams, starts to whimper.

Sam bends, grabbing a black dot, examining it before he sniffs.

"It's coffee," he mutters, standing. "It's not bugs, it's just coffee. Here, smell!"

"DON'T BRING THEM TO MY FACE!"

Sammy jumps back. "Dude, calm down!"

I fly into the kitchen, diving under the sink for the cleaning supplies.

We need soap, bleach. I think the steam cleaner is in the linen closet. Boil the water, Sammy. It has to be superhot. Where's my hair dryer? Can't sit on your bed, rip the sheets. I'll start the first load. We have some of those big black garbage bags, right? Let's put the furniture on the deck, I'll start scrubbing. Is it gonna rain? I don't think it's gonna rain. It can air out. Maybe save a mattress, seal off the room. What about Bud? I don't want him messing with the glue traps. We have to lay traps at each foot of the bed. Four traps, four beds, four times four is eight but we should double that to sixteen so we can do two rounds. Oh God, is that a bite? That's a bite!

"Mari? Mari, calm down. It's not bedbugs."

But it's too late. I'm sprinting up the stairs, yanking my clothes off as I go. Heart thumping, I strip the bed, checking for bloodstains.

FACT: Stains from blood or feces left behind by bedbugs usually appear on sheets and bedding as a rust color.

No sign of blood. Not on the sheets or the mattress. Maybe in Sammy's room? Or Mom's? Piper's? They could be anywhere. Everywhere. An infestation!

FACT: Bedbug eggs may be difficult to see with the naked eye since they are about the size of a grain of sand. Look for grain-sized eggs that are milky in color.

Downstairs, I hear Sammy on the phone.

"You have to come home! She's having one of her episodes again."

No, Mom. Don't come home. Stay away, we're infected. I'm infected. The linens, we need to wash all of them on the hottest setting, no, no, we need to boil water, steam clean, I think I brought our old one with us . . . wait, our old one? What if we brought bedbugs from Cali? What if they've been with us all this time?

FACT: Bedbugs can go without feeding for twenty to four hundred days, depending on temperature and humidity.

Bedbugs bedbugs bedbugs they'll follow us everywhere!

Piper hovers in her doorway, watching me.

"Piper! Strip your bed," I cry, throat dry. "We have bedbugs!"

Piper doesn't move. Just stands there with a smug smile painted on her face. As if we aren't under attack by mini demons; we'll never get rid of them. Never ever ever ever ever! They're multiplying, living in the walls, in the sockets, the carpet . . . on our clothes. I check over my body, every nook and crevice, in search of a bite. Nothing, nothing. But the eggs are there, in my arm hairs, invisible, microscopic. I knew it! I knew they were here! I knew it!

Shower. I scrub my skin with a new loofah. Hot water, soap . . . and rubbing alcohol. I jump out, slipping on the wet tile. Can't use the towel, might have bedbugs. Heat. Must use heat. Heat will get rid of them. I plug in my hair dryer, turn it on high, and blow-dry all my arm hair and leg hair. My skin is red and blotchy. Is that from the bedbugs or the hair dryer? Do I need another shower? More alcohol it stings, it burns, it stings, it burns. I have no clothes all of them covered in bedbugs they're everywhere, everywhere!

Downstairs, the front door slams.

"Sammy," Mom calls. "Where is she?"

"Mom!" I scream, running downstairs. "Mom! We have bedbugs again! I found them in the sofa."

Sammy covers his eyes as Mom grabs a blanket out of the living room.

"Marigold, my God," she shrieks, wrapping the blanket around me. My skin engulfs in flames.

"WHAT ARE YOU DOING!" I scream, shoving her off me, hard.

Mom crashes into the wall behind her, dropping her purse in shock. "Marigold!"

"I didn't wash that! It could have bedbugs!"

"You can't stand here naked!"

"Mom, you're not listening!" I scream through choked sobs, face sweaty, skin burning. "We have to call the exterminator. We need to book hotel rooms so they can do smoke bombs. We need to smoke them out!"

Everything itches. The scalp under my wet hair, my legs, my stomach, my arms my arms my arms they're everywhere oh my God please please please . . .

"I—I can't breathe. I can't breathe!" I gasp. "I can't . . . can't."

Mom's eyes flare as she scoops me up under my arms. "Sam, grab her inhaler! Come on, baby, come on outside with me."

Mom gathers the blanket and gently leads me out to the back veranda. The chilly air on my wet skin is a slap to the face.

"Come on baby, breathe," she instructs, slow and steady. "That's it, just breathe."

The patio furniture is covered in leaves that crunch under our butts. Mom rubs my back.

"Mom, we . . . we have to . . ." But I can't finish a single sentence. The building sitting on my chest weighs a million pounds.

"Marigold," Mom whispers, cupping my face. "Marigold, you need to relax, baby."

Sammy runs out to join us with Buddy on his tail. He passes me my inhaler and a bottle of water. Mom digs into her purse, taking out her medicine pouch. After about forty-five minutes of deep inhales and exhales, I could feel my heart rate start to slow by a fraction.

"Now in just a few, we're going to go inside and I'm going to show you what you saw."

"No," I whimper. "No, please, Mom! I can't. We need to go."

Mom smiles at Sammy. "But your brother has done all this work to make sure you're safe. Why don't you come see?"

Inside, the cushions and pillows are laid out on the floor like a giant thick rug. Mom tries to lead me over and I resist.

"No no no no no . . . wait, please!"

"Look, Marigold," Mom insists, turning on her phone's flashlight. "Look at their color, at their shape. It's not bedbugs, baby. Sammy's right, it's coffee grinds."

I blink and blink again.

"Coffee?" I parrot, as if I've never heard of the word before.

Mom talks to me calm and rationally, even places a few specks in my hand to examine. I sniff, recognize her morning rain forest brew. Not bedbugs. Just coffee. Tears spring up as I glance at Sam.

"I'm . . . sorry," I mumble with a shiver, clutching the blanket to my chest, painfully aware I'm naked underneath. How many times am I going to scar his childhood?

"It's all right, baby. I would've freaked out too," Mom says, holding me.

Shame swallows me up. I can't believe I shoved my mom. First, I made her have to move because of my addiction, because of my anxiety, and now I'm physically abusing her, when she's already done so much for me. Is this rock bottom? This has to be.

"We've been through a lot with those stupid bugs, haven't we," she says with a tender smile, wiping my tears. "They definitely left their mark."

Sammy brushes the sofa with a perplexed scowl. "How did coffee grinds . . . get in the couch?"

Mom shrugs. "I don't know. Guess maybe some spilled out when I took out the compost."

"Yeah, but in the sofa? It's almost like someone stuffed them down there."

She sighs. "I don't know, guys. But . . . it was an accident. Everything's fine now, right?"

I look over my shoulder at Sammy, his eyebrow cocking up, and know we're both thinking the same thing.

Piper.

Mom kisses my forehead. "I'm going to make you a cup of chamomile tea, draw you a nice oatmeal bath, and give you some melatonin so you can get a good night's sleep. That'll help you relax."

Resolve comes slipping back into my bloodstream, because there's only one thing I know that'll really help me relax.

Yusef is all smiles in the hallway by his locker, holding up a doughnut.

"Cali—"

"Not now," I grumble, blowing right past him.

I didn't change my clothes, brush my teeth, or do my hair. I rolled out of bed, grabbed my book bag, and took off for school in my pajama pants and Ugg slippers. I'm on a mission: trying to catch Erika before homeroom. I need some bud. I need to smoke a bong the size of my head.

My stomach cramps up. Did I take my pill yesterday? Or today? No more alarms on my phone. Too freaked out. My hands are shaking, sweat dripping down my face. Haven't been this bad since . . . I don't even know when. But if I don't find some bud soon I'm going to need something stronger. And I swore to myself . . . never again. I said the words in rehab, and I meant them. I know no one believes me and I don't want to give them a reason to be right. All I know is that Piper did this to me. She knew my greatest weakness and used it against me in the cruelest way possible. Don't know how I'm going to get her back, but I know I will.

Nearly running down the hall, I head toward Erika's locker but stop short at the sound of her voice coming out of the main office.

"That shit ain't mine! Yo, you can't do that!"

Through the scratched glass pane, I see Erika led out of the assistant principal's office in handcuffs.

"Nah! This shit's fucked up!!"

A crowd forms around me. The entire hallway of Kings High is at a standstill.

"Make room, back up," an officer orders, holding Erika's book bag in a large ziplock evidence bag.

My tongue dries out and I let the crowd swallow me as two officers carry out a screaming Erika.

"That shit ain't mine! You know it ain't!"

She lifts her feet, kicking a nearby locker. The crowd flinches.

"E!" Yusef screams from the other side of the hall, running toward her. "What's going on? What happened?"

"Yo, it wasn't me! Tell them! Tell them that shit wasn't mine!" Erika wails, making herself heavy as she dips to the ground, eyes filled with panic tears. I still can't move.

"What's going on?" a girl next to me asks in a whisper.

"She got caught slanging," another girl snickers. "They just searched her locker."

"Damn, another Fisher up to Big Ville. Is there any of them left?"

The hall is a swarm of voices, hot and sticky breath, shouting over one another as Erika resists.

A shell-shocked Yusef rubs his head, distraught. "What do I do, E? Tell me what to do!"

An officer yokes Erika up with a hard shake, slamming her face into the locker.

"Aye! I said knock it off!" he barks, inches from her eye.

It takes five girls to hold Yusef back from charging at them. They struggle, arms around his neck, chest, and legs. I cover my mouth with my hands, feet glued to the floor.

"Stop it," I cry, but no one can hear me over the chorus of shouting.

"Get off her," Yusef barks.

Erika takes a calming breath, nodding, tears rolling down her face. School security holds students back from following as she's led down the hall, toward the main doors.

"Yo, Yuey, take care of my grand for me, man! Take care of her. Tell her it wasn't mine!"

The walk home from school is dark and cold, the day a blur. Went to my classes, but I don't remember much more than moving from one room to the other. Didn't open a book or reach for a pen while the same thought kept repeating itself: Did she know I was there? Did she see me before they took her to jail?

Even the sentence felt strange in my head: Erika is in jail.

It was a strange déjà vu feeling, watching security comb through her locker, pillage through her things, tossing them in the trash like they didn't expect her to come back. Reminded me of the way they rummaged through my locker. They didn't find anything. But it didn't make me feel any less than a criminal. I put myself in Erika's shoes. Would I have to be dragged out the school kicking and screaming? I feel sick just thinking about it.

Yusef left school early, most likely to check on Erika's grandmother. That poor lady, now all alone. It doesn't make sense. Erika was the one who told me about the Sterling Laws. She knew them like you know every word to your favorite song. No way she would do something so careless.

Unless . . . they purposely planted something on her. But why?

A spark flares in me. Mom covered juvenile cases for the *LA Times*. She knows lawyers, knows the system. Maybe she can recommend someone. Help her with bail or something.

I sprint in my slippers, eager to make it home and explain everything to Mom. But as soon as I bust in, I'm greeted by the worst welcoming party.

"Ah! Marigold. Wonderful to see you!"

Mr. Sterling must have a billion new black and gray suits in his closet. He stands at the kitchen island, placing his mug of coffee down on the counter.

"Hi?" *What the hell is he doing here?*

"Hey, baby. You okay?" Mom's voice sounds . . . off. Why is she nervous?

"Yeah, I'm fine. Why?"

She gives Mr. Sterling an uneasy glance, then smiles.

"Well . . . um. I heard what happened to your friend at school today. Erika?"

Shit.

"Oh," I mumble, taking off my shoes, trying to find something to do with my hands.

Mr. Sterling smiles between us. "Yes, it's quite a shame, isn't it? Such a lovely young lady, with a bright and promising future. Too bad she was caught up in the wrong crowd. As soon as I heard, I decided to stop by here myself and check on the Anderson-Green family. I feel you're sort of my responsibility, given that I convinced you to move to our fair city."

"You didn't have to do that, really," Mom says sheepishly.

"No, no, I insist. Just want to assure you, these types of incidents will never happen again." He looks pointedly at me, eyes darkening above a gleaming smile. "Well, unless someone starts snooping in places they don't belong. Then she could find herself in a lot of trouble and others could be hurt by such careless actions."

My throat closes so tight, I can't even gulp.

He knows!

"Well, I'm off! Wife's cooking her famous roast chicken. Famous 'cause she picks it up from the store." He laughs at his own joke and nods at me. "Take care. Be safe."

He steps outside, Mom following, and they talk in hushed whispers on the porch.

Something dark hangs in the air in the words left unsaid. Still stunned, I linger in the hall before meandering into the family room.

He knows! But how? Are there mics planted around the house? Is he tapping our phones?

Still too spooked to sit on the sofa, I pace around the room, Buddy following. Wish I had weed to help me think, ease the scattering of panicked voices in my head. The secret garden . . . it needs tending, which shouldn't be a priority, but with Erika gone, it's my last resort. Can't trust anyone else.

I glance at the clock on the cable box, catching a glimpse of the modem's label, and gasp, running across the room to grab it—Sedum Cable.

Holy shit. They're monitoring our Wi-Fi! And Erika . . . oh God. It's all my fault!

I bring a trembling hand up to my lips, stifling a scream. They took her because of me, because of my snooping, because of something I did.

Mom enters the room with a look on her face that means

trouble. I put the modem down.

"I asked Alec to take off early so he can pick up Sammy and Piper," she says, her voice stony. "It's just me and you."

"Okay?"

"And I want you to tell me the truth."

I frown. "The truth about what?"

She walks into her office, then comes back with a piss cup. My mouth dries.

"Seriously?" Does she know what type of day I've had?

"Erika was dealing," Mom snaps, as if daring me to say she's wrong. "You knew, and that's the only reason why you were friends with her. You wouldn't be otherwise."

The sharpness of that truth is a fresh coating of guilt I wasn't expecting so soon.

"Mom . . ."

"We talked about this in group, remember? This is the addiction taking over what you know is right and wrong."

I cross my arms to hold myself tighter. The word *group* brings me back to Wednesday meetings inside a church basement. Memories I try hard to block out.

"But I'm clean," I say with a shaky voice. And it's true. Well, mostly.

Mom takes a deep breath. "Marigold, I love you. I also know you. And with the kids . . . we cannot have another incident like back home. I won't put Sammy through it. Again."

Using Sammy . . . a low blow. But I can't argue. That's the

thing that happens once you've OD'ed. You lose the trust of everyone and it feels impossible to get it back.

With a sigh, I grab the cup and head for the bathroom. The test is going to be negative, but just the thought that Mom felt she had to give it to me cuts deeper than a knife, burning me alive.

SEVENTEEN

THE GARDEN CLUB secured another donation for the beautification project in Maplewood. Today we are planting orange mums by the elementary school, in honor of Halloween. Ms. Fern said it was to inspire trick-or-treaters. The room's only response was silence.

Yusef attacks the patch of earth with his pick, uprooting and hacking anything in his way. I follow with large garbage bags, collecting trash and weeds. He works fast, trying to dig himself a hole straight to middle-earth. He hits a rock, deep in the soil. The pick rings like a bell, forcing him to stop and catch his breath.

"You okay?" I finally ask.

"Oh, I'm straight," he says with a sad laugh. "Except for the fact that my mom, dad, brother, and now E are all up at Big Ville and I'm just . . . here."

"Sorry, Yuey." And it's true. I feel so deeply sorry for him. But even more so for E. Mom's right, I'm only friends with people to get what I want, what I need. Yusef for his tools, Erika for her weed.

Yusef cracks a smile. "Told you not to call me that."

"Yeah, but I feel the need to fill Erika's shoes. Not that I ever could."

"You don't have to. I like you just as you are." His mouth curls up into a charming boyish smirk. No longer feeling worthy of his kindness, I turn away. This is all my fault. I cost a friend her freedom. But I can't tell Yusef that. Knowing what the Sterling Foundation is capable of, who knows what they'd do. I won't risk his life too.

"It was worth a shot," I mumble, stuffing more trash into a bag.

He squats down to rip up a handful of ragweed and shakes his head.

"She would've never brought that shit to school. I've known her my whole life; she wouldn't do something that stupid." He sighs. "They planted that shit on her. No question. Not that I can prove it."

Guilt floods my stomach and I'm ready to vomit anything that will relieve the pressure.

"My mom thinks I'm still an addict," I say, throwing more trash into the bag.

Yusef freezes, neck craning in my direction. To his credit, he tries his best to mask the shock, but I know this revelation was a sledgehammer to the idea he's painted in his head about me.

"Well . . . are you?" he asks in a measured voice.

"I haven't touched the Percs in months, and I don't plan on it. Problem is no one believes me."

He stands up, taking off his work gloves, and dusts off his shirt. "Maybe 'cause you keep lying, even to yourself."

I scoff. "Dude, I'm fine. I've changed, seriously, but weed, weed is nothing more than a plant. Like, medicinal therapy. Not even that dangerous."

"But have you actually tried giving it all up?"

"It's not that simple," I say, flustered. "I have these weird episodes and the medication I used to take back in Cali . . . just made me a foggy mess."

"And weed makes you a lying mess if you have to sneak around to do it."

It wasn't intentional, but being called a mess has an icy bite to it, enough to make me shiver.

"Weed . . . it really just stabilizes me," I start, trying to find a way to explain what feels so hard to put into words. "In, like, a way better way than those meds did. I have really bad anxiety. And if it was legal—"

"But it's not!" he shouts. "And anxiety? What you got to be anxious about? You have both your parents, ones with good-ass jobs, food in your fridge, a free house . . . no one around here got it as easy as you! They have a real-ass excuse to be strung out!"

I narrow my eyes, breathing flames. "Yusef, 'I have anxiety' is a full and complete statement. I don't have to explain the what and why to you!"

We glare at one another until the anger starts to fade from his eyes.

"You right. My bad, I guess."

Aside from wanting to smash his face into the ground, I'm pretty proud I stood up for myself, just like my guru taught me. Anxiety is a real thing. I wouldn't be this way for shits and giggles.

Yusef sighs. "Look, I hear you and all, but that shit locked up my whole family. My whole neighborhood, gone just like that. Folks still ain't right. We've lost everything, and I can't lose you too, because I like you!"

Heads snap in our direction, the entire garden club zeroing in. My mouth drops open and I quickly swivel away, trying to find something to do with my hands to ease the grossly embarrassing moment.

"Oh, I . . . um . . ."

Yusef winces. "Uh, I mean, not like you like that. I'm saying, you cute and all, but . . ." He takes a breath. "Okay, this is gonna sound . . . weird."

I snort. "Weird? In Weirdville? This must be good."

"You're, like, the first regular friend, that's a girl, that I've ever really had. Well, besides E, and she don't really count."

"Imma tell her you said that," I laugh.

He smirks, rubbing the back of his head. "It's just that . . .

all the girls here, they all want something."

"Ha! Dude, humblebrag much?"

"Nah, I'm serious," he says, seeming torn. "You know the statistics here after them Sterling Laws. Fifteen to one. I can't even look at a girl longer than ten seconds without her thinking we're together. I've even had girls claim they were pregnant, trying to trap me, when it's just impossible."

"Well, anything is possible, especially when you're having sex!" I laugh. "Unless you're not; then I guess that would explain it."

Yusef turns away, snatching up the pick. I cock my head to the side.

"Wait, are you seriously telling me you're a virgin?"

He shrugs, not meeting my eye.

"You mean, with all these girls . . . dude, you are literally sitting in a gold mine with blue balls! Treat yourself! No one would blame you. What's the holdup?"

He shrugs. "I dunno. I want to wait. For someone special."

"Yeah, right! I know guys who would kill to be in your shoes."

He eyes me. "Cali, not all guys are the same. Trust me on that."

We work in silence for a while and it feels good, just working with the earth, not thinking about school, Erika, Piper, the Sterling Foundation, or our creepy-ass house . . . until I glance at my watch.

"Shit. I have to go! Gotta stop by the library before it closes so I can finish and print my lit essay for tomorrow."

"Don't you have a computer?" he asks, genuinely confused.

"I do, or I did." I let out a delirious laugh. "But apparently Ms. Suga doesn't like technology."

I take off my work gloves, throwing them in my book bag with a yawn. The past week of sleepless nights is catching up to me. I turn to say goodbye to find Yusef frozen in place, his mouth gaping, eyes bulging.

"Wh-what did you just say?" he gasps.

"Huh? What I do?"

He gulps, moving closer to me. "How . . . do you know about Ms. Suga," he whispers.

A sinking feeling invades my chest. "Me? No, how do *you* know about Ms. Suga?"

"Shhhhhh! Keep your voice down!" he whispers, scanning around us. He grabs my elbows and leads me toward the corner, out of earshot from the rest of the group.

"Who told you about Ms. Suga?"

"Dude, I was totally joking. It's just some imaginary friend Piper's cooked up to blame shit on."

Yusef brings a fist up to his mouth. "Oh shit. I was just messing with you before, about the Hag and stuff. But now . . . now . . ."

He pales, and whatever I had for lunch threatens to come up.

"Yusef . . . what's going on?" I ask cautiously. "How do you know about Ms. Suga?"

His eyes dart around the ground, like a cat chasing a toy. "Well . . . maybe she overheard it somewhere. Maybe?"

"Would you just tell me what the fuck is going on!"

"Shhhh! Okay. Just . . . not out here. Let's go back to my house. I have to show you something."

Yusef's room is cleaner than I remember, the music still loud. I keep my distance from the wooden bed.

"You know this?" Yusef turns up his music with a smirk. Tupac's "Hail Mary."

I narrow my eyes. "Quit stalling. Tell me. How do you know about Ms. Suga?"

He sighs and turns down his music. "Okay. I'm going to tell you . . . but, damn, Cali. You can't tell anybody this, okay? Like, not even your folks."

I give him a sharp nod. "Fine."

He turns up the music again. "Come on. Follow me but keep quiet."

We slip out of his room, tiptoeing down the hall. I can see the back of Pop-Pop's head in his recliner, watching some old TV program. Yusef slowly clicks open the first door on the right and ushers me into a cramped room with baby-blue walls. Inside smells like shoe polish mixed with aftershave. A twin hospital bed sits in the middle of the room and I trip over a pair of orthopedic loafers, colliding into a walker.

Pop-Pop's room. What are we doing in here?

On a narrow nightstand is an old framed picture of a young Black couple, posing in front of Yusef's house. This must be Pop-Pop and Yusef's grandma. On the dresser is one of those classic cameras, the kind you need to load film into and have developed.

"Over here," Yusef says in a low voice, standing by a wall of old black-and-white framed photos, similar to the ones in the hallway. Except these aren't just of people; they're of homes, buildings, and skylines. Pop-Pop must have taken all these when he was younger. Yusef points to a photo, a wide shot of a quaint street with beautiful antique mansion-style houses on either side.

"This is Maple Street. Your Maple Street."

I do a legit double take.

"What? No way," I laugh, leaning in to spot our house, third one on the right. "Whoa!"

Yusef taps the photo. "The houses on your block were owned by the Peoples family. Joe Peoples and Carmen Peoples. The Peoples had five children: Junior, Red, Norma, Ketch, Jon Jon. Mr. Peoples was a carpenter who loved to play the numbers. Until one day, he actually won the freaking lottery, which like never happens to anyone around here. With all that money, he bought each of his children a home on Maple Street and bought Mrs. Peoples her own bakery across the street from the library. Folks called it the Suga Shop."

He takes a deep breath, pointing to another picture. A young Black woman, petite, with long thick black hair, stands in front of the shop in a ruffled apron, hands on her hips and a wide proud smile.

Ms. Suga . . .

"No," I gasp, recoiling.

Yusef nods. "She was known for making some of the best pies in the state."

"Wh-what happened to them?"

He takes a deep breath. "They say that Mr. Peoples died in some type of strange car accident. With him gone, all these white developers were lining up, trying to buy the houses from Ms. Suga, but she refused. One by one, three of the Peoples children ended up dying in some strange accident. Soon after . . . all these rumors started that the family actually got their money from selling drugs and the youngest son, Jon Jon, was going around, sneaking into people's houses and touching little kids. Folks stopped going to the bakery. The Wood gave Ms. Suga the cold shoulder. Then, after Devil's Night, after they found Seth Reed . . . some folks from the Wood . . . they cornered Jon Jon and set his house on fire. Ms. Suga, living next door, ran inside to save him. They never came out. Burned alive in the house . . . right next to yours."

My knees give in and I fall back on Pop-Pop's bed before shooting back up quick, dusting my jeans.

"Shit," I mumble. "The boarded-up house!"

Yusef struggles to continue the story. "But . . . it turned out all them kids were lying. Said some Russo mobsters paid them to make it all up. Jon Jon never touched any of them kids. But it was too late. Damage was already done."

"That's insane! They didn't just . . . wait, did you say 'Russo'?"

"Yeah. They used to run this city."

Still do, I think. Damn, this is a real-life nightmare.

"So, no one went to the police and told them that the kids were lying?"

He shook his head. "If anyone did . . . everyone in the Wood would've been up at Big Ville. So . . . there's a silent pact around here. Folks taking what they know to their graves. Only reason I know . . . well, 'cause . . . Pop-Pop."

I blink, realization sinking in. "No. Dude . . . he didn't."

Yusef rushes to explain. "He thought he was doing the right thing, you know? Thought he was protecting kids!"

The information eating me alive, I choke back a sob. That poor family. Yusef crosses the room.

"Anyway, after the house burnt up, they boarded it up, making it look like the others, so no one would ever know."

My jaw hangs open. "Oh God," I gasp, squeezing my eyes shut, thinking of what Erika said. How bodies were still in homes, left to rot forever.

"Folks been trying to ease the pain of their guilt for what they did ever since . . . in any way they can."

Drugs. That's what he means. It's why it hit this area so hard. And even after all that, most of the folks from the Wood still found themselves in Big Ville.

Speechless, I try to collect my thoughts. Because there has to be some reasonable explanation how Piper would know all this. "Someone at school must have told Piper about Ms. Suga."

"Maybe." He shrugs. "But . . . it's said that Ms. Suga has haunted all the homes on Maple Street ever since. That she was so angry about losing her family that she turned into the Hag. And if you talk bad about Ms. Suga or her children, she'll haunt you in your dreams. No one even walks down that street, there's been so many bodies found over the years. Folks are shook. Cali, if Ms. Suga is really haunting your house, you gotta be careful. She's out for blood."

"'And if you will indeed obey my commandments that I command you today, to love the Lord your God, and to serve him with all your heart and with all your soul, he will give the rain for your land in its season, the early rain and the later rain, that you may gather in your grain and your wine and your oil. And he will give grass in your fields for your livestock, and you shall eat and be full.' —Deuteronomy, chapter 11, verse 13–15. You see, it says right here how the Lord plans to make good on his promises of miracles. He put angels in the form of mayors, governors alike, to protect you from sin, so that you may live a life of prosperity."

We walk out into the living room and I'm in a haze. The idea I'm living in a house with so much tragic history, right next to one with dead bodies still inside, makes me want to vomit. A part of me wants to go running into Mom's arms. This should be enough of a reason to move. But I made a promise to Yusef not to tell anyone. Telling would only throw more people in prison. And I still haven't fessed up about Erika.

"You will always harvest what you plant in the Lord's will. As you sow, so shall you reap. Those who do not follow the Lord's will, will reap what they sow. That's why if you call now, I will send you these anointed HOLY SEEDS. . . ."

Pop-Pop is on a cordless phone, his voice light and chipper in a way I've never heard before.

"Ahh yes, this here is Mr. Brown, senior. Calling to put in this week's order."

We stand behind him, listening to him order five packets of Scott Clark's miracle seeds as the infomercial plays on.

"Why'd you let him waste his Social Security money on them stupid seeds?" I ask in a whisper.

Yusef shrugs, taking two sodas out of the fridge. "He's old. We let him do what he wants. Besides, he's been at it for years."

"Can't believe all these years and no one has gotten their seeds to grow. This man is running the biggest scam in Cedarville and the FBI hasn't scooped him up."

He sips, staring at Pop-Pop. "He thinks his seeds don't grow for him because of what he's done. So . . . he's spent his whole life trying to help other people grow their seeds, get their miracle."

I shake my head. "Scott Clark is setting people up to fail and have them pay for their own failure. But how does he expect anyone to reap if they can't sow those bogus seeds? It's total bullshit."

Yusef sighs. "Truth is, the ground is spoiled here, always has been." He looks at me. "And you can't grow where you're not wanted."

Thump.

Thump.

Thump.

Something hard hits the floor above me.

But that's impossible, because nothing is above me. Nothing but the roof.

Thump thump ba-thump.

There it goes again. Like a large sack of rice landed on the ceiling.

Or a body . . .

I stare up, willing my eyes to see through the plaster, and realize I've been trying to move my arms this entire time and can't.

Move, I order all my limbs, but they are defiant. It's like my body is asleep but my mind is fully awake. Something is pressing me into the mattress, making it harder and harder to shake free.

From the corner of my eye I can see a faint glow of orange

coming from my window. The glow becomes brighter, blossoming, setting the dark room aglow.

That's when I see her. Standing in the corner, dressed in her apron, her hair in pin curls, hands dusted with baking flour, arm burnt to a crisp, drool dripping off her lip.

I open my mouth, but nothing comes out. My lungs are cement bricks. Smoke drifts through the open window.

Thump. Thump.

She stands hunched over, a feral look in her eyes. The orange light grows brighter, revealing her face. And it isn't drool dripping down her lip. It's blood. It spills onto the floor by her bare feet. My stomach reels, gag reflexes pulling at the muscles in my neck, but I still can't move. She throws a limp arm across her chest, hitting the blackened arm, and peels her dead skin back like a banana, exposing bloody muscle.

The Hag! She's here! And she wants my skin.

As if reading my thoughts, she straightens, and I can hear every bone in her spine click into place.

"Fire!" Alec screams, footsteps racing down the stairs. "Everyone out!"

Wait. That's his real voice. This isn't a dream!

"Marigold, hurry," Mom calls as footsteps echo through the hall.

They're leaving me. They don't know I can't move! I can't move, I can't move. I'm . . . frozen. Stuck. Trapped.

Thump thump. The room glows brighter.

The stench of the Hag mixed with thick smoke makes my

eyes water and I'm afraid I'll choke on my own vomit before she kills me. She takes one step, her foot covered in black soot.

"Help," I scream, but it comes out as a strangled gargle.

Another step. It's hard for her to walk, but she's determined to have me.

I bite my tongue, holding my breath until I'm blue. She takes another step. The fire next door is jumping to our house, peppering the roof. The smoke is suffocating.

Heart thrashing, I focus on moving one limb, straining, contracting every organ inward. If I can just break free then I can . . .

Thump thump. THUMP!

A painful exhale shoots out of my mouth. I cough and hack up air. The pressure easing, my limbs now free, I flop out of bed, falling flat on my face.

Run! You have to run!

But as soon as I look up . . . she's gone. The room dark and freezing.

Thump thump.

Gasping, I stumble to my feet, legs like jelly, and pull myself to the window. The house next door is still boarded up tight . . . and not on fire. The giant tree that separates our properties looms above us; a loose branch tangled in vines dangles like a carrot, dancing on our roof. The wind must have knocked it free.

"Shit," I grumble.

Buddy treks downstairs into the kitchen with me. I refill the teakettle and click on the burner. No sense in trying to sleep after all that. Caffeine isn't the best cure for panicked nerves, but I never want to close my eyes again. If that was real, I could have died in the fire. I have to find some way to control this sleep paralysis.

I set the instant coffee, sugar, almond cream, and my favorite coffee mug out on the counter. With another few minutes to kill before the water boils, I stroll around the perimeter of the first floor, taking it in as if for the first time, massaging my temples, trying to rub the images of Ms. Suga's face out of my mind. The dream was so vivid. It felt like I was swimming through mud, sticks and branches caught in my throat. I could've died. . . .

Stop it, Mari! She's not real. This is all stress!

At the front door, I quickly peek through the curtains. Sweets smiles at me from her new home on the porch. And in the distance, the dark truck is parked in the same spot again. Too far away and deep in the shadows to peep a license plate. I move into the sitting room, hoping for a better angle but . . . why should I pretend not to see this jerk? Whoever it is should know that this weird-ass snooping isn't cool. Plus, after that horrible nightmare, I've had enough of the creepy bullshit.

I yank open the front door and burst into the street at full speed. The truck flips on its brights, blinding me, then makes a shrieking U-turn, speeding away. Too fast for me to sprint after in my flip-flops.

"Fuck!" I scream, at the corner, heart pounding and winded.

Missed him again. Yusef said no one comes to our block but this asshole has no problem with it.

A shadow catches my left eye. Someone just slipped out of sight, behind the secret garden. Or I think it was someone. The bushes are blocking my view. Could've been just a random shadow. Or maybe . . .

"Hello?" I call out in a panic. Bugs shriek in the night air. A breeze ruffles the tops of the trees, leaves shower down on me. I flinch as one touches my shoulder and run back to the house.

Buddy whines from the porch, unaccustomed to being outside without a leash. I grab his collar and pull him into the house, closing the door.

Inside is silent. It takes a moment to process that I'm standing in darkness. The lights, they were on when I left. If someone turned them off, wouldn't they wonder why I'm running through the streets in the middle of the night?

Slowly, I wade through the hall and flick a switch. The teapot is off. It never whistled, never even boiled. The instant coffee, cream, and sugar I had taken out are all gone.

And my mug is now sitting in the middle of the kitchen floor.

EIGHTEEN

OKAY. SO MAYBE I'm in the middle of some super-cheesy horror movie. I've watched enough of them with Sammy to know the drill. We have all the basic elements: family moves to a new town and into an eerie house with a dark past.

But something doesn't feel right; it's like the formula is . . . off. By now, we should've seen a levitating chair or at least heard some giggling dead kid in the walls. For the most part, nothing outrageous has happened.

Well, except that whole basement door incident. And the wrinkled hand reaching into the shower. And the lights going out. And my mug . . .

I can't believe I'm about to do this.

Thumbs tapping away, I start my research. It's not that I don't believe in ghosts; I'm sure they exist. But I'm not jumping up to tell other people that. Especially when those people already think I'm crazy, seeing bedbugs everywhere I go. This will only make it worse.

Outside, the rain is pouring. I've checked several times to

see if we're in the middle of a hurricane, the way the wind is slapping the trees around.

"Hey, Sammy," I shout toward the door. "Can you take out the flashlights? Just in case."

Mom and Alec are on a double dinner date with Mr. Sterling and his wife, at Alec's suggestion, leaving me home to babysit again. Piper hasn't emerged from her room all night and Sammy has discovered some new series on Netflix, refusing to leave the sofa.

But in my room, wrapped in my weighted blanket, I'm googling "how to know if your house is haunted." If you had told me three months ago I would be moving to the Midwest, researching hauntings on a dark and stormy night . . . I would've asked for whatever bud you're smoking, 'cause I want to be that baked too. But here we are!

First article: "6 Telltale Signs Your House Might Be Haunted."

1. UNEXPLAINED NOISES OR SMELLS

Welp. We definitely have that. That funky stench is not just coming from the basement. We've experienced it on the second floor too. I keep reading.

2. MOVEMENT OF INANIMATE OBJECTS

Doors opening and slamming on their own, the cabinets in the kitchen . . .

I take a steady breath and scratch the inside of my arm. Okay, two out of six.

3. EXTREME COLD OR HOT SPOTS

Hm. Well, nothing too extreme. But then again . . . I'm always cold in here, so how would I even know the difference? Can't count.

4. STRANGE ANIMAL BEHAVIOR

I glance up at Buddy's spot on the bed, now empty as he cuddles with Sammy. Buddy has been acting weird since we've moved in here. The barking, whining, staring at nothingness . . .

Three out of six. Not the worst.

"Mari! Mari!" Sammy yells from downstairs.

He probably can't find the flashlights.

"Yeah, one second," I say, and keep scrolling.

5. FEELINGS OF BEING WATCHED, TOUCHED, OR EVEN PHYSICAL ASSAULT

Yes, no, and . . . no. Other than my pride, no physical harm. And even I can admit my paranoia can be a little . . . intense.

6. ELECTRICAL PROBLEMS

My blood turns into snow, thinking of the night I hung out with Yusef and Erika at the beach. The way all the lights clicked off. I brushed it off as faulty electrical work. Still could be.

At that very moment, the lights flicker, static hissing.

Okay. Soooo . . . maybe our house is haunted.

With a deep breath, I open a new search tab: "What to do if your house is haunted?" Scanning an article, I zero in on a line midway through . . .

If not done properly, burning sage can aggravate spirits. You may even see more activity. Proceed with caution.

Crap.

"Mari! Mari, come here! Quick!" Sammy yells.

What is he up to now? And damn, why is it so cold in here? Is the boiler broke?

"Mari, are you coming? Hurry up!"

"Coming, I'm coming!" I grumble, locking the screen.

The rain roars outside, clapping against the windows. Sammy has every light on in the house, something he does when he's scared but doesn't want to admit it. I chuckle and head down the hall.

"Yeah? What's up?"

But the first floor is empty. The TV is on, episode five still playing, and Sammy . . . nowhere to be seen. No sign of Buddy either. They couldn't have gone upstairs without me noticing. Those stairs would let us know ants were climbing up them. He definitely called me from down here . . . although he did sound far away. Farther than usual. I turn off the TV and take in the room.

"Sam?"

Silence. The kind of silence that feels heavy and loaded. On the sofa, a bowl of popcorn is tipped over, kernels spilled onto the rug, the throw blanket still warm. An icy sensation crawls up the back of my neck as rolling thunder makes the glass cabinets shake.

Something is wrong.

"Sam," I call, louder this time, patting my pockets for the phone that's still upstairs on the charger. Maybe he took Buddy for a walk? Which makes no sense, but nothing has been making sense lately. Lightning flashes, the back windows like a wall of black mirrors reflecting the stillness of the house: a silver teapot on the gas stove, pans hanging from the ceiling rack, a metal basket of Red Delicious apples on the table bathed in warm light. Pulse throbbing, I approach my reflection in the deck door, cupping my eyes to peer out into the darkness. Trees violently whip in the wind, a hectic dance. Inside, the house is calm, picturesque. Then something clicks behind me.

CREEEEAK

In the reflection, I watch the hallway closet door slowly swing open and the look on my face belongs on a movie poster.

"Sam?" I whisper, peering over my shoulder, the tremor in my voice identical to the one in my hands.

The house holds its breath.

I shouldn't check, I know I shouldn't check, everything inside me screams I should just make a run for it. But . . . where's Sammy?

Lightning strikes, the gold doorknob catching its spark. Keeping my steps light, I creep closer. *It's nothing, it's nothing, relax,* I chant to myself, entire body now shaking. With two quick steps, I wrench the door open wide, jumping to face whatever's behind it. But there's nothing there. Just some hanging coats, random shoes, and a mop.

"Sammy?" I cry out, now desperate. "Where are you!"

Suddenly, a hand shoots out from between the coats and yanks me inside by the collar. I let out a shriek, forehead hitting the back wall of the closet, the door slamming behind me. Balance skewed in the pitch darkness, I whip around, thrashing at the air, clothes, hangers . . . ready to fight for my life, until a flashlight clicks on, illuminating his face.

Sam.

"Sammy!" I snap, shoving his shoulder. "What the hell are you doing?"

Sammy digs his trembling nails into my forearm, eyes wide and glassy, pure terror painted across his face.

"That's not me!" he whisper-shouts, lips quivering. "That's not me!"

"What? What are you talking about? Are you—"

Then I hear it. His voice. Sammy's voice. Calling me from outside the closet door. And everything inside me curls inward, hardens, and I stop breathing.

"Mari! Mari! Come downstairs!"

NINETEEN

"MARI! MARI!"

In the narrow hallway closet, my mind struggles to untangle the thoughts trying to make sense of it all. My little brother is standing in front of me, his mouth closed. But his voice, the voice I'd know anywhere, is calling me from outside the closet door.

"Mari, are you coming?"

"No fucking way," I gasp.

Sammy trembles, the flashlight dancing in his hands. Acid fills my mouth. There's someone out there, pretending to be Sammy. There's someone in the house!

"Mari! Mari, come here! Quick!"

Something touches my arm and I flinch. A coat sleeve. The cramped closet seems to be shrinking around us. Tightening. Strangling. And if someone's out there looking for us, they could easily find us in here. I focus on Sammy.

"Turn that off," I whisper quickly.

Sammy does what he's told, gripping my arm in the darkness, the only light shining through the door sill. Buddy sniffs our feet, confused by our little game as I press an ear to the door. No movement. The voice . . . Sammy's voice . . . sounds muffled and far away, yet close. Too close.

"What is that?" Sammy whispers.

"I . . . I don't know," I mutter, and begin blindly feeling around for something to protect us with—a bat, golf club, shovel, anything. But no luck. My hand hits a narrow box on the top shelf. The sneakers Alec bought; he never returned them. I slip them onto my bare feet.

Sammy's grip tightens before he whimpers, "Mari . . ."

Below us, the floor rumbles as if we're sitting on the belly of the house and it's hungry. Then, silence. Until there's a loud thud of a foot hitting hollow wood, then another.

Someone is coming up the basement steps!

Sammy's eyes bulge and I place a hand over his mouth to keep him from screaming.

With a loud clack, the basement lock clicks and the door creaks open. I push Sammy behind me, backing behind the coats, blood surging.

"Mari! Mari!"

Sammy's voice is louder now. Closer. Almost as if it's right next to us. Real Sam's tears spill over my hand.

"Mari! Mari, come here! Quick!"

His voice sounds muffled and has a slight echo. Real Sam

trembles against me. Suddenly, Buddy growls, and I quickly grip his mouth to keep him quiet. But it's too late. The house stills. The house heard us.

Heavy steps, the steps of a slow-moving dinosaur, shuffling, heading our way.

A wave of panic hits me and I lurch forward, grabbing hold of the doorknob, placing a leg on either side of the frame, and lean back. A rotting stench, like dead rats baked in a heat wave mixed with . . . piss, engulfs the closet. I lean away farther, suppressing a gag.

That's when a shadow appears in the door sill and the footsteps stop. My breath hitches. Sammy wraps his arms around me, squeezing his face into my back, and I'm nearly convulsing in fear.

Please . . . please God please . . .

The shadow huffs like a horse and moves on, passing the door, and heads down the hallway. Now loud above us, we flinch with every step as it makes its way to the second floor.

Which means downstairs is clear.

I whip around to Sammy. "Okay, on the count of three, I'm going to open the door."

"No," Sammy whimpers, eyes flaring. "No, Mari. Let's just stay."

"It knows we're in here," I explain carefully. "We're sitting ducks if we don't move."

He sobs quietly. "I can't. I'm scared."

"You have to."

"He'll follow us!"

"No it won't. Ghosts only haunt inside of houses. It can't hurt us once we're outside."

"Ghosts?"

I squeeze my eyes. Shit, the thought never even occurred to him. Even as I say the words, I'm praying I'm right and it's not some rando maniac squatter making himself at home.

"When I open the door, I want you to run as fast as you can outside. You run and you keep running no matter what."

"Please, Mari. No."

I lean into the door, hand on the knob, and bend slightly into a starting position.

"Ready? One. Two . . ."

On three, we burst into the hallway, the lights blinding after sitting in the dark for so long. I charge ahead, Buddy skittering next to me. I yank the front door open wide, glancing up the empty steps behind us as Sammy slams his shoulders into the screen door, and jumps down the porch steps with a scream. Feet hitting the pavement, I'm in sprint mode when it hits me.

Piper.

"Wait, Sam!"

Sammy turns, rain pummeling us.

"What!" he shouts.

"I have to get Piper. I can't leave her here!"

"Screw her!"

I shake my head. "Go! Run and call the police."

"Mari, no! Wait!"

With no time to argue, I race back to the house, leaping up the porch, and fumble inside.

"Piper!" I call up the dark staircase, heart hammering. "Piper, where are you?"

A door creaks open upstairs. Light steps amble down the hall. Piper stops on the first landing. It's hard to see in the shadows but she's glaring down at me, like she's never seen me a day in her life.

"Come on! We have to get out of here," I press, waving her on. No telling where they . . . or it is. "Run! Come on!"

Piper's expression doesn't change. She doesn't move, just stares. Face cold and hard like a marble.

"What are you doing? We have to go!"

Piper rolls her shoulders back then her head suddenly snaps to the right, as if someone had called her. But I didn't hear anything. She takes one last look at me before slowly stepping out of sight.

"Where are you going? Piper, get back here," I yell, chasing after her, taking the steps two at a time.

Halfway there, a raspy voice wails, and it's so disorienting, I nearly freeze mid-stride.

"THIS IS MY HOUSE!"

Then, as if someone leans over the top banister, something swings out from the darkness and I catch a glimpse of a soaring broom.

What the . . .

The broom whacks me in the face, and I fly backward down the stairs with a scream. My head bangs against the hardwood floor, tailbone hitting the bottom step.

"MARI!" Sammy screams from outside.

"Uhhh, shit," I moan, rolling to my side, pain exploding, tiny white dots taking over my vision.

Buddy barks hysterically, scratching at the screen door.

The voice screams again, a shrilling sound. "GET OUT MY HOUSE!"

Lungs shriveling to raisins, I almost piss on myself as I stare up the dark staircase at . . . nothing. No one is there.

"Mari, get up! Please, get up," Sammy begs from the porch, reaching for me, rain splattering around him.

There's soft movement in the shadows and I can't pull my eyes away. Leaning forward, I try to make out the shape in the blackness, just as something sails down fast toward my head.

"Ah!" I shriek, flipping onto my stomach, a quick dodge as it clatters beside me with a loud smack.

"Mari!"

I roll over, coming face-to-face with a broom head. The same broom Mom was looking for.

"Shit," I gasp, shoving it away with my foot, scooting back against the wall.

A door slams upstairs, followed by hard footsteps. The house huffs.

"Mari! Mari, come here! Quick!"

Scrambling to my hands and knees, I crawl outside, then I'm up on my feet, limping off the porch.

"Come on! Come on!" Sammy cries, and he's like a blue streak in the wind he's running so fast. My muscles manage a light jog down the street until my body feels too heavy to carry. The distant streetlights start to blur, the pulse in my ear the only sound I can hear.

Shit, I'm going to pass out.

"Sammy," I gasp, swaying to the right, the ground tilting under me.

Sammy doubles back. "What's wrong?"

With a stumble, I drop to my knees, breath ragged and slowing.

"Mari," he cries, catching my head before it hits the pavement. He whips around, frantic, and starts to scream. "Help! Heeeeelp us!"

No one will hear him. Not in this rain.

"Sammy, go get Yusef," I mutter, my eyelids fluttering, the world is going dark.

"Mari! Don't go to sleep, Mari, please," Sammy cries, shaking me. "Help! Help!!!"

Buddy circles us, barking and whimpering.

"Next block . . . over," I slur. "The house with the roses."

Sammy sniffs, nodding. "Buddy, down. Down, Bud!"

Buddy lies on the wet ground and Sammy softly places my head on him.

"Stay, Bud! Stay! I'll be right back!"

Sammy takes off running, I can't tell which direction, the street is so dark. The abandoned houses . . . they seem so large from this angle, as if they grew twenty feet higher, leaning inward, windows like angry eyes staring down at me. Buddy whimpers, his cold nose nudging my face. I close my eyes, the pouring rain kinda relaxing, like taking a cold shower after a hot day of track practice. Not quite, but close enough. Until I feel Buddy tense under me, a low growl deep from his belly.

"Buddy?" I mutter, unable to open my eyes.

He jumps to his feet, and the back of my head slaps the concrete. Crying out in pain, I manage to roll to my side. Buddy stands over me, furiously barking. The kind of ferocious barks he saves for strangers or intruders coming too close. Someone's here.

"Buddy," I gasp, opening my eyes.

A set of beaming headlights pop on, blinding me. Footsteps. Hard ones, like the ones from the house.

Oh God, it wasn't a ghost!

Panicked, I beg my body to move, to cooperate, hand grabbing for anything around me.

"Help," I croak in between sobbing tears, then think of Sam. He got away and he won't be here to witness his sister's murder. A strange relief fills me as my arms give up and I roll over, readying myself.

Then the rain stops. Or I think it stops, it's no longer

hitting my face, but the sound is still surrounding us. I force my eyes open and for a brief second, I see a shadow standing over me with an umbrella. Not a shadow, a man.

Mr. Watson?

Too weak to scream, I gasp before everything fades to black.

"Aye, aye. Cali! Come on, Cali, wake up!"

I'm underwater, Yusef's voice calling from the surface. My eyes struggle to focus, the darkness still edging as my brain floats, coming up for air.

Yusef is leaning over me, tapping my cheek. "There you go! Open your eyes, come on."

My head is lying on something soft. And kind of dry. The rough cotton scratches my neck.

"Mari," Sammy whimpers, and I realize he's gripping my hand.

I want to say "Don't cry, Sam" but I can feel myself fading fast again and glance at Yusef.

"The . . . the house," I utter, my arms limp, trying to point. Piper is still inside.

Yusef scoops me up off the ground, cradling me in his arms before it all fades to black again.

• • •

The color yellow is the first thing I see. For a moment, I think I'm staring into the sun. Then I notice how cold I am, how soft the sun feels, and my eyes pop open. A pattern of little red flowers on faded fabric stares back at me. A sofa cushion. My face is on some random . . . sofa?

FACT: Bedbugs have not been shown to cause or spread diseases. Some people will react to bedbugs bites, and excessive scratching can lead to secondary infections.

I sit up quick and the room spins, causing me to lean sideways. Need to get up, need to get up. I could be getting an infection at this very moment. Is that something on my arm? A bite? An egg? Soap, alcohol, bleach . . .

"Yo, hold up," Yusef says next to me and gently eases me back down. "Not so fast."

His arm weighs a thousand pounds on my shoulder and I'm too weak to fight him. Doesn't stop my skin from flaming up, making me want to scrape it off with a peeler. I want to scratch, I need to scratch. I want to smoke. I also want to just be a regular, normal person. Not such a basket case in front of strangers. Tears drench my eyes.

"Hey, Cali, it's okay," Yusef says, leaning over me, stroking wet hair out of my face. He smells so good, even in his wet clothes. I cave, softening into him, and for the first time tonight, I feel safe.

"You're okay," he whispers, holding me. "Look, Sammy's right here."

Sammy, wrapped in a blue towel, sits in Pop-Pop's recliner,

staring at the floor. His face drained of blood, eyes wide and unblinking as if he's seen something . . . crazy. The same look he had when I woke up in the hospital, puke in my hair, stomach pumped clean. The memory is a knife twist.

"Here, drink some water," Yusef says, offering me a glass. "How's the head? Unc says we need to keep you awake. In case you have a concussion."

Across the living room, Mr. Brown is talking in hushed whispers on the phone, glancing at me every few seconds. By the kitchen, Pop-Pop stands in a blue fuzzy robe and leather house slippers with a suspicious glare. Suddenly, memories of the headlights flood in.

"Hey, where's . . . where's Mr. Watson?" I ask, searching the room. "Did he leave already?"

"Mr. Watson?"

"Yeah. He was with me."

Yusef raises an eyebrow, glancing at Sammy. "Cali, when we found you, you were lying in the middle of the street, knocked out cold. And alone."

No way . . . the headlights . . . I couldn't have imagined that.

"But he . . . he covered me, with an umbrella," I whimper, exhaustion creeping in again. "He gave me a blanket for my head. You didn't see him? Seriously?"

Yusef's face goes slack, lips a straight line. He's trying not to give away what he's thinking. But it's too late. I know that look. He thinks I'm baked, high off some drugs and seeing things. Which would explain everything that happened in the house. And if it wasn't for Sammy being there with me . . . I would also question my own sanity. But I know what I saw. Or heard.

"Yo, what were y'all running from?" Yusef asks. "Sammy said someone was in the house?"

I have no idea where to even begin. My head is throbbing, a sharp aching pain. My clothes are starting to stiffen, the rain and muddy water drying onto my skin.

Sammy's knee is bouncing. He has that look, where he's trying to solve a super-complex puzzle.

"It sounded just like you, Sam," I mumble, gripping the towel Yusef swaddles me with, a shiver ripping through me. "Your exact voice."

Sammy, still in a state of shock, takes a long blink.

"Unless . . . someone was doing some kind of impression of me or something," he says, voice flat.

Yusef's eyes toggle between us as Mr. Brown enters the living room, clearing his throat.

"Your parents are back. Come on, let's get you two home."

The rain has eased by the time Mr. Brown drives us back home. Inside, Alec wears a pained expression, clutching Piper tight to his chest in the kitchen, police lights flashing off their shared pale skin.

As we approach, I catch the end of Piper's story.

"And then they just left me," she sobs. "They yelled at me and ran out the door."

Alec's lips form a hard line when he spots me. He places Piper on her feet as Mom rushes toward us.

"Mom!" Sammy shouts, running full speed into her stomach, clutching her. "Mom, the house is haunted!"

With that said, the police take their cue to leave. My steps are slow, still dizzy and in absolutely no rush to walk back into this place. Wonder how long it'll take to pack a bag before we leave for a hotel. Because we definitely can't stay here. Not one more night. The house is angry, you can feel it in the air.

"Where the hell have you been!" Alec roars, his tone explosive.

"They. Left. Me." Piper chokes out the words again through hysterical sobs. "I was so scared, Daddy."

Through the intense pain, a flash of anger boils.

"What are you talking about?" I spit. "You saw me at the bottom of the stairs, calling you! You walked away!"

"No I didn't," she says, the corner of her mouth slipping into a cruel smirk before rubbing her face into Alec's side.

The simple act of her denial makes my stomach turn. I sway, the fridge catching my fall.

"You pushed Mari down the stairs!" Sammy cries, Mom holding him back from charging at her. "She could've died!"

"No I didn't." She glances up at her father, and in a sugar-sweet voice says, "Daddy, I was just in my room and then I heard them shouting."

"Unbelievable," Alec yells. "I can't leave her alone for one freaking night."

I stare at Piper. Or really *through* her, with a different set of lenses. The extra pale skin. The dead tired eyes. The weight loss. The weird talking to walls. Ms. Suga. The thought smacks against my throbbing head and it all becomes clear.

"Oh my God," I whisper. "She's possessed."

"WHAT?" Alec screams, positioning Piper behind him.

"That's the only explanation. The Hag got her!"

Sammy is staring at her now, eyebrows pinched. "She just . . . stood there," he mumbles.

"Okaaayyyy! You two have been watching way too many movies!" Mom snaps, shaking her head.

That's the thing, I didn't remember what all those movies had taught me, reasoning everything away instead of facing the truth: our house is haunted. And Piper is possessed by the Hag. The Hag named Ms. Suga.

I was ready to tell everyone everything I knew about the place, but one look at Alec's burning-red face made me go silent.

"Raquel, this is the last straw. You told me she had her problems under control."

"Alec—"

"What excuse are you going to give her this time? She's put both Piper's and Sammy's lives in danger!"

Mom sighs and walks into her office, procuring a pee cup.

You've got to be fucking kidding me right now!

"Mom! What are you doing?" Sammy shouts, standing in front of me, arms stretched protectively. "I was here! I heard it too! She's not lying! She's not . . . not on drugs! Mari wouldn't leave without Piper. She ran up the stairs to go get her. She was trying to save her!"

Piper's face slips into a confused scowl, eyes softening.

"Sam . . . are you sure you weren't hearing things?" Alec asks.

"We *both* heard it," Sammy snaps.

"And there were only three of us in here," I add, leaning against the counter. "Unless Piper became a ventriloquist overnight."

Alec ignores me and stares right at Sammy.

"Look, I know this is tough, pal, but is it possible your sister might . . . not have been herself . . . again? Maybe tripped, and just fell down the stairs?"

Mom straightens. "Alec," she warns. A weak warning at that.

"Then how did I hear the voice *too*?" Sammy shoots back. "Am I high?"

Mom tears up, crossing her arms. "Oh, Sammy."

With a pounding head and losing all will to fight, I pat Sammy's shoulder.

"It's all right, Sam. Forget it. I'm not taking that stupid fucking test because I'm leaving."

"Leaving?" Alec and Mom balk.

"Yeah, I'm ready to go back to Cali and live with Dad."

"What? You can't just make that decision on your own," Alec scoffs.

"Yes I can," I say, looking directly at Mom. "That was the agreement with Dad, right? If things don't work out with Alec, I can move in with Dad. It was the only way he'd allow you to take us out of the state. And things are clearly not working out if my stepfather is accusing me of being on drugs when I'm not. Not exactly ideal conditions for a recovering addict."

Alec blinks, turning to Mom. "Is this true?"

Mom takes a steadying breath, not breaking our stare. "Yes."

Baffled, Alec searches his hands as if looking for the right words to say. Piper clutches him tighter.

Sammy huffs, standing next to me. "Well, if she's going, then I'm going with her!"

"Sam," Mom gasps, with a trembling lip. "Baby . . ."

"No! Mari's right. And I hate it here! I want to go home!"

TWENTY

THE NEXT MORNING, I call Dad to make immediate arrangements. Don't care who it may hurt, I can't stay here. These ghosts are violent, and I have the lump on the back of my head to prove it.

Since Dad's still in Japan finishing a project, we have to wait another two weeks before he can fly out to bring us home.

Which means we just have to survive the night, as they say. Make that several nights.

Sammy fortifies his bedroom with booby traps and an infinite number of flashlights. I no longer sleep, surviving off a diet of coffee, caffeine pills, and candy. I burn so much sage we're practically living in a low fog.

But the house has been quiet for days. No weird smells, voices, or strange footsteps. It's as if it knows it's done its job and is satisfied with the results. We're leaving, like it wanted us to. Well, some of us.

Alec and Piper mostly keep to themselves, eating out and

playing in her room. Mom hides herself away in her office working, until Saturday morning, when she knocks on Sam's door.

"You two feel like taking a walk?"

The Riverwalk is a redbrick-style promenade off the Cedarville River with plenty of restaurants, shops, food trucks, and kiosks, bookended by casinos and an eat-in movie theater. The place is all decked out for Halloween. We pass a pumpkin-carving contest at the pavilion along with signs for the Halloweenie puppy parade.

Sammy picks out a booth by the window at Johnny Rockets so we can watch the steamships sail by. It hasn't been just us three in months and it is relieving not having to walk on eggshells.

"So, Sammy," Mom says, after placing three orders of veggie burgers and Tater Tots. "Did you decide what you're going to be for Halloween?"

He plays with the straw of his lemonade. "I was going to be a zombie . . . but that's a little too close to home."

I snort, the first time I've laughed in days. Mom shoots me a look and I slide down in my seat.

"Guys," she starts, hands folded on the table. "I know things have been . . . rough. There's been so much change this year."

She looks pointedly at me and I don't back down. I'm tired of my mistake being used as a weapon against me. She sighs.

"You know, my entire life, I've never won anything," she says, kissing the side of Sammy's head. "Well, aside from you two. But really, never been first place in sports, never got a scholarship to college or anything like that. So when I was accepted for this residency, I was excited. More than excited. I thought this was a chance for a fresh start, not just for me after a divorce, but for all of us."

I blink. "So . . . you just didn't want to move . . . because of me?"

"No! Of course not. I wanted to go. I wanted a change. And when I brought it up to Alec," she continues, "he was fully on board. He knew how important it was to me, and knew it would be a great opportunity for you two. The man just moved with Piper to our town and was willing to relocate with her again. So regardless of what you may think, he really does love you two."

"Well, he has a funny way of showing it," I scoff.

"Yeah," Mom says, her eyebrow cocking up. "So do you. You're not exactly a walk in the park."

Eyes growing big, Sammy glances away, sipping his drink, which means he agrees.

I want to counter but I can't because they might have a point. I haven't been exactly welcoming to Alec. Aside from the fact that within months of him moving in I was coding on my bedroom floor. Not exactly the best way of making a first impression.

"To be honest," Mom continues, "he's a little hurt about our secret contingency plan. Because families don't have that. Families stick together no matter what and help each other."

I think of Yusef and sigh.

"But . . . he doesn't believe us about the house being haunted," Sammy mumbles.

Mom straightens, her lips pressed together. She doesn't believe us either.

"You made your decision about leaving and . . . I respect that," she says. "I'll always respect your wishes. But I just think . . . this place could be really good for us. For our future. Plus, I don't want to live without my babies." She cuddles Sammy. "So maybe just . . . think about it some more. For me? Please?"

"Mr. Watson! What are you doing here?"

Mr. Watson meets us in the driveway as we pull up from lunch, carrying an old toolbox and small stepladder.

"Irma called. Said you were having trouble with the lights."

Mom nods, zipping up her jacket as Sammy and I unload some groceries.

"Oh. Right. Alec must have . . . told her. Find anything?"

He shakes his head. "I checked what I could and everything seems to be working all right."

"So you went into the basement?" I ask bluntly.

He looks at me for five seconds too long. "No."

"Of course not," I mumble, snatching a bag out of the trunk.

There's something I just don't trust about Mr. Watson. Every answer he gives seems dense and cold. He knows more than he's saying, not that I can prove it.

"Maybe you should talk to Irma about calling an electrician," Mr. Watson says to Mom. "Should anything come up again."

"You're right," Mom says. "And thank you. Sorry for the trouble."

From the porch, I watch Mr. Watson pack up his Volvo. Not a truck.

But I know what I saw.

Sammy's room is just like mine except with way more stuff and a hell of lot less eerie. His door doesn't open or close on its own and after spending the last few days camping out on the floor, I can also confirm I have yet to see one stranger standing in the corner. Could my room be the haunted epicenter of this house?

I can't believe I even have to ask myself these types of questions. But I've been researching nothing but info on demonic hauntings, even ordering holy water from the Vatican, not caring who sees anymore—that's if someone is still monitoring our internet use. The Sterling Foundation must know what's going on in here. They specifically put us in Ms. Suga's house. But why? Why try to scare the shit out of us if their goal is to make this community great again?

Cupping the back of my head, I lie on Sammy's bed, staring up at the ceiling, wondering what life will be like, living with Dad? At least I'll be closer to Tamara, only a four-hour drive. But . . . we'll be thousands of miles from Mom. All this time, I thought she moved because of me, when really, she wanted a change just as much as I did.

Change is good. Change is necessary. Change is needed.

Sammy sits cross-legged on the floor, playing a video game. He hasn't said much since we came back from lunch. We've both been quiet. Mom's words still running through my head on repeat.

"I feel shitty," I finally say aloud.

Sammy pauses the game and looks up with guilt-drenched eyes.

"I . . . I don't want to leave Mom," he says, his voice hesitant.

I sigh. "I know. Me neither. But I can't stay here. It's not safe."

"But . . . if Piper pushed you down the stairs, imagine what she'll do to Mom if we're not around."

There's a million ways Piper could hurt Mom. The thought is gutting. I roll onto my side.

"She won't come with us, Sam. No matter how much we beg."

He rubs Buddy's head, thinking. "Yeah. But . . . maybe we can make her."

I laugh. "Have you met Raquel? We can't make that woman do anything she doesn't want to do."

He shifts closer to me. "If we can prove that the house is haunted and that Piper is possessed, she'll have to come with us."

"And how do you plan on doing that?"

Sammy crawls over to his desk, digging through a bottom drawer. "With these!"

In his hands, he holds two GoPro cameras, a couple of rechargeable batteries, and cords. I sit up.

"Where'd you get those?"

"They were Dad's. He used them for some old construction project. Said I could have them."

I pluck one of the cameras out to examine it.

"And what are you going to do with them?"

"Set them up around the house. If we can show Mom proof that Piper is crazy-town, she'll totally come be with us . . . and Dad."

There's an eagerness in his voice, for Mom to be with Dad again, and I feel a twinge for his heartache.

"Sam," I say gently. "She won't leave Alec. That's her new husband, remember?"

Sammy diverts his eyes, shoulders curling, fidgeting with the cameras.

"I know that," he mutters. "And I guess maybe Alec can come too. But this is the only way they'll believe us. Plus, we'll need proof Piper's possessed or the church won't perform an exorcism on her."

"How the hell do you know that?"

"Duh! *The Conjuring*. You fell asleep before the end."

Okay, that's probably true. I fall asleep during most movies. But if I had known that movie would be the key to my survival here, I would've drunk some coffee.

"Come on, Mari. We at least have to try. It's our only shot!"

Well, a plan is better than no plan.

"Okay. Let's do it."

"What you doing here, Cali!" Mr. Brown says with a laugh as he unloads his truck. "I thought y'all would be long gone by now."

"Nope, my parents insist on torturing us," I say, walking up the driveway.

He chuckles. "Yusef's inside, cooking dinner."

"Domesticating him," I say with an impressed nod. "I like that."

"As it says in first Corinthians, chapter three, verse eight . . . 'The one who plants and the one who waters work together with the same purpose. And both will be rewarded for their own hard work.' And children of God, I'm here to provide the seeds that you will plant, and you will do the watering. Do not forsake his words. For the devil is among you! He has poisoned your minds, makes you feel you can't trust the very people he put to care for you. . . ."

As usual, Pop-Pop is in his chair, faithful to the program. Yusef throws some potatoes in a pot of boiling water, wiping his hands on a dish towel.

"I've come with gifts," I announce, placing a case of soda on the kitchen table. "You know, for saving my life and everything."

Yusef cracks a smile. "Aw, you didn't have to do all that." He raises an eyebrow, with a mischievous smirk. "Seeing how it was Mr. Watson who really saved you."

I purse my lips. "Are you seriously going to make fun of a girl with a concussion?"

He laughs and reaches for my hand, interlocking our fingers.

"Sorry, guess you're not the only one who cracks jokes when you're uncomfortable." His voice turns serious as he gently rubs the inside of my palm. "I was . . . really worried about you."

The tenderness, I could just melt into him, I need a hug so bad. But . . . I step back, bumping into Pop-Pop's seat, and scramble away.

"Yeah, well. I didn't drown." I cough out a laugh, stuffing my hands in my hoodie to keep them hidden just so he doesn't reach for them. Then I can pretend I don't want to reach for his. I'm queen of making awkward moments more awkward.

Yusef rolls his eyes with a smirk. "But what was up with all that? Mr. Watson lives all the way on park side. What would he be doing around your block? And that late at night."

"I don't know. And he's the least of my worries with a demon running loose in my home."

"Well, can't say I ain't try to tell you." He gives a sympathetic smile. "Wanna stay for dinner?"

"Sure. Can I also camp out in your garage with Sammy? We won't be any trouble. We just need an extension cord and the Wi-Fi password."

He fake thinks, tapping his chin. "Um, not sure how that'd go with the neighbors. Maplewood got enough rumors floating around."

Yusef opens the oven and stuffs a seasoned raw chicken inside. "And if I didn't say it before, I'm proud you went back to get your sister. Means you ain't as heartless as you think."

He winks and my stomach tenses, appetite gone. I came here on a mission to tell the truth but I'm already having second thoughts. Depending on how he reacts, I may not have a friend left in Cedarville by the end of this convo.

"Um, hey . . . I have to tell you something," I blurt out. "It's about Erika."

"All you have to do is call the number below, place your order, and we will send you one pack of seeds absolutely free. Follow the instructions in the detailed letter I will send to you. . . ."

Yusef straightens. "Okay, what's up?"

I crack open a soda and take a sip, buying myself some time.

"Yes, hello. This is Mr. Brown, putting in this week's order."

I glance at Pop-Pop, catching the tail of the rolling credits on Scott Clark's program, and almost choke.

"Wait! That girl!" I scream.

Yusef jumps, looking out the back window. "What girl? Where?"

"Would y'all keep quiet," Pop-Pop snaps. "I'm on the phone!"

"That girl in the picture frame," I say, pointing to the TV. "Can you rewind?"

Yusef nods, rushing into the living room.

"Pop-Pop, lemme see that real quick," he says, snatching the remote out of his grandfather's hand.

"Hey! What you doing with my TV!" Pop-Pop shouts, helplessly trying to get out of his chair.

"Just a minute," Yusef says, rewinding back a few beats to the outro of Scott Clark's program.

"Right there! Stop!" I shout.

He freezes on a picture frame sitting on Clark's bookshelf. I lean in to take a photo of the screen, then nod at Yusef.

"Thanks, Pop-Pop," he says quick as we race back into the kitchen.

"What's going on?" Yusef asks, leaning over my shoulder.

I zoom in to the blurry family photo, the kids all with white-blond hair. Judging from their modest clothes and hair-styles, the picture was taken a long time ago, but the girl's eyes are a familiar crystal blue. Haunting with a soul-sucking stare.

I remember thinking the same thing when I noticed her eyes before.

"Can I look up something on your phone?" I ask, breathless.

"Uh, sure," Yusef says, a question lingering while he's passing his cell.

The Foundation may be watching our Wi-Fi, but maybe not watching his.

I google Scott Clark and a Wikipedia article comes up first. I scroll down to the personal life section.

Scott Clark has five children: Scott Clark III, Kenneth Clark, Abel Clark, Noah Clark, Eden Clark. . . .

Eden! That's the woman who sits on the board for the Sterling Foundation. Eden Kruger. Her maiden name is Clark. Scott Clark is her father. Scott Clark, the magic seed pusher, the Cedarville scammer.

"Holy shit," I mutter.

If I had dug a little deeper, searched a little harder, I would have seen the forest for the trees early on. But once I knew what I was looking for, it was all easy to find. The connections . . .

—*Patrick Ridgefield, heart surgeon*

Also part owner of Lost Keys, the contracted architecture firm hired through the city for the redevelopment project, and city board member, approving budget.

—*Richard Cummings, retired football player and community activist*

Also the owner of Big Ville, a for-profit prison.

—Eden Kruger, philanthropist

Also the daughter of Scott Clark, magic seed scammer.

—Linda Russo, partner at Kings, Rothman & Russo Law

Connected to the Russo Empire mafia.

—Ian Petrov, CEO of Key Stone Group Real Estate

His name is on the deed for over fifty properties in Maplewood. All of which are abandoned. And he has kept them that way for over thirty years, leaving the Wood to look like it's in shambles when it could be so much better.

Dad was right; this is a game of chess. And all the pieces have been moved in place to checkmate Maplewood.

"Dude," Tamara says over the phone. "This is like major true crimes–type investigation shit we're doing here. A haunted house and now this . . . you can come live on my floor for the rest of high school. My mom won't mind."

Knowing the Foundation was watching, I placed a call from one of the Riverfront casinos' free phones to the only person I knew who could rock this research stuff.

"There's another thing," Tamara says. "You mentioned something about Devil's Night, right?"

"Yeah."

"Dude, it's, like, all over Instagram. You don't see it?"

I pull out my phone again and try. "No. Nothing under the hashtag. It's empty."

"Hm," Tamara huffs. "Well, then . . . I think it's been shadow banned."

"What's that mean?"

"It's when a certain hashtag is blocked from people seeing any content related to it. So, like, I'm looking at photos of Devil's Night in Cedarville here in California, but you don't see them at all. Which means . . ."

"They're banning the content so no one can see what's happening in Maplewood! But why?"

Tamara clicks her tongue. "Dude, you have to get out of there. And judging by the pictures I'm about to send you, you better be out of there before Halloween."

Snuggled in a bed made of blankets and pillows on the floor next to Sam, Buddy snores beside me as I stare at the ceiling. I can't even pretend to sleep. Not after seeing the eight photos of Devil's Night Tamara sent. Each one worse than the one before. Fires raging on almost every street corner, homes massive fireballs turning the sky orange. Sobbing neighbors, standing in front of their own well-lived-in homes, desperate to save them. Seems they got the shitty outcome of a very shitty situation. I know, not super eloquent, but it's the truth.

Some of the houses I recognize from my morning runs. The charred remains barely standing, now surrounded by weeds, like warped monuments to the past. The more recent photos of Devil's Night didn't have many burning homes, just a few lit-up trash cans.

But it all seems so tenuous, like we're sitting in a false sense of safety. This place could easily slip back into old habits.

CREAK

I've been up enough nights to recognize the different sounds the house makes. And I know without question the bathroom door just opened down the hall, yet no one walked in there.

Buddy tenses, his ears perked, staring at the door, a chair and rope tied around it, keeping it locked.

CREAK

Sammy suddenly sits up, scrambling for his flashlight. Fear tightens its hand around my throat and squeezes.

"Did you hear that?" I whisper.

Slack-jawed, Sammy only nods in response. And I'm not going to lie. It feels good, having someone else experience this with me. Feels good not being so alone. But I hate that it has to be Sam. He's already been through so much. And I'm partly to blame.

Thump. Thump.

Footsteps outside. Something is walking downstairs. I can't believe Alec or Mom doesn't hear this. They can't be *that* tired.

The footsteps thump down the hall, into the kitchen. Water trickles out a faucet; cups clink. Buddy leaps to his feet, his fur bristling, and I grip his collar, holding him back. Don't want him to chase the noise away.

This time, we welcome it.

In the morning, Sammy collects all the hidden cameras set up in the kitchen and family room.

"We definitely caught something last night," Sammy says, grinning. He takes the cameras over to the TV, playing with the various wires, and I find myself impressed by his nerdy techy skills, how handy they've become in times of need. I can barely charge my phone without assistance.

"Okay, I think I've got it," he says, switching inputs, and in pops a frozen image of the kitchen with night vision.

"Can I just say . . . this is very *Paranormal Activity.*"

Sammy glares at me. "Don't say that."

"Why?"

"You clearly didn't see the end of that movie either."

My back tenses. *Oh boy.*

"Mom! Alec!" Sammy calls upstairs. "Can you come down here for a minute?"

After somehow corralling our parents onto the family room sofa, Sammy stands proudly next to the TV, camera in hand.

"What I'm about to show you is going to blow your minds," he announces like the opening act of a magic show. "It's the proof that we need."

Mom and Alec share a curious glance and chuckle.

"Proof of what?" Mom asks.

"You'll see! Mari, hit the lights."

In the darkened room, Sammy speeds up the playback for the kitchen camera. Most of the night, no activity. Then, at the 2:52 a.m. mark, something moves in the corner. The light pops on, the kitchen empty. Mom and Alec sit up straighter. I hold my breath, watching them study the screen, just as eager to see the face of the monster that's been haunting me for the past two months. But it's only Piper in her powder-blue pajamas, entering the kitchen, reaching over the sink, filling a cup with water.

Sammy's mouth drops.

We watch Piper stop in the middle of the room to take a big sip, and though it's somewhat hard to tell, she seems to be looking directly into the camera.

I whip my head around, finding Piper standing in the hallway, staring right at me. A laugh on her lips.

She's playing us.

Mom's frown deepens. "What are we supposed to be looking at here?"

In the video, Piper wipes her mouth and places the cup on the counter. Almost in the same spot I've found cups before.

Sammy stumbles over his words. "But . . . we heard something last night."

Alec raises an eyebrow. "Why were you spying on Piper?"

Quickly, I leap over to grab the remote and turn off the TV.

"False alarm," I blurt out, before the conversation could go left. "Taking Buddy for a walk. Sam, come on!"

"Hey, Sam! Marigold! Get back here."

I grab Sammy's wrist. "Whoops, can't talk. Gotta run!"

On the corner outside the secret garden, the fall wind slips through our jackets. Sammy, deflated, kicks a nearby rock.

"She must have heard us talking about the cameras," he

groans. "Sneaking around like usual. What do we do now?"

For a moment, doubt slips in. All this time, could it really have just been Piper grabbing a cup of water late at night? But . . . how did she reach the glassware? And those footsteps . . . they were too heavy to be Piper's. Unless she was purposely walking that hard. So many questions, and a video might be our best bet of answering them.

"Let's take another crack at it," I say. "Set the cameras up in different spots this time. We have to catch her doing something! Dad will be here in a few days so we have one more shot."

Sammy, resolved, nods. "Okay. But what about Piper?"

"I'll distract her while you set the cameras up again."

"How are you going to do that?"

I chuckle. "Easy. I'll just talk to her."

From my room, I watch Sammy tiptoe down the stairs, giving me a thumbs-up. He needs at least ten minutes to set up all the cameras. I take a deep steady breath and walk across the hall. Piper is lying on the floor dressed in her pajamas, drawing on sheets of printer paper, her lava lamp turning the room blood red.

"We need to talk," I say, closing the door behind me.

Piper frowns, dropping her crayon before sitting back on her heels. "About what?"

"You know what. This little game you're playing. I've had enough of the bullshit."

At first, Piper plays coy, as if she has no clue what I was referring to. Then her face darkens.

"I told you," she hisses. "This is Ms. Suga's house and she wants you gone."

I cross my arms, inconspicuously checking the time. Two minutes.

"So what's in it for you, being Ms. Suga's guard puppy?"

She raises her chin. "She's my friend!"

"No, you don't have any friends because you keep talking to this fake one! She isn't real."

The corner of her mouth twitches. "I have friends. Ms. Suga is my friend. She cares about me! Not like you!"

"What? What makes you think I don't care about you?"

"You've never been nice to me. You were always making fun of me behind my back. And you called me annoying."

"What? When?"

"The day before you . . . you . . ." She pauses. "And then you went away to that hospital."

Shit. I have a vague memory of that day. I remember that I was exceptionally high, didn't even make it to track practice. Piper came in my room to show me . . . something, but I shoved her out.

"Is that what this is all about? Piper, I know we didn't really know each other back then. I mean, you'd just moved in, but . . . I've changed."

She jumps to her feet. "No you haven't. You're still mean to me! You're still smoking that stuff that makes you sleepy. And

Ms. Suga doesn't like it. This isn't your house. It's her house and her rules and she said she doesn't want you here. She said, when you guys are gone, she's going to make an apple pie for me and Daddy just like Grandma used—"

She cut herself off, knowing she's said too much, exposing her real mission: to replace her grandma. The only friend she really had. My heart softens and I can't even be mad. She's hurt. And she's acting out on that hurt.

"Piper, I—"

I stop short, the drawing by her foot catching my eye. On the paper are stick figures of her and Alec standing outside the house, all the windows in hectic flames. Then in the corner, by what I guess is the street, I see another person. A woman with brown skin, strands of white hair . . . wearing a pink apron with a pie on the front. My mouth goes dry.

Piper snatches up the paper and shoves it behind her back.

Be cool, I tell myself, rubbing my temples. Though I was ready to run, screaming. Five minutes.

"Piper," I say gently. "Listen to me. Ms. Suga . . . she's not real."

"That's not true," she whines.

Six minutes.

"It *is* true! And this isn't her house anymore. This is *our* home now. She needs to let go. We need to help her let go, move on. And we can do that . . . together."

Piper is flustered. "She *is* real. And she says you need to leave! You're a junkie and you need to go!"

"She's not real, you idiot! You're just a pawn in some game she's playing. Don't you get it, she's using you!"

The words left my mouth before I could stop them. And it took a fraction of a second for me to realize I fucked up.

Piper's eyes narrow, her hands rolling into fists. "You're going to be sorry that you said that."

Zzzzzz POP!

The lights click off and we're thrown into darkness, the fear instantaneous. I reel back, hitting her accordion closet door with a yelp. The door shakes, hangers clacking, and I jump away.

Did . . . did that damn door just push me?

I turn to Piper and she doesn't move, her little face a shadow. A scream is stuck inside my throat, legs desperate to flee. But I can't move. Don't know what's out there. Then I look at Piper and realize, I don't know what's in here either.

I yank open the door to the hall and hit a wall of stench so foul it makes my eyes water. It's spoiled meat, sour vomit, and shit. The coldness makes the scent sharp, stinging my nostrils.

Something is here. Alert and aware. It's like the house can hear our every word, knows what we're thinking. . . .

Oh no!

I take off running, trying not to trip down the stairs.

"Sammy!" I shout, sprinting through the hall.

Sammy is in the family room, a flashlight pointed up to his face.

"You okay?"

He nods, holding Buddy steady, and gives me a thumbs-up. He's safe . . . for now.

The basement door huffs, metal jiggling.

"Did you hear that?" I whimper. The house . . . it's coming alive.

Wide-eyed, Sammy slowly drags the light across the empty room, into the corner.

Alec's bright blue shirt hovers by the basement door, the light bringing out the natural red highlights in his hair.

"Who locked this?" Alec asks, yanking the handle again.

A heavy gasp escapes and I deflate against the sofa.

"Where did you come from?" Sammy asks, voice cracking.

"I was in the office fixing Mom's printer."

So he was just down here in the dark? That's weird.

Mom trudges downstairs carrying a flashlight.

"Why aren't you in bed?" she asks as she shines the light in the corner for Alec. He wiggles the knob, examining the lock.

I push Sammy behind me, backing into the windows, watching Alec attempt to open our only protection from the demon living below.

"Maybe . . . maybe we shouldn't do that," I offer, muscles clenching.

Alec pauses to glare at me. "Well, if I can't get into the basement, I can't access the circuit breaker and get the power back on."

Whatever lives in the basement, it wants us to come down

there. It's been trying to lure us from the very beginning. Sammy grips my shirt.

"Mari . . ."

Mom glances at us, frowning. "What's wrong with you two?"

Alec steps into the kitchen and opens a drawer. "Where's the key?"

"Key? What key?"

"The key to the basement," he says, as if it's a stupid question. "I put it right in here after storing the moving crates."

There's a freaking key? Has he been going down into the basement all this time?

Buddy stiffens, a low growl rumbling from his throat.

"Daddy?"

We whip around, shining all our lights in the direction of her voice. Piper stands in the hallway, wincing at the brightness, hands shielding her eyes.

"What's going on?"

"It's okay, sweetheart," he says, taking a flat-head screwdriver to the lock. Piper blinks, looking stricken.

"Daddy," she whispers hesitantly. "Don't."

Shit. Even possessed Piper doesn't want him to go into that basement! And if he opens that door, I'm not standing around here to see what's on the other side.

"Make a break for it," I whisper to Sam. "Hurry!"

Sammy nods, skittering down the hall with Buddy. I circle, widening the distance between the basement and myself, before gently touching Mom's elbow.

"Mom," I whisper. "Mom, we need to go."

Mom doesn't notice the seriousness in my tone, too preoccupied watching Alec.

"Let's just call the electric company," Mom decides, pointing her flashlight on the table to find her purse.

I'm going to have to drag her out of here. I won't leave her.

"Mom—"

Zzzzzz POP!

All at once, the lights flick on and we flinch. Sam is already outside, the porch light shining above him.

"Well, there you go," Alec says with a grin, dusting his hands. "My job here is done!"

"What was that all about?" Mom laughs, resetting the stove clock.

"Old house, old problems," Alec says with a shrug. "But if I could get downstairs, I could check it out to be sure. Will have to call a locksmith tomorrow."

"Mom! Come look!" Sammy shouts. "I think the lights are still off down Maple Street."

We congregate on the porch, the night air brisk. Sweets sits on the ledge, facing the street. Alec shuffles down the walkway, straining to see.

"I don't think it's just Maple Street," he says. "I think it's all of Maplewood."

It's easy for us to gather in the middle of the street when

cars never drive this way. From our view, you can see that Maple, Sweetwater, and Division are sitting in pitch-blackness. Houses in the distance blend with the night sky. Our house is a tiny candle in the middle of the dark woods.

"I'm sure they'll get power any moment now," Alec says, full of optimism. "Look, we can stand here and watch it happen! Like fireworks!"

We wait and wait and wait and wait. Nothing. The trees seem to cave in, shadows growing around us, wind swirling leaves into the street. I glance up at Piper's window and can't shake the eerie feeling that we're being watched.

"Daddy, I'm cold."

Mom, playing with her cell phone, grumbles. "I can't find the number to the electric company. It's like they don't exist. Oh, wait. No service? What the hell is going on?"

Sharp thorns prickle down my back and I shudder. We need to get out of here.

"Daddy," Piper says, pointing down the street. "Someone's coming."

Not just someone. Many someones. A steady storm of foot-steps, heading our way.

Alec frowns with a bemused chuckle. "Wonder what they want."

Mom stares for a moment before a light bulb clicks.

"Everybody inside," she orders, pushing us back toward the house. "Now. Let's go!"

"What's happening?" Sammy asks as she pulls him down the walkway and up the stairs.

"Inside! Hurry!"

A crowd of people emerge from the darkness as they near the house.

"Raquel," Alec says, oblivious as usual. "What's wrong?"

"Aye!" a voice barks behind us, and we freeze.

Mr. Stampley stalks onto the grass, pointing a finger at the house. "Why you got power and we don't!"

The parade of neighbors that followed him spreads out, making a semicircle on the front lawn, faces contorted in scowls, the air charged and hostile.

Alec, genuinely confused by their presence, shrugs. "Don't know. You'll have to ask Cedarville Electric."

Mom, standing in front of us on the porch, discreetly dials 911. Still no service.

"Shit," she mumbles.

"Oh I see, so you think you having power in your new fancy home makes you better than us!"

"Fancy?" Alec chuckles. "Have you seen this block?"

Someone gasps, the outrage visceral.

"So the Wood ain't good enough for you?" a man yells.

Curses are thrown, steaming-hot burns. In the far back, Yusef is standing in the street, seeming puzzled by the sheer size of the crowd. We catch eyes and he shakes his head, disappointed in our neighbors. Neighbors I recognize from my runs, school, and the library. People who know us but seem hungry to attack.

"What, you don't like living with Black people?"

"He didn't say that!" Mom snaps, stepping down to join him on the bottom step. I glance at Piper, standing beside Sammy, shivering in the cold. She peers over her shoulder into the house, as if she's waiting for someone to come out.

"Ain't nobody asked you, sis," a younger woman shouts, neck rolling. "And you need to watch it with that one! He's been trying to get with every female he come across."

"What?" Alec shouts. "What are you talking about?"

"It's true," another woman says. "I've seen him spitting game to all the sisters at the office. That man's a flirt!"

Alec turns to Mom. "This is ridiculous. I'm not flirting with anyone!"

Mom gives him a curt nod. She believes him. And honestly, I do too. Alec seems too stupid to cheat.

"He probably not going after no females," Mr. Stampley says. "Too busy going around stealing people's stuff from they houses!"

The crowd roars with agreement.

"We told you before," Mom says in an even tone. "We don't know how your belongings ended up on our porch."

"Maybe your boy took them!" a man yells, pointing at Sammy. "I see him walking that dog around!"

"That's what people do," Alec snaps back. "They walk dogs!"

A woman shouts, "Then they got their little girl trying to get the kids to come play with her in them abandoned houses."

Piper takes in a sharp breath, flinching, grabbing hold of Sammy's arm, then quickly lets go.

"Yeah, they all been hanging out in them houses. That older one be smoking up in there too."

I stiffen at the reference, my legs going numb.

"Mmhhmmm. You know she got a problem," someone snorts. "Been to rehab and everything!"

Tears pool, the shame instant and cutting. Sammy steps near, gripping my hand tight. Mom glances back at me, hurt in her eyes. Hurt for me. I know she didn't tell anyone. So, how do they know?

"Yup. I've seen her sneaking into that house on the corner," another man shouts, another nameless face.

The secret garden. Crap! How could I have been so stupid to think no one would notice. *Deny deny deny . . . no one has proof.*

Yusef frowns, watching the comments ping-pong around the crowd before meeting my gaze. I shake my head, mouthing, "It's not true."

Yusef only stares back, face void of emotion.

"Yup. She still got that monkey on her back," someone cackles.

The crowd laughs and it's several gut punches, the wind knocking out of me each time.

"I'm sorry," I whimper to Sammy, knowing how much of an

embarrassment I am to him. To my whole family. Mom takes the stairs two at a time, throwing an arm around my shoulders.

"Come on, baby," she whispers. "We don't have to listen to this."

"Hey!" Alec barks, stepping off the stairs. "You leave her out of this! You have no right to talk about her that way. She's a kid!"

I've never seen Alec defend me about anything. It's almost comically relieving.

"Look, I work for Mr. Sterling," Alec says, pulling out his cell. "I can give him a call and ask about the power. But I'm just like you! I have no idea what's going on. I'm not in charge here!"

"Damn right you're not. You didn't even pay for this house," Mr. Stampley snaps. "You living here free, acting like you better than us!"

"Yeah!" the rest shout with agreement. How freaking dare they come at us when they've done so much worse! They burned a family alive! Or, well, their families did. Most of them are probably dead. I look next door, to the boarded-up house with the bodies inside and gulp. As if reading my thoughts, Yusef shakes his head, warning me. And he's right, they may kill us for even knowing about the Peoples family.

The angry crowd is tightening, shifting closer to the house. It's a mob, my panic mind starts to process, glancing at the house next door again.

We could end up just like them.

If I run inside now, I could grab the van keys, and we may have less than five seconds to make it to the car.

Then, without even a sound, the streetlights spring to life on the sidewalk, one by one, startling the crowd.

"There! See, the power is back," Alec snaps, pointing down the road. "Now would you get off my property and stop harassing my family? Please!"

After some grumblings, the crowd begins to disperse, receding into the street, heading home without one apology. Mom exhales the breath she'd been holding as Piper races down the steps, hopping into Alec's arms.

Yusef looks on before stuffing his fists into his pockets and follows the crowd. And in the distance, tucked in the shadows, Mr. Watson quickly hops into a truck on the corner. A truck I recognize because it's been parked on our block for several nights.

TWENTY-ONE

BEFORE SUNRISE, I throw on my running gear and slip out the front door, relieved to see the lawn empty. It hurt, having my worst mistakes used as punch lines by strangers, embarrassing my family all over again. We only have four days left in this place, and I don't want to give these people a reason to keep me. I have to move the pots somewhere and destroy any evidence I step foot in the secret garden. Should've done this sooner, like after watching Erika get dragged away. Guess I was too . . . desperate. But weed isn't worth spending my life in prison with the rest of Maplewood.

Through the overgrown path, I push aside the door and duck under the tarp, coming face-to-face with a man standing in the middle of the kitchen.

Yusef.

"Shit," I gasp, gripping my heart. "Dude, don't you think I've been scared enough?! What are you doing here? How did you . . . ?"

Yusef touches one of the blooming buds, his face stoic.

"So is that what you've been using my tools for? My fertilizer? You've been growing this shit!"

Crap.

"Um, well . . . I just—"

"You lied to me," he hisses.

A part of me wants to tell him to mind his business. That he had no right to come barging in like he owned the place. He didn't even stand up for me when the entire neighborhood dragged me for filth. But another part of me wants him to scream louder, tear me apart, because I deserve it. I deserve all his heat and rage. For this and many other things.

"I'm sorry," I mumble.

"Get rid of it," he snaps.

That was my plan all along. But one look at the budding pots, my proud work of art, and I have second thoughts.

"But it's so close. It's almost ready to be harvested. Yusef, I'm not a dealer or anything. This just . . . really helps me. And, well, you give Erika a pass!"

"Are you fucking serious right now? You trying to compare yourself to E?"

I wince, brain not functioning enough to know not to bring up such a sore spot. Desperate, I try another angle.

"Okay, but maybe we . . . together . . . can make a little money and . . ."

The look on his face stops me cold. His eyes narrow, jaw clenching.

"You know what, Cali, you actually belong up in Big Ville.

You so thirsty for this shit that you don't even see what's going on right in front of you! How we all are hurting! No wonder everyone calling you a junkie. And they right. The way you be scheming on everybody, even your own family. Who could trust someone like you?"

His sharp ice pick pokes right through my chest.

"Yusef," I breathe, fighting back tears.

He pinches the bridge of his noise and huffs. "I ain't no snitch. That's not me. But if you don't get rid of this shit, I'm turning your ass in myself. And I won't give a fuck what happens to you after that."

It's hard to put into words what it's like throwing perfectly good cannabis plants into a compost bin. It's like a starving child forced to throw away fresh food. There was no way to burn it without drawing attention to the scent, and it was too risky leaving it in a regular trash can for someone to find. Mom's compost bin was the safest place.

I uprooted the plants, ripping them from the pots with tears in my eyes. Not because of the loss, which should have broken me after all the work I put in. It was the combination of . . . everything.

Junkie. The word had such a cruel bone-deep meaning, leaving no room for understanding or compassion. No one knows why I am this way. They're not even interested in knowing. They just see the surface and that's enough for them. But of all people,

I never thought Yusef would be so shallow. He knows me, more than anyone around here. Can't believe he could be just as cruel.

My muscles ache for a long run. The kind that could have me lapping this entire city, twice. I'm not ready to face any of my neighbors, but without weed, a run is my only outlet. So after school, I blast my music, keep my eyes focused, pretending I'm in the middle of a race and that every person I fly by is a tree. I push myself, harder and harder, breathing through the intense stares, pain, and tears. I would've kept running, if Tamara didn't call.

"Dude," I pant, slowing to a stop at the edge of the park. "My life sucks for so many reasons."

I explain everything, full-on diarrhea of the mouth about the house, Piper, Erika, Yusef . . . no detail left unturned. She listens in silence, then chuckles.

"He's right."

"Damn, not you too," I groan.

"You're my girl and I love you but . . . you can be a self-centered asshole sometimes," she says, in a sorry-not-sorry kind of way. "Like, do you even notice you only call when you need something? Seriously, when's the last time you asked what's going on with me? Everything seems to be happening to you, as if you didn't have a part in it."

I open my mouth, but once again come up empty with excuses. It's what happens when you haven't slept in a week.

"And I told you before, put yourself in Piper's shoes for a

change," she says. "If you were her, and your new sister did something hella shitty to you, what would you want?"

I sigh. "An apology."

"Right. So how about you start there!"

Change is good. Change is necessary. Change is needed.

"But that's not why I called you," she says, brightening. "You don't need to grow your own shit anymore. You're about to be saved!"

"Huh?"

"I just read they actually legalized recreational marijuana statewide last year. Cedarville has just been waiting to hand out licenses for dispensaries. One was finally approved and it's a national chain!"

"Are you serious?" I gasp, a smile blooming.

"Yeah. Sending you the article."

> City leaders have approved its first dispensary license to Good Crop Inc, allowing Cedarville the opportunity to participate in an industry that's estimated to yield $5 billion in annual sales. Good Crop currently operates dispensaries in Arizona, Connecticut, California, Florida, Maine, Maryland, New Jersey, Nevada, and New York.
>
> CEO Nathan Kruger says, "We're excited about bringing new jobs to the city of Cedarville!"

"Dude," I groan, closing my eyes.

"What?"

"Please tell me Nathan Kruger isn't related to Eden Kruger in some way, right?"

Tamara goes quiet, typing hectically before muttering an "Oh. Fuck."

—*Eden Kruger, philanthropist*

Daughter of Scott Clark, magic seed scammer. Also, married to Nathan Kruger, weed pusher.

Back at the house, Mom waves from the car pulling out of the driveway and I find Sammy in the kitchen.

"Hey, where's Mom off to?" I ask, grabbing a water out of the fridge.

Sammy pops a bowl of oatmeal into the microwave and shrugs.

"Some meeting with the Foundation people. She was waiting for you to come home first. Piper's upstairs."

I lean in close and whisper, "Did you check the cameras yet?"

"Not yet. Was waiting until the coast was clear. Plus, I haven't had my snack yet!"

Right. After-school oatmeal was top priority.

"Okay, I'll grab them while you eat. Cool?"

"Cool," he grins as the timer dings.

Shedding my sweaty shirt, I run upstairs to change and just as I reach the top, my bare foot lands on a nail.

"Ow!" I scream, gripping the banister to keep from falling, hopping on one foot, the pain blinding.

"You okay?" Sammy calls.

I manage to sit on the top step, propping my foot up to inspect the damage. No blood drawn, only a deep imprint left. Thank God. Last thing I need is a trip to the ER. I search for the culprit and there, a few steps down, is not a nail but a tiny beige pebble.

"Ugh," I groan, reaching down to grab it. "This is why Mom says no shoes in the house!"

The pebble pricks my thumb as I hold it between my fingers and upon closer inspection . . . I blink twice, eye twitching. It's not a pebble either, it's a tooth.

"What . . . the fuck," I mumble.

The tooth is sharp, yellow, blood dried black flaking on the bottom. Sammy's already lost all his baby teeth. Only person left would be Piper.

I knock on her doorframe. "Hey."

Sitting on the bed, Piper meticulously folds her laundry, taking her time to make each shirt a crisp square, then adding it to a neat pile. Just like a little old lady would.

The tooth, sitting in my palm . . . it's too large and worn down to be a kid's tooth. But where did it come from?

"Daddy says you're leaving," she sneers without looking up.

Quickly, I shove the tooth in my pocket.

"Um, yeah. Guess you're getting what you wanted after all."

Lips pressed together, she lifts her chin and shrugs. "Well . . . good."

Thinking of Tamara, I suck up my pride.

"So look, I just wanna say, I'm sorry for what I said yesterday. About you being a pawn. And for what I did . . . when I was high."

Piper's head snaps in my direction. I've surprised her. Not sure if that's a good or bad thing, so I keep going.

"Back then, that had nothing to do with you and it had everything to do with me. You and your dad, you were just meeting me in a different time in my life. But I've changed, whether you believe me or not. Just hoping we could, you know, have a sort of truce these last few days."

She frowns. "What's that?"

"It's like when you agree to stop fighting and arguing for a certain period of time. So can we do that? Have peace for the next four days?"

Piper mulls it over. "And then . . . you'll leave?"

"Yup."

She hesitates, nibbling on her lip, then nods. "Oh. Okay."

Why does it feel like that's not what she really wants?

I'm about to ask when something clatters downstairs. I step into the hall.

"Dude? What are you doing?"

No answer. Just Buddy barking.

"Sammy?" I call, taking the stairs slowly, trying to ignore the prickling in my stomach. I make the corner, the kitchen empty, a cup of water spilled on the counter, knocked over. A fresh wave of panic covers my bones in ice.

Shit. Where's Sammy?

Instinctively, I glance at the basement door, still shut. Buddy barks wildly, prancing by the table. Something moves; a squeaking fills the air. I stagger toward Buddy, gulping, and find Sammy sprawled out on the floor behind the kitchen isle.

"Sam!" I scream, diving for him.

Sammy claws at his throat, eyes frantic, legs kicking. I pull him into my lap.

"What, what's wrong, what's . . . ?"

Then I smell it. A scent I'm not always used to. One that hasn't been in our home since Sammy was four. Sweet yet savory, coming from the bowl of oatmeal lying beside him.

Peanut butter.

There's being scared and then there's being completely petrified. And I hadn't hit that level until this very moment.

Sammy strains, helpless and desperate. His sneakers squeaking against the floor.

"It's okay, it's okay," I reassure him in a shrill voice. "I got you!"

Piper comes running in and stops short. "What's happening?" she yelps. "What's wrong with Sam?"

Sammy's lips are swelling, cheeks puffing. Mom made us run practice drills for moments like this. I know what to do, just hope I don't screw it up.

"He's having an allergic reaction," I cry, lying Sammy on his back and running to the fridge. "He's going to go into shock. Call 911!"

Eyes widening, her mouth moves, but no words come out.

I leap, fishing around the top of the fridge for the cup. Didn't Mom put them up here? I know she did, I saw her! But there's no cup, no EpiPen. Instead my fingers graze against something sharp and plastic, like Legos. I reach, grabbing a ball of them and as soon as I open my hand, my stomach drops. It's the GoPro camera, smashed into pieces.

"Shit," I mumble, glancing at Piper, standing frozen in shock, watching Sam struggle, her eyes flooding with tears.

"Piper, please!" I beg, my own tears exploding as I head for the stairs. "Call 911!"

In Sammy's room, I rummage through his backpack. Mom always puts an emergency pen in the front pocket. But the pockets are empty, in all his bags.

"Fuck!" I scream, waves of panic keep crashing into me as I try to dial Mom, thrashing around her room. He needs his EpiPen. He won't make it to the hospital alive without it. Where the hell are all the pens?!

Wait!

In my room, I dive under my desk, pulling out a file box. I dig around until my hand hits it. The extra EpiPen I threw into my self-care kit before we left Cali. It made me feel safe, knowing I could take care of my brother. I almost forgot about it. But . . . how long has it been in here? Do these things expire?

God, Mom, pick up the phone!

Something black on my bedspread makes me take an impulsive step back, whimpering. I drop the pen, body going rigid.

FACT: Wait . . . no!

I take a step forward and on second glance . . . more Lego pieces. The remains of GoPro camera number two crumble in my hands.

Focus! There's no time.

The stench near the bathroom is violent as I race by. Ghosts. Demons. They're all trying to kill my brother. This house and everything in it has been trying to kill us from the start.

Back in the kitchen, Piper is standing over Sammy, shaking and crying.

"He. Can't. Breathe," she sobs into the phone, leaning over him.

Is she really on the phone? Is this all an act?

"Get away from him!" I scream, shoving her aside. She shrieks, her cries ear-piercing. I need to get Sammy out of here. The house can't hurt us once we're outside.

Sammy's face is blue as I drag him by the armpits out the door, onto the porch. He strains, the gurgling noises horrific before he goes limp.

"Okay, okay, okay," I mumble to myself, positioning him.

"Grasp the pen. Orange tip down. Remove the cap. Swing, jab, three seconds, click."

God, I hope this works!

Piper drops to her knees beside me, phone still pressed to her ear.

"He's not breathing!" Piper shrieks.

"Please please please," I whimper before lifting the pen in the air and stabbing it into Sammy's thigh.

"He has always been so careful about his allergies," Mom sniffs outside Sam's hospital room. "Always looking at ingredients . . . he doesn't even take trick-or-treat candy. Just pretends! I don't know how this could've happened. And I wasn't even home! I'm the worst mother! I can't do anything right!"

Alec rubs Mom's back, his forehead sweaty, tie undone.

"Babe, it's okay. He's fine. Mari got to him in time, she knew what to do, just like you taught her. You're a great mom."

Piper stands off to the side, staring at Alec but for a change, not interrupting our parents' tender moment. Dried tears cover her face, her eyes red and puffy.

"Are you sure it was peanuts?" Mom sniffs. "We've been buying that same brand of oatmeal for years! He just had it yesterday and was fine!"

"Positive," the doctor says, her tone clipped. "We'll monitor him until the morning. For now, he's safe and in stable condition."

Mom cracks with grief and Alec consoles her.

Piper opens her mouth then closes it, twisting her fingers. She glances at me, then quickly diverts her eyes, staring at the floor in a daze. Maybe she felt the waves of hot anger radiating off my skin. Because if she takes one step in this direction, I might kill her. She has something to do with this. She knows it, I know it. Only a matter of time before we'll be alone. Fuck an exorcism, I'll deal with her myself.

Dad is on an emergency flight from Japan. He cursed and shouted all the way to the airport. He, too, knows Sammy. Knows he would never mix peanut butter in his oatmeal. Something . . . or someone did this to him.

I'm so busy staring at Piper I don't even hear my name being called.

"Marigold," Mom repeats. "Your brother is asking to see you."

The hospital room smells like it's been drenched in rubbing alcohol, the fluorescents blinding, and I'm immediately brought back to the last time I found myself strapped down to one of these beds. Puke in my hair, dried piss on my thighs . . . stomach cruelly empty.

"Mari," Sammy moans, and I rush to his bedside. He's wrapped in a clean white sheet and hooked up to a monitor. His face is so swollen that his eyes are almost shut.

"Hey," I whimper, holding back tears. "Are you okay?"

He tries to shrug, words slurring over a swollen tongue. "I feel gross."

"Sammy, I'm so sorry. I should've been watching you. Should've never left you alone in the house, not even for one second. I'm such a screwup."

"Dude, you can't watch me every second of every day."

I sniff with a laugh. "Yeah. But I'll die trying."

"It's not your fault," he says, trying to reassure me.

I lean onto the bed and hold his hand. "I keep thinking . . . about how all you wanted was to *just* spend time with me or play video games with David. When really, you were missing Dad."

Sammy quickly looks down at his stomach, not responding.

"You're always hella chill," I continue. "Who would even know if something was up with you? And what did I go and do? Blow you off, again and again, until you had to scrape me off the floor so I wouldn't choke on my own vomit." I hold back a sob. "You . . . deserve a better sister."

"But I don't want another sister," he mumbles, trying to smile. "I saved you, then you saved me. So we're even."

I chuckle. "Dude, not even close."

Wincing through a deep breath, Sammy glances over my shoulder at the closed door.

"Did you find the cameras?" he whispers, his voice hoarse.

"Yeah," I sniff. "They were both smashed. Piper must have found them again."

Sammy tries to swallow. "There was one more."

It takes a moment for the words to register. "What?"

"There's one more camera. One I didn't even tell you about, 'cause it's really old and I wasn't sure if it would work. It's in the glass kitchen cabinet, behind Mom's china."

Hope blooms. "Sammy! Dude, you're a genius!"

He nods, trying his best to smirk. "There has to be something on there this time. It'll either prove there really is a ghost . . . or that Piper tried to kill me."

TWENTY-TWO

IT'S A SILENT ride back to Maplewood. Alec doesn't even turn on the radio. It feels unnatural, us four without Sammy. But he's alive, that's all that matters. And I'm going to get him justice. Only reason why I was even willing to leave the hospital and not sleep in the corner of his room.

Piper stares out the window, playing with the hem of her jacket, silently sobbing. She doesn't look at me. Not even once. Probably too full of shame and guilt. That camera is going to prove everything! And when it does, I'm going to murder this little brat. Rage courses through me, searing my veins.

Alec pulls into the driveway, the house looming over us. Piper's lava lamp is on, the window glowing red. Was that on when we left? I can't remember; everything was such a blur when the ambulance arrived.

"Is . . . anyone hungry?" Mom asks weakly as she heads up the porch steps to unlock the door. Normally, I would be full of dread at just the idea of stepping foot in the house again.

But this time . . . I'm pumped with adrenaline. I bounce on the balls of my feet, stretching my calves. All I need to do is run into the kitchen, grab the camera, and book it before anyone can stop me. What to do after that, I don't know. I don't even know how it works but I can't keep it in the house. Things have a funny way of disappearing and it may be the only proof we have to catch Piper.

As soon as Mom pushes the door open, I practically bulldoze past Alec and am halfway down the hall when I hear a sharp wheezy cough. We all freeze, the darkness hiding our faces.

"What's that?" Mom gasps.

I listen to the silence then hear it again. A loud, wet hacking. Someone's in the house!

Alec holds a finger up to his lips, a hand outstretched in front of Piper.

"Everyone outside," he whispers, ushering us to the door.

I tiptoe toward him, then straighten, spinning around in the threshold.

"Mari, what are you doing?" Mom whispers.

"Wait," I utter, muscles hardening. "Where's Buddy?"

There's never been a day that Buddy isn't jumping for joy within five seconds of us walking in. He should be here by now.

Stunned, Mom has the same thought and runs inside. "Buddy!"

Alec turns on the lights.

"Buddy!" he calls.

I hear it again, a wet hacking right above our heads.

"Buddy," I shout, racing upstairs, Mom trailing me. As soon as I reach the top, I trip over a pillow left in the middle of the floor and fall flat on my face.

"Oh my God!" Mom yells, and I whip around.

Buddy lies on his side in front of the bathroom, panting and wheezing, an almost identical scene to Sammy. I lunge, frantically crawling over to him.

"No, no no no . . . ," I whimper, stroking his head. "Buddy, it's okay, boy. I'm here. I'm here!"

Mom examines him, trying to open his mouth. "Come on, Bud, what did you eat?"

Buddy struggles, the hacking so much worse up close, eyes rolling back into his skull.

"Mom, he can't breathe!"

Alec gently pushes Mom aside and scoops Buddy up in his arms.

"Good boy, I've got you," he coos. "Raquel, you drive!"

I stumble down the stairs after him. "Wait, I'm coming too!"

"No, Mari," Mom says, grabbing my arm. "You stay here with Piper!"

"Buddy?" Piper sobs in the foyer, covering her mouth with both hands. "Daddy, what's wrong with him?"

"It's okay, sweetheart," Alec shouts over his shoulder,

heading for the car, Mom sprints ahead of him to open the door. "We're just going to take Buddy to the doctor. You stay here with Marigold! Buddy is going to be fine."

From the porch, I watch Mom back out the driveway and speed down Maple Street before turning back to the house. Piper stands in the doorway, her little face red and puffy. She meets my gaze, taking a step back, and for the first time, she seems genuinely frightened of me. As she should be.

"You did this," I hiss, hands balling into fists.

Piper violently shakes her head. "NO! It wasn't me. I swear!"

I shove past her, stalking into the kitchen.

"What are you doing?" Piper cries, chasing me.

In the cabinet, behind the plates, I find the last GoPro camera, so inconspicuously placed, no one would notice it.

Piper stares at the camera in my hand, breathing heavily.

"Mari," she quivers. "I think we should—"

"Let's see you get out of this one," I snap, and storm toward the door.

"Where are you going?" she begs.

"Getting the hell away from you!"

"Wait, please! I didn't know Ms. Suga was going to hurt Sammy. I didn't know!"

"Cut the bullshit, Piper! You knew!"

Piper bites her lip, her sobbing tears an insult to injury.

"Please don't leave me," she begs, grabbing my sleeve. "Please! I'm scared!"

I shake her off, staring into her terrified eyes.

"Good!" I bark, and slam the door behind me.

Yusef opens the door in a white T-shirt and dark jeans.

"Yeah?" he says peevishly, his eyes cold.

I try to slow my breathing and keep calm, despite being far from that.

"Can I come in?"

He sniffs, face blank. "It's late."

"Please," I say, voice cracking. "I just . . . I need to talk to someone."

Glancing over his shoulder, he rolls his eyes. "Aight, come on. Just for a minute. Then you gotta get gone."

In the living room, I'm surprised to see Pop-Pop still awake in his chair, watching some old black-and-white TV show. He gives me the stank eye as we walk past, into Yusef's room.

"You okay?" Yusef asks, without an ounce of real care.

I sigh. "No, not really."

He huffs, turning down his music, and we stand in silence.

"Heard Sammy's in the hospital. He good?"

I nod, nervous that if I open my mouth, I may burst into tears, the images of him too fresh and raw in my head. But then I remember what he told me and pull the GoPro out of my hoodie.

"You know how to use this thing?"

Yusef raises an eyebrow at the camera and steps back. "Just

need to talk, huh? So you want my help *again*? Why am I not surprised?"

A fresh rush of shame comes crashing in.

"It's not for me! It's for Sam. It might be the only thing that'll help answer what happened to him. Please!"

"You something else," he grumbles, shaking his head, then motioning to the bed. "Have a seat. Once we done, you can be out."

I glance at his bedframe, my arm inflaming. "Can I, um, borrow a chair from the kitchen? Or I can just stand."

He follows my eyes and flinches. "Oh! Uh, yeah. I'll get another chair. Here, have mine."

Yusef's computer chair is leather and rather new compared to the rest of his room. I sit, not totally at ease, but after the day I've had, I can't stand on my feet for much longer.

He places a kitchen chair next to mine, then begins nervously playing around with the wires behind the monitor.

"You know . . . ," he starts. "I'd, uh, never try something with you or nothing like that."

I frown at him. "Huh?"

He doesn't meet my eye. "That's why you didn't want to sit on the bed, right?"

Seconds pass before I let out an exhausted laugh. "Dude, it's not that. I'm . . . afraid of bedbugs."

He cocks his head to the side. "What?"

As he sets up the GoPro, I give him the rundown on my bug

phobia, and honestly, it feels like a weight off my chest, telling the truth, sharing a glimpse of the world through my head.

Change is good. Change is necessary. Change is needed.

"But I don't get how weed helps you. Doesn't that make you more . . . paranoid?"

I shake my head. "There's two strands: sativa and indica. Indica is good for relaxing and pain relief. Doesn't have the hallucinogenic effect."

"You sound like a professional," he muses. "Never tried the stuff."

"Yeah. And I don't blame you for hating it. It's not right, what happened here, with your family. Especially when weed is legal everywhere else. I should've been more sensitive to that. I'm sorry. Sometimes I forget what's important to me. Or . . . who."

Yusef blinks back surprise, and just as he opens his mouth, an image pops on the screen.

He frowns. "Isn't that your kitchen?"

The camera gives a bird's-eye view of the kitchen and family room in the background, part of the fridge blocking the hallway. Yusef nods, impressed.

"Yo, you ever see that movie *Paranormal Activity*?" he chuckles, leaning back in his chair.

"It's one of Sammy's favorites. He loves the whole series. Too boring for me. It's like watching paint dry, waiting for something to move every fifteen minutes."

Yusef cackles. "It speeds up at the end."

Thinking of Sam, I glance at the GoPro and catch a sob in my throat.

"I always miss the ending. We . . . Sammy and I . . . we used to watch movies every Friday night. Ever since he was five, Sammy would always pick horror movies since he never wanted to watch them alone. He needed others around to feel safe. Last year, I started missing movie nights, 'cause of track meets or whatever. Truth is, being at home was . . . uncomfortable. I'd see black spots everywhere, finding bites no one could see, scratching all the time. Felt like I was going crazy. You know, I haven't slept more than four hours a night in years. It's why I always fell asleep during movies. That and the Percs, made me so damn sleepy. Then, one day, Sammy made me promise that I'd do movie night with him. And I wanted to keep that promise, so I went the whole day without taking one pill. But . . . by the last bell . . . I felt like I was ready to fling myself into the sun, I was so itchy. So I thought, no Percs, I'll just smoke some weed. Figured, if I just take a quick hit then maybe I could last through the entire movie for once. I was out of my stash and my connect got pinched. My ex . . . said he knew a guy and I trusted him. Last thing I really remember was walking into my room. Sammy found me foaming at the mouth. Turns out the weed was laced with fentanyl."

"Damn," Yusef mumbles.

"School expelled me pretty fast after that. My ex said he

was going to come clean, say I got the weed from him, but . . . he never did. My parents dumped their entire savings into helping me get better. People started treating us like social lepers. Parents wouldn't even let their kids come over to play with Sammy and he was already so . . . alone."

Yusef stiffens, setting down the camera. On the screen, the kitchen is still empty, no movement, and no sign of Piper. I sigh.

"OD'ing is the type of mistake you never shake. Because the only person who believes you're really better is you. But I guess I deserve it. 'Cause at the end of the day, I wanted to be high more than I wanted to be home hanging out with my little brother. I chose the high over Sammy. I embarrassed my family, put us in debt, forcing us to move here. So I don't deserve nice things like colorful dresses, friends, boyfriends, or even track. I deserve to just be miserable. But . . . when we were still in Cali, all those days of me doing homeschooling and rehab, locked up in my room, Buddy and Sammy they were there for me, you know? They never treated me like a fuckup, even though that's how I felt. Well . . . feel, even now."

Yusef nods slowly, inching forward as if to catch me.

"I can't lose Buddy." I cough out the sob, the dam crumbling. "I can't lose Sammy. They're the only ones who don't care what kind of fuckup I am. They think I'm awesome! Do you know what that's like? Someone who thinks you're hella dope no matter how many times you screw up?"

Yusef sighs. "I don't think you're a screwup."

"Yes you do," I cry. "You hate me! And I deserve it."

"I didn't say all that. Just 'cause I'm not feeling you, don't mean I ain't feeling you, feel me?"

I blink. "That . . . makes absolutely no sense."

We laugh, his forehead leaning against mine.

"You're not a screwup, Cali," he breathes, tracing a finger along my jaw.

I shudder at his touch, shutting my eyes as fresh tears well up.

"Yusef . . . I don't deserve someone like you."

"Why do you keep trying to punish yourself just because you made a mistake? That's the opposite of what anyone who cares about you would want you to do."

"How do you know that?" I whisper, desperate for answers.

"Because I . . . wait. Wh-what was that?"

"Huh?" I say, eyes fluttering open.

Yusef stares at the monitor, examining it closely.

"Yooo," he whispers, a fist to his mouth, pointing, and I follow his finger.

Back in the kitchen, everything remains seemingly still. But in the far left corner, the bottom cupboard door near the sink waffles slightly before opening on its own.

I gasp, grinning at Yusef. This is it! The proof we need to show Mom that there really is a ghost. That I'm not seeing things or just being a nutcase. Yeah, it's hella creepy, but I could almost burst into tears the relief is so sweet. I gotta call Sammy and tell him we did it!

"Wait a second," Yusef mumbles, squinting. "What's that?"

At the top edge of the cupboard door, a small hand appears, gripping the wood tight. My heart flies up to my throat. I recognize that hand. The gnarly knuckles, the dark burnt skin, the fingernails . . .

"What the fuck?" I mumble, leaning closer.

Another hand appears, then a bare foot touches the floor, as if steadying itself, crooked toes drumming . . . before an old woman crawls out of the cupboard, limb by limb.

"Oh shit!" we shout in unison, flying back in our chairs.

The woman is small, her thin hair choppy sprouts of gray, face haggard and back hunched. She glances from left to right, stretches, then moves gingerly in tattered rags posing as clothes. On the apron tied around her bony frame, you can just make out the pie stitched on the front.

"She's wearing my sweater," I mumble in absolute shock. The cream cable-knit one I thought the laundry had eaten, so filthy it's almost unrecognizable.

The woman opens the fridge and takes out the oat milk, drinking straight from the carton, then mashes a banana into her mouth. Next, a yogurt, followed by handfuls of my guacamole, and I'm ready to vomit.

"I gotta get Unc, he needs to see this!" Yusef says, fumbling out of the room.

The woman seems comfortable, in no rush, as if she's done this plenty of times before. She tries biting into one of the apples we brought back from the farm and winces, holding a hand to her cheek.

I think of the tooth in my pocket as Piper enters the frame, unfazed by the woman's presence, and my blood turns to ice. They talk, calmly at first, but Piper seems confused, shaking her head . . . refusing something.

Just then, my phone rings. Mom.

"Mom, I was about to call you. You're never going to—"

"Mari! GET—RIGHT—NOW!"

"What?" I say. The line is terrible.

"Someone—house! Get Piper—GET OUT!"

Piper says one final word to the woman before padding away. The woman watches her, then takes a key out of the pocket of her tattered apron and heads down into the basement.

Piper was telling the truth, all along. No one believed her. And now she's in that house . . . alone.

"Found—in Bud—OUT! NOW!"

The woman's voice springs to my memory.

"GET OUT MY HOUSE!"

The phone slips out of my hand as I bolt toward the door.

"Cali!" Yusef calls to my back. "Wait!"

But I'm already down the driveway, arms pumping, trying to beat my own record . . . back to Maple Street.

TWENTY-THREE

THE LIGHTS ARE on. Every single one. The house is a torch in the distance. The front door wide open, dry leaves blowing inside.

"Piper!" I scream, taking the porch stairs two at a time, noticing Sweets is smashed into a pumpkin pancake. "Piper, come on! We have to go!"

I charge toward the kitchen, where I last left her. The TV is on, Scott Clark spitting his vitriol. The entire floor is empty. But the basement door is open.

Oh no.

"For vengeance is in the hands of the Lord but as he makes you in his liking, he expects you to act on his will and do what he deems necessary. He speaks through his angels, the prophets and community leaders who have been anointed . . ."

I stare down into the abyss. It's not as black and never-ending as it usually is. A soft light glows below.

"Piper?" I say in a trembling voice. Silence. But she has to be down there.

With ragged breath, I tiptoe down the steps. The thin wood creaks and moans under my weight. I grip the aged railing, afraid a board will give in and I'll fall right through, breaking a leg or worse.

"Piper?"

A wall of broken wooden chairs and tables surround the bottom of the steps like a dam, towering to the ceiling, Alec's moving crates tucked in the corner. But behind it all, the light glows brighter. I slip through a narrow entry, my insides a chaotic mess, and find the rest of the basement . . . sparse. A near empty space, the floor dusty, the air damp and cold, smelling of rotting food. A thick coating of dust blankets the bare bookshelves. My foot kicks an empty can and it rolls off to the side, where other empty cans of soup and vegetables lie near a rusted tricycle. And in the far corner sit two makeshift beds, made of charred rags and sheets, a bedbug paradise. The single candle flickers as I stop short.

On one mat is Mom's zucchini spiralizer. Along with Alec's watch, the hammer with the red-and-black handle . . . the list goes on. A treasure trove of stolen goods. Something familiar catches my eye. Near a pillow made of faded curtains is an old tape recorder. Similar to the one Mom used to use reporting for the town's journal when I was little. She would let me record notes and funny voices on it. Which is the only reason why I know how it works. I press play.

"Mari! Mari, come here! Quick!"

My stomach drops, the recorder slipping out of my numb hand and landing on a tin can of . . . peanut butter.

Oh my God . . .

"Piper," I whimper, backing away. I run up the stairs, barreling around the corner and up to the second floor.

"Piper, where are you?!" I cough out a cry. Her room is empty. Maybe she's hiding; she has to be in here somewhere, she just has to! I dive under the bed then shove open her closet. On the floor are blankets, stretching out from a hidey-hole in the corner, along with empty chip bags, juice boxes, and Lunchable containers.

She was living in here!

Head buzzing, I run into the bathroom, throwing back the shower curtain. No Piper. The guilt is heavy, weighing down my lungs as tears bubble up. I left her alone and now the Hag—or whoever that is—has got her!

The sour smell hits me like a brick to the face. I cover my mouth, gagging, bending over the sink to catch any chucks, as I finally recognize it. It's human. Raw body odor mixed with shit and . . . blood. The metal copper scent is so strong, it's unmistakable.

Behind me, something shifts. It's slight but noticeable. I freeze, gazing up into my reflection. The large bathroom is still, sparkling clean, nothing out of place. But the linen closet door is cracked open. And in that dark crack, one giant yellow eye is staring back at me.

Holy. Shit.

The contents in my stomach curdle as I stand paralyzed for what feels like eternity. I bite my tongue to smother a cry, then attempt to play it cool, casually looking away, pretending I saw absolutely nothing. I turn on the faucet and splash some cold water on my face. But my heaving chest and trembling hands must be giving me away.

She knows I can see her! Shit, shit shit . . .

A thin river of blood slowly snakes out of the closet, flowing down the grooves in the checkered bath tiles toward my sneaker. It pools quickly at my heel and I stiffen into wood. The door slowly creaks open wide. And behind it is not a little old lady . . . but a giant man. The same man who was standing in my room the night of the party.

"Demons hate anything happy."

My body won't turn around. Nothing in this world could make me turn around. We lock eyes in the mirror. Half of his face has the texture of dark molded clay. The fire seared meat out of his cheek, neck, and hair, skin misshapen around muscles and veins, his left ear gone. Beside him, blood rains down onto the floor with soft thuds. Two of his fingers are missing, as if ripped off . . . or bitten.

Buddy . . .

Light catches something metal by his boot and I crumble. In his one good hand, he grips the handle of Mr. Stampley's ax.

An ax. He's holding a got damn ax!

Silent fire alarm bells ring through my head as he places a single finger over his lips. Then, in one blink, he charges, shreds of clothing flying behind him like dangling streamers, the ax scraping the tiles. The scream that escapes my mouth is bloodcurdling as I bolt out of the bathroom.

"W-w-w-wait," he yells.

He speaks. He has a voice! He's real. And that realization makes it all so much worse. The size of a bison, his heavy steps are like earthquakes chasing after me. He smells revolting but familiar and even in my panic as I run for the door, I realize . . . it's the stench from the basement, leaking through the vents. We've been smelling him all along.

Down the stairs, I slip and slam into the wall, and he jumps in front of the exit. I skirt around him, toward the kitchen, picking up speed. I'll run through the glass back door if I have to, then I'll . . .

Something ropes around my throat, yoking me, and I catch air before landing on my back. I gurgle up a scream and he yanks me by the collar, dragging me into the kitchen. I flail and kick wildly.

"NO!" I scream, elbow connecting with the back of his leg. He stumbles, toppling like a tree, his giant fist ramming into my stomach, knocking the wind out of me. My eyes are blinded by stars as I curl over.

"W-w-wait," he stammers, rising to his feet, his eyes panicked, the ax still in his hand.

I look up into the face of my soon-to-be killer just as another set of steps run into the house.

"Marigold!" Yusef screams from somewhere as a shovel swings through the air and whacks the man across the head. He winces, drops the ax, and covers his one good ear. Yusef swings again and I scramble from beneath him. The man tackles Yusef to the ground with a grunt.

I'm up on my feet, grabbing Mom's cast-iron skillet hanging from the ceiling, and swing at the man's head, but it merely ricochets. I hit again and again until something cracks behind us and the hall closet door flies open.

"LEAVE MY BABY ALONE!"

The old woman bursts out the closet, screeching, her arms flailing. Stunned by the sight, I'm frozen in place until she leaps, sinking two sharp teeth into my shoulder.

"Ahh!" I scream, jerking left, then right, trying to shake her off. But she clings to my body like a monkey, convulsing and gnawing, nails digging into my neck. I pull at her hair and it comes out in handfuls.

"Helppp!" I cry, slapping her head, her hands, anything I can reach.

Yusef dodges the man, jumps up, swings the shovel and hits the old woman in the face. She falls hard on the floor with a clunk, leaving my shoulder slick with spit and blood.

"MA-MAAA!" the man screams.

Mama? I think, just as he charges at us, his face contorted in rage.

"Watch out!" Yusef yells, pushing me aside.

WHOOSH!

The ax cuts through the air, the blade singing. I duck and it slices into the counter with a crack.

WHOOSH!

I roll out of the way, the man swinging the ax left and right, aimlessly.

"Back off!" Yusef shouts, holding a chair up as a shield. "Run, Mari!"

The man shoves him one-handed and Yusef's head whiplashes into the wall, his body going limp.

"NO!" I cry, running for him, but slip on a pool of blood from the man's missing fingers and eat the floor.

WHOOSH!

The ax slices into the hardwood, inches from my head. Panting and sobbing, I quickly roll and army-crawl behind the sofa. He stalks over, the house shaking with each footstep. He throws the sofa aside like it was made of cardboard, holding the ax over me, ready to hack me into pieces.

This is it. I'm going to die.

I think of Sammy and Mom as I close my eyes, bracing for impact.

POP POP

Gunshots make us all whip around to the open front door.

Mr. Brown stands in the yard, smoke swirling from his gun, pointed in the air. He stares inside the house, bewildered by the sight.

"Ms. . . . Suga?" he gasps, his eyes wide.

The old woman coughs, flopping over like a rag doll.

By the counter, Yusef moans, and I spring for him.

"Shoot him! Shoot the man!" I scream, diving over Yusef. But when I look up, there's no one there. The back door is open.

The man is gone.

TWENTY-FOUR

MS. SUGA IS sitting on a chair placed in the middle of the family room, EMTs and police surrounding her. She stares transfixed at the floor, dead behind the eyes, drool dripping out the side of her mouth. The Hag is not as terrifying as my imagination made her to be. In the light, she's nothing but a pitiful old lady. Being that she's barely ninety pounds soaking wet, they don't handcuff her. But they didn't see the way she popped out of that closet.

"Definitely going to need stitches," the EMT says to me. "And a tetanus shot."

In the dining room, the EMT treats my shoulder bite while another gives Yusef a once-over, holding an ice pack to his head.

"Did you recognize him?" I overhear the officer ask Mr. Brown out on the porch.

"No," Mr. Brown says. "But judging by his size . . . he has to be Jon Jon, the youngest boy."

"The one they said was touching kids?"

"Um. Yeah," he mumbles.

Yusef and I share a look.

"Did you see which way he went?" the officer continues.

"No. I was . . . damn. Is that really Ms. Suga in there?"

Pain flares as the EMT applies pressure to the bandages on my bite.

Police searched every room of the house. Every closet, under beds, and in the basement. No Piper. And the man, or Jon Jon, vanished right before our eyes. He wasn't a ghost. Just like Ms. Suga's not a ghost. They're real, and they've been living with us this whole time.

"I just . . . can't believe she's still alive," someone whispers in the kitchen.

"Me either. What, she gotta be eighty by now, right?"

Alec paces around the dining room, hands on his hips. "You can't just *make* her tell us where Piper is?"

Mom folds her hands together, tears in her eyes.

"Sorry, sir, she's still not talking. But we have several units canvassing the area. We'll find your little girl."

In the lobby of the twenty-four-hour animal hospital, Buddy somehow managed to hack up the two fingers he ripped off Jon Jon's hand. Mom took one look at the fingers and bolted for the car. They raced back to the house, arriving just as Mr. Brown let off a warning shot.

"Alec!"

Mr. Sterling stands in the doorway, dressed in another sharp black suit, as if he sleeps in them.

"Mr. Sterling?" Alec says.

"I came as soon as I heard," he says, his voice chipper. "Thank God you are all okay."

"Piper is still missing," Mom corrects him, an edge in her voice.

"Oh my. How horrible. But I'm sure she's fine. Our police force is the best in the country. They'll find her." He glances over his shoulder. "You have quite the big crowd out there, waiting."

Outside, dozens of neighbors stand behind the caution tape, gawking at the house. A hum of nervous voices travel inside. Our once-isolated block looks like an outdoor concert.

"And they can keep waiting," Mom snaps. "We need to find Piper!"

"If you want, I can go talk to them," he offers casually. "Tell them the situation and put their minds at ease. Maybe they can help with the search. They know this area better than we do."

A stricken Alec only nods, tears in his eyes.

"That would be great, thank you," Mom says, holding Alec.

Mr. Sterling tips his head into the kitchen. "Wow, imagine that. Some woman . . . living in the basement. All these years."

Ms. Suga's head pops up at the sound of Mr. Sterling's voice. With a croaky scream, she's up on her feet, charging, arms aimed for his neck.

And the throng of police surrounding her learn the hard way that she's more agile than she appears.

The crowd falls silent as the EMTs wheel a strapped-down Ms. Suga out on a stretcher. They stare in pure astonishment at the physical embodiment of their urban legend being rolled away. Ms. Suga scowls at the crowd, but then she glances up at the house and the anger melts out of her eyes, the expression on her face morphing into deep sadness, chin trembling. This may be the farthest she's been from her home in over thirty years.

Beside me, Yusef grabs hold of my hand, giving it a gentle squeeze.

"Take it easy," someone says. "She's just an old lady." And yet, she was so much more than that.

An officer approaches Mom and Alec on the porch. "We're going to take her to the hospital, have her checked over and try to get her to talk. Hopefully, she'll tell us where your daughter is."

Ms. Suga doesn't take her eyes off the house, even as the ambulance doors close.

I look up at the house next door, at the ivy vines rustling in the breeze.

"How did they survive the fire?"

Yusef glances at me, his eyebrow arching. "Huh?"

"You said the house was set on fire with them inside. So how did they get out and no one noticed?"

He gazes up at the house, roping an arm around my waist. I lean into his intoxicating warmth and safety.

"Friends, I know you're all scared. I'm scared too." Mr. Sterling addresses the crowd from the porch as if it is his pulpit. "But we have to be rational here. This man is very dangerous. He's kidnapped a child, a little white girl named Piper. So we have to let the authorities handle this."

The crowd stirs, enraptured. They hadn't heard about Piper yet and the words he uses seem purposefully inciting: Kidnapped. Scared. Dangerous. Little white girl.

Someone shouts, "We got a maniac in the streets!"

"Remember when he was touching those kids?"

"That was a rumor, y'all, remember?" Mr. Brown says from his truck, trying to ease tempers.

"Have the police found him yet?" a woman asks, a shrill of hysteria in her voice.

Mr. Sterling stuffs his hands in his pockets, looking mournful. "I'm afraid not. And I won't lie, I'm not sure they are going to. This man has eluded us for decades."

The crowd gasps, now talking in fast whispers. "What? Why? How?"

"They need to get him before he gets us!"

"What are we gonna do?" someone yells.

Tensions simmer, the air charged. I shift closer to Yusef, his arms tensing.

"Well, the police can only do so much," Mr. Sterling says.

"That's where you come in. After all, who can keep their streets safe better than the people who live in them."

"What the hell is he doing?" Yusef mumbles.

I glance back at Mom and Alec, watching Mr. Sterling with the same confused scowls.

"And, oh. I don't know," Mr. Sterling ponders, playing coy with a shrug. "Maybe, to help find him, we should do what we did back in the old days." He pauses. "Smoke him out."

The crowd is stunned by the suggestion, but they slowly nod in agreement.

"Shit," Yusef mumbles.

"Yeah," Mr. Stampley shouts. "Let's light him up!"

The crowd cheers in unison.

"What the hell are you doing?" Alec shouts, grabbing Mr. Sterling's arm. "My daughter is out there and you're egging on a mob!"

Mr. Sterling smiles, patting Alec on the shoulder.

"Now, now, Alec, I wouldn't be so worried about that. I'm sure she'll be just fine. The good people of Maplewood will be careful. They won't let anything happen to your daughter. But we can't have some maniac running around the streets. Just think of the children."

"I am! I'm thinking of *my* kid!"

Mr. Sterling says nothing, only glancing from face to face on the porch, then smiles.

"Well. Doesn't seem like there's much left for me to do here.

Guess I'll . . . head on home."

Alec lunges for his neck and Mom struggles to restrain him.

Mr. Sterling grins at me and strolls back to his car.

He played us.

Meanwhile, the crowd intensifies.

"Well, what y'all standing around here for," Mr. Stampley shouts. "Let's find the son of a bitch!"

"I got some gas at my house," someone offers.

"No. Oh no," Yusef mumbles, racing into the crowd, and I follow.

"We got some fireworks!"

"He can't be out on the streets like this, no way."

"The girls, they won't be safe," a woman warns at a feverish pitch. "Y'all have to do something! Y'all gotta take care of this!"

"Y'all wait!" Yusef says, climbing up on his truck bed. "Don't do this! You've seen what them fires can do. They can wipe out the whole neighborhood!"

"What you doing, man?" Mr. Brown shouts at Mr. Stampley, grabbing him up by his collar. "What if them fires spread! Folks around here barely making it by as it is. We can't go burning everything down, we'll having nothing left!"

"You know he can't live," Mr. Stampley says in a low voice, wiping his hands off him. "You know he can't. Unless you want your father up at Big Ville."

Mr. Brown's eyes widen. Something passes between them.

He backs away, just as the crowd disperses. The hunt for Jon Jon is on.

As Yusef continues to plead with everyone, I spot Mr. Watson in the crowd, staring at Ms. Suga's ambulance driving away. I run over, blocking his line of sight.

"You knew," I hiss.

Mr. Watson opens his mouth, then palms the hat in his hands. "I . . . I wasn't sure."

"How! There was a whole family living in our basement and you didn't know?"

"The Foundation . . . they told us to never go in the basement. Made us all sign these papers, said they had it wired and if we went down there, they'd sue us for everything we got. But . . . something about it just didn't sit right with me."

"Is that why you were parked on our block at night?"

He eyes the ground in shame. "Yes. Was wondering if y'all saw or smelled some of the crazy things I did. Couldn't sleep at night thinking about it. If it was really a ghost, I thought you'd leave by now."

Suddenly, the police officers that once swarmed into the house are now running out the same way the construction workers would at the end of their shift.

"Hey!" Mom shouts. "Where are you going?"

An officer stops to face them on the lawn. "We've been told to fall back and evacuate the area."

"What? Why would you leave? There's clearly something

about to go down around here!"

The officer shrugs. "Following orders. If I was you, I'd leave too. This place is about to be up in smoke. The way these people riot . . . they're like animals."

"These people?" Alec shouts, joining Mom. "They're the citizens you're supposed to serve and protect! You can't just go!"

He shrugs again. "Like I said, I suggest you get out of here while you still can."

Alec shakes his head, furious. "Not without my daughter!"

"Suit yourself. There are talks of roadblocks. No one in or out of Maplewood for the night."

On the street, only a pocket of people remain. Yusef rushes over to me.

"We're gonna go get the fire department! They won't come unless we stay on their asses."

"But what about Piper? We have to find her!"

He points at my parents. "Y'all should split up and look. Cali, I can't let my city burn. It's all we got!"

I know that more than he realizes. Mr. Brown marches over, sweat on his brow.

"Yusef, you drive over to the east side. I'll go over to Midwood. We need all the help we can get." He turns to the remaining crowd. "The rest of you, you know what to do. Pull together your things in case you have to leave. Use them hoses."

The crowd disperses, jogging back to their homes. Yusef

grabs my hand, pulling me into a tight hug.

"I promise," he whispers, "as soon as I get the fire department, I'll be back to help look for Piper. We'll find her."

I nod, holding back nervous tears before letting go of my only piece of safety, watching him barrel down the street.

"Marigold," Mom shouts behind me, keys in hand as they run to the car. "Alec and I are going to drive around and try to find Piper. Stay here, in case she comes back."

"No," I bark, chasing them. "I'm going to look too!"

"No, Mari," Alec insists, eyes brimming red. "It's not safe."

"We need to divide and conquer," I shoot back. "We have to work together to find her before it's too late!"

Mom stares into my eyes and nods, relenting.

"Okay, fine! Don't leave Maple Street and call if you run into any trouble."

"Please, Mari," Alec begs. "Please be careful."

As they hop in the car, I hang on the driver's-side window.

"I'm sorry," I blurt out. "I should have never left her alone."

"Listen to me," Alec says, holding my hands. "This is not your fault. We're going to find Piper. And then we're going to get the hell out of here. Together. Okay?"

I nod, mouthing the word "okay," before he peels out of the driveway.

As soon as they're out of sight, I suddenly remember my phone was still at Yusef's. But Piper could be in any of these houses. And who knows when the mob will be back. I have to try.

• • •

Inside the house, Mr. Stampley's ax is still on the floor where Jon Jon left it. I snatch it up along with a flashlight and run full speed for the secret garden. I need to check every corner of every house on this block. She couldn't have gone far.

The temperature dropped, my breath fogging, and if at all possible, the houses on Maple Street seem creepier than ever. Maybe because I don't know who else could be lurking around like shadows we can't see. My steps echo in the strange throbbing silence. I jump around cracking sidewalks, and right as I'm about to charge into the brush, something up the block catches my eye. A pallet covered with a beige tarp sits on the corner of Sweetwater like a large forgotten birthday present. The brightness jarring, it stands out among the rubble and trash on the street.

I move closer to investigate, pulling back the tarp. It seems like random supplies—a stack of bricks, firewood, kindling, and a giant can of gasoline.

A firework screams up into the sky, lighting it up red.

Two blocks over, a similar pallet sits under a lamppost. All the brand-new necessary tools you need to burn down your own city. Then it hits me: this was the Foundation's plan all along. They knew Ms. Suga and Jon Jon were still alive. They knew the people in Maplewood would do anything to keep themselves safe. And letting them burn down their own homes is an easy way to get rid of an entire community, giving them the perfect opportunity to build a whole new Cedarville. But first, they had to find someone foolish enough to move onto Maple Street to get the ball rolling. Someone not from here and in desperate need of a free house. They used our family as bait. Pawns in their game.

Checkmate.

The night air smells like burning firewood. In the distance, I see the glow of the first house smoking. A crowd cheers. The mob is moving quick. Too quick. They'll be back on this block soon. I need to find Piper. And fast. If Yusef can't convince the fire department to come, we may not make it out of here alive.

Inside the secret garden, the pots are empty, and my makeshift tools in a pile by the door.

"Piper," I call. "Piper, are you in here?"

I shine the flashlight downward, noticing a set of footprints in the dust, heading toward the front of the house.

These footprints aren't mine.

Following the steps, through the kitchen, dining room, past the stairs, I turn a corner and am surprised to see a set of bookshelves in what appears to be the sitting room, windows facing Maple Street. Just like in our house. Except one bookshelf sits tilted from the others. Which is exactly where the footprints seem to stop. I knock on the wall then stomp my foot. Hollow.

Using the ax head, I push the surprisingly light bookshelf aside, finding a utility hole with a metal ladder.

"Piper?" I say, and my voice echoes back.

Shit.

I swallow the fear, stuff the flashlight in my shirt, and climb down the ladder. One step, two steps, into a one-man catacomb. The tunnel is tall and narrow, walls made of various materials—rocks, cement, brick fragments, glass, and thousands of tin bottle caps. I shine a light down the tunnel, but it only goes a few feet. After that, pitch-blackness.

"Hello?"

Water drips and echoes from somewhere close. Gripping the ax, I start walking, the tunnel widening as I go along. I reach a clearing, with two separate entrances, a fork in the road. Which one has Piper?

"Shit," I mumble, and my voice echoes. Something moves ahead of me in the darkness and I whip in its direction.

"Hello?" I shout. "Piper?"

Bravery leaking, I'm ready to make a run for it when I spot a faint glow of light in the distance. I race for it, flashlight bouncing, the tunnel narrowing, my breath growing shallow.

Please be here, please.

At the end, there's a short set of stairs, and a door made of thin warped wood, opened just a crack, light bleeding out. I stare at the door, heart racing, hand held up, frozen.

You walked through a dark tunnel leading to nowhere and you're scared of a piece of wood?

"It's just wood, it's just wood," I chant softly, swallowing back every bedbug fact threatening to bubble up.

I push the door with my shoulder and stumble into . . . a

basement. Not just any basement . . . the basement in our own freaking house! The makeshift beds are exactly where I saw them earlier, the candle burning to a stub. I spin around, staring up at the large bookcases hiding the secret tunnel.

That unmistakable familiar smell reeks behind me and my eyes water, the tears instant.

Oh no.

I spin around and there, hunched in the corner, blending in with the darkness, stands Jon Jon. A towering giant, ready to kill me.

TWENTY-FIVE

THIS IS WHERE I fucked up, See, I assumed Jon Jon would be long gone by now, running away from the mob trying to burn the city down. That's what I would do. You know, something rational.

But we're not talking about someone rational. We're talking about a guy who's spent several decades hiding in our basement with his mother. This has Alfred Hitchcock's *Psycho* written all over it.

Jon Jon's yellow eyes drift to the ax in my hand, jaw wiggling. In an instant, the basement shrinks to the size of a closet, my lungs tightening. He could easily overpower me, snatch the ax, chop me into bits. Blood drains from my head as I realize this is the second time I'm about to die today.

But I won't go down easy. I raise the ax like a bat, shifting my stance, and push the words out through clenched teeth.

"Where's Piper?"

He winces, sticking his neck out as if to hear better.

"Please," I beg. "Just . . . tell me where she is!"

He blinks several times before raising his arms, his bloody hand now wrapped in a piece of curtain. I grip the ax, backing away.

"I don't want to hurt you. I don't," I say, shaking my head, voice trembling. "But . . . please. She's just a little kid."

Jon Jon steps forward and I yelp, arching the ax back.

"W-w-wait," he begs, flinching. "Y-y-you looking for your sister, right?"

My mouth cracks open, gearing up to correct him. But he needs to know how important she is to my family . . . and to me.

"Yes," I gasp. "I'm looking for my sister."

Change is good. Change is necessary. Change is needed.

"I can take y-y-you to where she is," he says, nodding, motioning for me to come closer. I eye his dirty hands and long fingernails caked with mud and grip the ax tighter.

"How do I know I can trust you?" I spit, inching my way to the steps, just in case I have to make a break for it.

A noise outside makes both our heads snap toward the basement door. Voices shouting. Jon Jon runs up the stairs.

"Wait! Where are you going?" I shout, following him. For a big guy, he can move pretty quick and silently when he wants to.

Glass shatters so close it sounds like it's inside the house.

Jon Jon zips through the hall, creeping into the sitting room. He hugs the wall and peeks through the blinds.

"Look," he whispers, calling me over. I nibble on my lip before following his lead, keeping close to the wall and peering out the window.

Outside, a crowd gathers around the secret garden house. They found the pallet and are making good use of it. Throwing bricks through the already broken windows, lighting gas-soaked kindle.

"That was my sister's house," Jon Jon says tonelessly, his face unreadable.

Inside, smoke billows, the flames growing larger, fire eating up the moldy curtains. I touch the window, watching it burn. *It was mine too*, I want to say. My secret garden, a place I planted my dreams, however ridiculous they were.

Jon Jon pushes away from the wall. "W-w-we gotta hurry!"

He races through the hallway, light as a feather, back into the basement, and I run after him. He shoves open the last bookcase. Another tunnel.

"Come. Come," he insists, trying to usher me inside. "It's this way."

"No!" I snap. "Where is Piper!"

"I try to tell you," he says, fumbling through his words. "Tell you to wait. Come. I'll show you."

I peer inside, then point my chin at the entrance.

"You go first." No way am I going to let him have the upper hand on me.

He nods real fast, hunches over, and enters. I grip the ax

tighter and follow. The tunnel is narrower than the other, but somehow tidy and warm. A string of old Christmas lights dangling along the rock-bed wall lights our way. Still, I keep six feet of distance between us.

Jon Jon looks back at me with a nervous smile as he shuffles forward. "This better, right? Better?"

Is he really looking for approval right now? I have an ax aimed at his head.

"Yeah," I mumble. "Better."

"Daddy built the tunnels a long, long time ago."

"Why?" I blurt out, unable to control my curiosity.

"Daddy hated the cold. Made these tunnels so we all had a way to move around in the wintertime. Took him almost two years."

He stops suddenly, spinning around with a frown. I flinch, backing up, tightening my grip on the ax.

"Where they taking Mama?"

Keep cool, Mari.

Have to be strategic here. Any mention of his mother could send him into another Hulk Smash fit and there's not enough room to fight him off.

"Um . . . to a hospital."

"Oh. Is she coming back?"

I swallow. "I . . . I don't know."

Jon Jon rubs his hands together, thinking hard.

"Mama . . . she ain't what she used to be. I told her to leave that little girl be, but she couldn't. She's still mad. She didn't mean it, though."

I narrow my eyes. "You were in my room."

Jon Jon blinks several times. "I was? Oh. Uhhh . . . Mama says I sleepwalk sometime. That . . . used to be my room, when I was young."

"Why were you trying to scare the shit out of us all this time? What the hell was that about?"

Jon Jon stuffs his hands in his holey pockets, not meeting my eye.

"The man said, if we run you off, we don't gotta go away. We can stay."

"What man?"

"I dunno. Mama just told me. Said he own lots of houses."

Mr. Sterling . . . it has to be. Maybe that's why she tried to attack him.

"But . . . how did he know you were still alive?"

He shrugs. "Dunno. He just . . . knew. For a long time."

Still skeptical, I take another step back. "So why are you helping me now?"

He squirms, shoulder twitching. "Mama just . . . went too far. Hurting that little boy. We don't hurt children. But . . . she my mama."

Jon Jon's eyes dart away, mouth trembling. In the light, I notice the little hair he has left is all gray. Then I remember the story about Jon Jon being accused of touching kids in the neighborhood. How they all turned on him only for it to be a lie. He was so young when it happened. I take a deep breath and lower my ax, reminding myself he isn't the real monster here. The real monsters made him this way.

"I know," I murmur.

Jon Jon bites his lip and quickly shuffles forward, the path inclining. I snug the ax under my arm. At the end of the tunnel, he pushes against a wall painted to look like the rocks. It creaks, swings open, and we step into darkness.

"Be careful," he warns. "Wood ain't so good."

Eyes adjusting, I take in my surroundings. We're in another house, different but with a similar blueprint, feels like we're inside a giant brick chimney. The walls are blackened, furniture charred, and wood soggy. What little light there is shines through the cracks in the boarded-up windows, vines crawling inside.

We're in the house next door.

I take a step and Jon Jon's hand shoots out to stop me. He points to the ceiling, at the massive hole where the second floor, third floor, and roof have caved in, dumping the house's contents into the foyer. The air, thick with mold, still has a hint of smoke in it, even after all these years.

Staring up at the stars, I glance back down into the tunnel. So this is how they survived the fires. They escaped, never to be seen again.

The boarded-up windows muffle the voices outside, but the

mob is close, and this house would be next on their list. We need to hurry.

"Where's Piper?" I ask quickly.

Jon Jon flusters, searching around the room. "Mama took her in here, but . . . I don't know where she put her."

"Piper?" I shout, voice echoing.

Thump. Thump.

The noise makes both our heads snap up. I shrink away, my arms going numb.

The same thumps from my dream.

"Is someone . . . else . . . here?" I murmur, spine tensing.

Jon Jon shakes his head. "No. It's just me and Mama."

Right. His whole family is gone. All these years, they've been alone . . . until we moved onto Maple Street.

Outside, the voices are louder now. "THIS IS WHERE IT ALL STARTED!"

Jon Jon ducks as if they can see him through the walls.

"No no no no," he whimpers. He covers his ears, balling up on the floor.

Maybe I should tell them we're in here. Maybe they can help us find Piper. But then I take one look at Jon Jon and realize they won't listen to a word I have to say. They're operating in fear; they're out for blood.

Thump. Thump. Thump.

I pace around Jon Jon. Despite the hole, the rest of the floor looks relatively stable, the wood solid. But the front staircase is a heaping pile in the middle of the foyer, so there must be another way up.

"Jon Jon, how do I get upstairs?" I whisper.

"No no no no," he whimpers, rocking back and forth.

A shrilling shriek then a boom echoes around us. Fireworks shoot off above and the room glows red. Jon Jon covers his head as if a bomb was set off. He's babbling too loud. They are going to find us. And I need him in order to find Piper.

The light of the mob's torches bleed through the cracks in the boarded-up windows.

"Jon Jon, please. We have to move."

He closes his eyes, shaking his head. The voices, the fire, the smoke . . . he's terrified, reliving his worst nightmare all over again. I bend in front of him.

"Jon Jon, I swear. I won't let them hurt you. I'll get you out of here. But we need to find Piper!"

He shakes his head, hard. "No, no, no . . . I deserve it. I deserve it."

"You don't deserve any of this. You don't deserve to hurt yourself after they hurt you."

He cries. "No, no, no. We killed that little boy. We just wanted our house back. And we killed him."

"Who? Sammy? Sammy is alive! You didn't kill him."

Jon Jon stops rocking long enough to look up at me.

"He's alive, I swear," I say again. "You didn't hurt anyone. But if we don't get out of here, Piper could die. I could die. Is that what you want?"

Jon Jon pauses to think it over. Finally, he stands, wiping his face, and points to the back.

"O-o-o-over here," he stutters, shuffling down the hall. Behind us, bricks come hurtling in. We run deeper into the house, hiding behind a wall.

In the kitchen, a set of stairs leads to the second floor. We climb, keeping our steps light. I peer down the hole at the first floor. Two of the boards are ripped off in the living room. Glass shatters and the room erupts in flames.

Oh no. . . .

"We gotta go," Jon Jon utters.

"No! Not without Piper. Where would your mama put her?"

Jon Jon looks around, overwhelmed.

"Piper!" I call.

Thump thump. Thump thump.

She must hear us. We're getting warmer.

"What's over there?" I ask, pointing to a door to the right of the hole.

"That's Daddy's study."

We hug the wall, tightrope walking across the remaining floor, rising flames threatening to lick our heels.

Another two Molotov cocktails are thrown in, the fire scorching. Black smoke fills the house. Jon Jon stares into the flames, weeping. He's terrified. I shouldn't have made him do this.

"Jon Jon, you can go," I offer. "I'll find her. Don't worry!"

He shakes his head and keeps moving, sweat dripping down

his face, the heat sweltering.

"She's in here!" Jon Jon says, and busts into the room. But the office is dark and empty. A window broken, bird feathers blanketing a large mahogany desk. I step back out into the hallway and listen.

"Let's split up!" I cry. "You look down there, I'll check this room."

Jon Jon nods and makes his way around the hole. I open up the next door, ramming right into a four-poster queen-sized bed, soup cans on the dusty mattress. I glance at the ground. Footprints.

"Piper?"

THUMP THUMP

"Wait! She's in here!" I cry out into the hall.

The sound . . . it's coming from behind the bed, which is blocking a door behind it.

"Piper, hang on! I'm . . ."

And just as I grab the mattress, I see them. Bedbugs. Real ones this time, an entire family gathered on the corner, bloodstains a scattered black painting.

"Ohh, ohhh God," I whimper, dropping the mattress and slamming into a wall, clutching my wrist, hand frozen into a grip. I stare at my hand, the invisible eggs now on my skin, try to fix my mouth to call for help. Where's Jon Jon? Is he gone? Did he run away? I don't even blame him.

THUMP THUMP THUMP THUMP

Run, run, run, get out of here, they're on you now, you need bleach, blow-dryer, burn your clothes, can't breathe, need air, no, need hot water, run, run, run . . .

But Piper . . . I can't leave her.

With a babbling sob, I suck in a breath, grab the mattress, and push it off the frame. Then, using my whole body weight, I shoulder the bedframe aside, screaming, dying for this nightmare to be over. *Wake up! Wake up!*

Jon Jon rushes in, stepping behind me, easily pushing the frame over, freeing a path to the door.

"Piper, I'm here," I gasp, coughing up smoke and wiggling the handle. Locked. "Piper, stand back!"

I arch the ax up and bring it down on the handle with one swoop. Then another. The handle breaks off. Jon Jon jabs his fingers in, wiggles, and yanks the door open. And in the corner of the closet . . . is Piper. Wrists and ankles bound, mouth gagged. Her eyes bulge as she screams through the dirty rag. We work quick to free her, then she leaps into my arms, sobbing.

"I'm sorry, I'm sorry," she cries, then coughs, then we're all coughing. The smoke is rising, filling the boarded-up house, suffocating us as we file into the hallway.

We're closer to the front of the house. I can look up into the night sky, fireworks sparkling blue above us, black smoke swirling.

"This way," Jon Jon says, opening another door down the

hall, ushering us in and slamming it closed. The room is pitch-black. I can't see my hand in front of me. Piper clings to my waist.

"How are we going to get out of here?" she cries.

I have no clue. The fire is too massive. We may burn up trying to make it back to the tunnel.

BOOM!

Piper yelps, gripping tighter. "What's that?"

Another BOOM and the sound of splintering wood.

"Jon Jon?"

BOOM! Jon Jon slams his shoulder into a boarded-up window. The board flies into the night and sweet air slips in.

"Come on," I say to Piper, holding her hand, and CRACK! The floorboard breaks under my foot, swallowing my leg, and I fall through before grabbing hold of the sides. Flames scorch my legs and I tread the air.

"Ahhh!"

"Mari!" Piper shrieks, clutching my arms. "Noooo! Help!"

Jon Jon leaps over, one-handedly pulling me back up. Little flickers of fire sprinkle down my leggings. I kick furiously, patting them out, my ankle covered in blood where the wood sliced into me. Jon Jon tears a piece of his shirt and wraps it around the wound. The pain is blinding; I bite my arm as he ties it tight, trying to stop the bleeding. A crack splits down the room like we're standing on a thin ice-covered lake. The fire sizzles below us. This whole floor is going to cave at any moment. I swat Jon Jon's hands away.

"No time! We have to get out of here!"

Jon Jon nods and helps me up to my feet. I scream through gritted teeth, blood dripping into my sneaker, and hobble across the room. Piper coughs and I push her near the window. It's a two-story drop, the back of the house a jungle of vines and trees.

"Easy now, little one," Jon Jon says to Piper with a prideful smile, lifting her onto the windowsill. He pulls a nearby branch. "Grab hold of this."

Following his thinking, I climb onto one of the lower branches, my ankle screaming as I scoot forward and hug the trunk of the tree mercifully. I can't climb down, not like this. Piper makes her way to me and we sit side by side.

"Hold on," I pant, wrapping an arm around her. "Don't let go."

Face covered in a thin sheen of sweat, Piper looks back up at the window.

"Come on, Jon Jon," Piper says, reaching for him.

But Jon Jon shakes his head. Not in a petrified way; his face seems more resolved.

"What are you doing? Come on!"

He shakes his head again. And I know what he's thinking.

"No," I snap. "You're coming with us! They'll understand. We'll help you!"

Suddenly, a bright white light flashes on Piper's face and she flinches with a scream, nearly falling.

"Hang on!" I shout, gripping her arm as the flashlight pings between us.

"Hey!" a man's voice yells from the ground. "Hey, y'all! There's some kids back here!"

Jon Jon backs away from the window, staying hidden. He won't come. If we go out together, they'll catch him, and the way the mob is riled up, they may not turn him over to the police.

"Hide!" I whisper, clutching Piper. "You have to hide!"

His eyes toggle between Piper and me, before running into the blaze, skirting around the edge of the giant hole, back down the stairs.

"Jump, girls!" the man below shouts, the crowd now with him. "Jump! We'll catch ya! Just jump!"

I take one more look through the window, catching a glimpse of Jon Jon, running toward the tunnel . . . his clothes on fire.

TWENTY-SIX

POP-POP IS THE one who answers our desperate knocks at the door. He eyes us through his trifocals, unmoved. Piper scoots behind me, burying her face.

We reek of smoke, our clothes covered in black ash. The bite on my shoulder is bleeding through and my ankle is a bloody mess. Down the street, a mob is setting fire to another house, cheering as it burns. I wrap an arm around a shivering Piper and raise my chin.

"May we come in? Please."

Pop-Pop mutters and widens the door.

Quickly, I shove Piper inside and limp straight to the bathroom. Yeah, our house wasn't on fire (yet), but I definitely didn't feel safe staying there alone. Pop-Pop shuffles into the living room, slippers scratching the floor, TV on the local news.

"Shouldn't be letting in strangers this time of night," he grumbles, slumping into his chair. "It's crazy out there right now. Bunch of hoodlums running the streets."

I take my sneaker and sock off, remove Jon Jon's makeshift bandage, and dip my ankle into the tub, turning on the faucet. Air whistles through my teeth as bright blood swirls down the drain.

Piper sits on the edge of the tub, watching me, her face pale, eyes glassy.

"I thought she was my friend," she sniffs.

"Yeah," I sigh, grabbing a wad of toilet paper to dab the cut. "I know."

She glances down at her hands before her voice breaks. "Why doesn't anybody like me?"

The sight of a bawling Piper crushes my heart.

"Piper, I like you," I say, sitting beside her.

"No you don't! You hate me," she cries. "I should've died in that fire. Sammy and Buddy got hurt and it's all my fault."

"It's not your fault. She tricked you. Why should you hurt yourself because of a . . . mistake?"

The words ring true. Even for myself.

"But I don't have any friends." She hiccups a sob.

"Well, I'm more than just your friend. I'm your sister. We're sisters. Which means we gotta look out for each other. We both gotta do better now because it's us against everybody. Okay?"

She nods softly, drying her eyes, then points to my ankle. "Grandma says you need to clean boo-boos so they don't get dirty or you'll get sick."

I smile. "That's very true. You want to help me?"

We rummage through the sink cabinet and find some rubbing alcohol. I bite down on my fist as I clean the wound, then Piper wraps a towel around it, taping it. No sense in trying to make it to a hospital. I pop three Tylenols and pray my foot doesn't fall off by the morning.

Back in the living room, I sit Piper on the sofa with a blanket and grab two cups of water from the kitchen.

Exhausted, my ankle throbbing, I fall into the sofa, vaguely aware of the bedbugs laying eggs on my arms but too weak to fight them.

On the news, the Wood is like a war zone, houses engulfed in balls of fire. A helicopter circles overhead, zooming in on people throwing bricks and neighbors trying to put the fire on their roofs out with water hoses. Not a fire truck or police car in sight. The headline reads: "Riots in Maplewood."

A newscaster says, "Devil's Night has come early to the Maplewood area of Cedarville. . . ."

Exactly what the Foundation wanted.

"Is Daddy okay?" Piper asks, staring at the screen, gripping the blanket.

That's a good question; no telling where Mom and Alec are in all this mess. I was supposed to call when . . . oh crap!

The phone is still on the floor of Yusef's room. No service. Can't even send a text and the last one received was from Tamara.

DUDE? Are you okay? Maplewood is burning!

"Shit," I grumble, rubbing my temples, slumping back on the sofa. My shoulder hurts and my ankle is bleeding through the towel. I can't move again, need to keep it elevated. One thing's for sure, I won't be running anywhere anytime soon.

"Animals," Pop-Pop mutters, staring at the screen. "Don't believe in the Lord."

The look I give him could fry the remaining hairs off his head. *They're not animals*, I want to snap, not just at him but at anyone who would listen. This is all a game! Why can't anyone see that?

Maybe that's it. Maybe they can't see what the Foundation blocks the world from seeing. How can you see above it when you're drowning in it? But that ends today. I'm going to make sure, if it's the last thing I do, that everyone knows what happened here tonight and why. I'll let people know the real deal about this place, tell the truth the media left out, scream it from every corner. I'll share all Tamara's research, publish my own book if I have to. I'm going to save our home, our city, from being taken over. My mission is fireproof and it feels good.

Change is good. Change is not always necessary. But the right change is most definitely needed.

"Did they catch that Jon Jon yet?" Pop-Pop asks without looking at us.

Piper tenses and I tap her leg, shaking my head discreetly.

"Nope," I say to Pop-Pop. "Not yet."

"Hmph," Pop-Pop grumbles, and changes the channel to Scott Clark.

"'So that the genuineness of your faith, more precious than gold, which though perishable is tested by fire.' First Peter, chapter one, verse seven. Children of God, what you plant in faith, do not dig up in doubt. The Lord looks to you to spread his gospel, his righteous word. How do you expect your seeds to grow if you do not do the Lord's bidding. . . ."

Piper leans in closer and whispers, "Do you think he's okay?"

Tears spring up and I nod.

"Yeah." And if not, he will be. I'll make sure of it.

She thinks for a moment, then says, "We should leave him sandwiches before bedtime now. So he doesn't get hungry. He likes tuna fish."

It's such a small, tender gesture, and then I realize . . . it's something she's been doing all along. Keeping them hidden, keeping them safe.

"Yeah," I agree, smiling, pulling her close. "That sounds like a great idea."

"'And I will raise up for them a prophet like you from among their brothers. And I will put my words in his mouth, and he shall speak to them all that I command him.' Children of God, the Lord has asked me to speak to you tonight, to do his will . . . for weeping may endure for the night, but joy cometh in the morning. I would not lead you astray. Trust me."

ACKNOWLEDGMENTS

A couple of things:

1) This was my first official venture into horror—a genre I've been in love with my entire life)—yet I was still able to keep a toe in the psychological thriller space. Best of both worlds! I hope you've enjoyed it.

2) Season one, episode twenty-two of my favorite TV series of all time, *The Twilight Zone*, is the book's iron spine. The closing narration of "The Monsters Are Due on Maple Street" depicts the theme flawlessly:

> *"The tools of conquest do not necessarily come with bombs and explosions and fallout. There are weapons that are simply thoughts, attitudes, prejudices to be found only in the minds of men. For the record, prejudices can kill, and suspicion can destroy, and a thoughtless, frightened search for a scapegoat has a fallout all of its own—for the children and the children yet unborn. And the pity of it is that these things cannot be confined . . . to the Twilight Zone."*

Not only was this a pandemic book, this was also the first time I'd ever experienced true writer's block. I fussed, whined, and threw fits like a toddler. So I want to give major props to my editor, Ben Rosenthal, for working through the kinks and struggles with me.

To my lit agent, Natalie Lakosil, thank you for always tirelessly fighting for my needs and being my cheerleader. I appreciate you more than I can say. To my film agent, Mary Pender, thank you for seeing my potential and asking for what I'm worth plus interest.

Erin Fitzsimmons and Jeff Manning, thank you for such a stunning cover. It really is an iconic classic!

Huge shout-out to the publicity and marketing team at HarperCollins. I know you all had to pivot in a major way while juggling a million projects during a global pandemic, and your efforts do not go unnoticed. Thank you for your continued support of my career.

Props to my beta readers and fellow horror lovers, Mark Oshiro and Lamar Giles, as well as Kwame Mbalia and Justin Reynolds for being apart of the writing council. Thanks to Dhonielle Clayton, Nic Stone, and Ashley Woodfolk for encouraging me to not settle for less than I deserve.

Thank you to all the bloggers, reviewers, Instagrammers, and TikTokers who shouted out my books and for the endless support. You bring me so much joy.

Thank you to my parents for watching my naughty dog child while I got my swagger back at writing retreats and for being never-ending book marketers.

Most importantly, to R.L. Stine. I am honored to have your name on the cover of this book. I would not be the writer I am today if I didn't have you to inspire me. Trying not to cry while I write this, so I'll just simply say thank you for saving me.